MILITANTS, ARTISTS, POETS

MILITANTS
ARTISTS
POETS

JIM BURNS

PENNILESS PRESS PUBLICATIONS

www.pennilesspress.co.uk

Published by

Penniless Press Publications 2020

ISBN 978-1-913144-12-8

Cover: Some books reviewed

CONTENTS

ACKNOWLEDGEMENTS

Many of these reviews were written for the on-line *Northern Review of Books*. The appropriate details are listed below:

St Ives: The Art and the Artists. October, 2018

Creative Tensions. November, 2019

Arthur Caddick. September, 2019

Impressionism in the Age of Industry, June, 2019

Pin-Ups: Toulouse-Lautrec. December, 2018

Van Gogh in 50 Paintings. June, 2019

Colour and Light: Henri-Edmond Cross. November, 2018

The Women Who Inspired London Art. June, 2019

Lotte Laserstein. January, 2019

Sophie Taeuber-Arp. February, 2019

Into the Night. November, 2019

Creative Gatherings. July, 2019

Artist Quarter. July, 2019

Provisional Avant-Gardes. August, 2019

The Institutions of Russian Modernism. March, 2019

Darkness: A Cultural History. April, 2019

Whitechapel Noise. March, 2019

Staging Life: The Manchester Playwrights. November, 2018

Street Songs. May, 2019

Tony Roberts: The Taste of my Mornings. April, 2019

Writing from 19th century Prague. October, 2019

Dreamers: When the Writers Took Power. June, 2019

The 19th century Underworld. May, 2019

Vice, Crime and Poverty, August, 2019

More Rivals of Sherlock Holmes. June, 2019

The Popular Front Novel in Britain. July, 2019

Cold Warriors. September, 2019

Prague Spring. August, 2019

The Lost Girls. September, 2019

Blitz Writing. October, 2019

Other acknowledgements are listed below:

Jack Kerouac: Lonesome Traveller. *Beat Scene 94,* Coventry, Late-Summer, 2019

Looking for Kerouac. *Ambit 102,* London, 1985

Underground with the Hippies. *Tribune,* London, 21st May, 1969; 9th January, 1970; 20th March, 1970

Easy Living. *Beat Scene 93,* Coventry, Summer, 2019

Mimeographing *Move* 1964-1968. Written for the "Art of the Mimeograph" Conference, Westminster University, London, February, 2019

London in Verse. *Ambit 98,* London, 1984

Some New British Poetry, 1988. *Ambit 116,* London, 1989

Some Poets. *Ambit,* London, 104, 1986; 105, 1986; 113, 1988; 116, 1989; 117, 1989; 118, 1989; 120, 1990

From the Forgotten Forties. *Jazz Journal,* London, February, 1975

Who Remembers Doug Mettome? *Jazz Journal,* London, June 1975

The Good Old Days. Published as "Julian" in *The Ant's Forefoot 1,* Toronto, 1967, and in *Types,* Second Aeon Publications, Cardiff, 1970

The Barmaid. *Grosseteste Review,* Lincoln, Winter, 1968, and in *Notes From a Greasy Spoon,* University College Cardiff Press, 1980

Sweet Saturday Night. *For Bill Butler,* edited by Eric Mottram and Larry Wallrich, Wallrich Books, London, 1970

Corporal Ollerton. *Cells,* Grosseteste Press, Lincoln, 1967

On the Scene. *Types,* Second Aeon Publications, Cardiff, 1970

The Drifter. *Types,* Second Aeon Publications, Cardiff, 1970

My thanks to the editors concerned and to Ken Clay and Joan Mottram

INTRODUCTION

It's difficult to get away from Paris when writing about art, and several reviews in this collection inevitably refer to the city, though not only for art but also for the cafés, cabarets and other locations where artists and writers met to socialise. Paris wasn't the only place where such activity happened, so London, Berlin, New York, and several other cities also come into view. As a background to what went on artistically in Paris there is a review of a book dealing with the "vice, crime and poverty" which shows that it was all there while the painters and poets and their patrons carried on their conversation. This isn't to single out Paris for its perversities, and the review of writing from nineteenth century Prague shows that prostitution and its perils thrived there.

St Ives hardly rivals Paris as a centre for artistic innovations, but it has since the late-nineteenth century attracted painters. And for a period in the 1940s and 1950s it did provide a base for some artists who gained national and international attention. Bryan Wynter, Peter Lanyon, and others created work comparable to what was being produced in New York. A few poets settled in St Ives around the same time, most prominent among them W.S. Graham. There was also Arthur Caddick, about whom little has been written in recent years. I'm not going to claim that his humorous poems are on a par with Graham's poetry. They're not, and it would be foolish to say they are. But they are entertaining, and Caddick deserves to be remembered as a light-hearted poet, as well as a St Ives character.

It is a fact that, as noted above, wherever painters and poets congregate, cafés, clubs, and cabarets open to cater for them. Three reviews look at such places and the people who frequented them. Paris again occupies the centre ground, but Berlin, Prague, London, Zurich, and other locations also had their coteries clinging together around a café or bar. There is a myth of the solitary genius working alone, but I would guess that most practitioners of the arts like to get together with fellow-artists to talk, drink, debate, and occasionally fall out. There is the story about the painter Sven Berlin knocking Arthur Caddick to the ground in a pub in St Ives.

Prague when the communists were in control probably wasn't a city that had a flourishing café culture. It didn't seem that way to me when I was there for a few days in the early-1980s. Was there some sort of "underground" that I didn't know about? There had been a brief period of relative openness when Dubček launched the Prague Spring, but it was soon crushed after the Russians brought in their tanks. This was during the so-called Cold War, and as well as looking at what happened in Prague in 1968, there is a review of how writers on both sides of the Iron Curtain were caught up in the literary struggle between the major powers.

While Prague was experiencing invasion, the hippies in American were in the news as they swarmed into San Francisco and occupied themselves with drugs, sex, and rock music. I thought at the time that what was happening in Prague was of more interest and importance than what was taking place on the West Coast, but books were written about the hippies and several of them are reviewed. Some say that the Beats were precursors of the hippies, but I've never thought that was true, and Jack Kerouac, the subject of two reviews, didn't see things that way, either.

Artists' models are not often written about, but their role in inspiring painters in London is covered. Also in London, there are reviews of books about Jewish singers and comedians in Whitechapel during the era of mass immigration in the late-nineteenth and early-twentieth centuries. And books about what it was like to be in the city during the war years.

Manchester gets a look in with a book about Annie Horniman and the Manchester playwrights of the early 1900s. Most of their plays are long-forgotten, apart from *Hindle Wakes* and *Hobson's Choice*, but they're fascinating to read about. There are reviews of a number of poets from the 1980s or thereabouts, many of them probably now overlooked. It could be a fact that most poets are fated to be forgotten, but that seems to me a good reason to try to revive interest in at least some of them.

As before, I've taken the liberty of including a handful of short prose pieces. They're not stories, in the strict sense of the word, and perhaps "sketches" best describes them? And there are a couple of articles about forgotten individuals from the world of jazz. The period they came from, the mid and late-1940s into the early-1950s, had its influence on me. As Gilbert Sorrentino put it, "Bop, for me, was the entrance into the general world of culture".

ST IVES: THE ART AND THE ARTISTS

St Ives, a place, and also a name that resonates with stories about the "school" or "movement" associated with it. And the artists, of course. There have been artists around St Ives since the late-nineteenth century, but it was, perhaps, only from the 1930s on that the notion of a group which could have something in common in relation to what might be called "modernist art" appeared to have substance. Prior to that, most of the artists worked in a style that largely documented the town and its residents, with an emphasis on the sea and the men and women employed in various aspects of the fishing industry. Not all of the painters lived in St Ives, and for a time Newlyn was important, with Stanhope Forbes and Walter Langley located there. But St Ives soon started to dominate in terms of a broad awareness of art in Cornwall. And the name St Ives is certainly associated with movements in art largely starting in the 1930s

I suppose it's reasonably accurate to say that it all began with the arrival of Ben Nicholson and Barbara Hepworth in 1939. They were refugees, in a sense, from the Second World War and the threat of London being a prime target for German bombers. They were quickly followed by the Russian sculptor, Naum Gabo. Nicholson was not completely new to the area, having visited it with his first wife, Winifred Nicholson and their friend, the ill-fated artist, Christopher Wood. The story of their "discovery" of the naïve painter, Alfred Wallis, and their advocacy of his work, is fairly well-known, though it eventually led to accusations of Nicholson exploiting Wallis and making money from paintings he bought for next-to-nothing from him and re-selling them in London at much higher prices. All that would come later.

Bernard Leach was already in St Ives, though Chris Stephens says that "while the artists' colony was an attraction" Leach found it a "disappointment until the arrival of Hepworth and Nicholson". The war years weren't easy for any of them, and the post-1945 period, with the country locked into an austerity as harsh as that experienced during the war, didn't improve quickly. There was initially a feeling that a better society might evolve from the election of a Labour Government committed to radical changes. But the spirit of "make do and mend" persisted well into the late-1940s, and artists like Peter Lanyon, Margaret Mellis, and John Wells, had to improvise and produce constructivist works from whatever material they could find, including old piston rings, pebbles, knitting needles and string.

Bryan Wynter moved into The Carn, a cottage near Zennor Hill. It was isolated, and had no electricity or running water. It wasn't just painters that were being attracted to the area around St Ives, and Stephens particularly refers to the poet W.S. Graham, who was to establish friendships with Wynter, Peter Lanyon, and a later arrival, Roger Hilton. But Graham wasn't the only poet to settle in Cornwall, though the others didn't stay as long as he did. George Barker, John Heath-Stubbs, and David Wright, also put in an appearance. Sven Berlin, painter, sculptor, writer, suggested that: "Among them was an almost conscious degradation through poverty, in which poverty became a vice and was used as a form of depravity". Berlin would become a controversial figure among the St Ives community, particularly when his 1962 novel, *The Dark Monarch*, had to be withdrawn from circulation after several people threatened the publisher with libel prosecutions. The full story of who these people were, and why they claimed to recognise themselves in the book, is told in its 2009 reprint.

There was a St Ives Society of Artists which had been founded in 1927, but Peter Lanyon started the Crypt Group, along with Sven Berlin, John Wells, Bryan Wynter, and the printer, Guido Morris. The Group held three exhibitions between 1946 and 1948, with other artists besides those named also participating. The aim was clearly to establish the fact that the newer arrivals in St Ives had different ideas about what they wanted to achieve as artists. It should be noted that exhibitions were also held in the Castle pub, where the landlord's brother was the painter and sculptor Denis Mitchell, and in George Downing's bookshop.

That there was a steadily growing development of a community is evident from other activities beyond those of the painters. Guido Morris was producing leaflets and catalogues for the exhibitions, but was also printing small collections of poems by, among others, Norman Levine and Arthur Caddick. Levine later turned to fiction and works like the novella, *The Playground*, and the novel, *From a Seaside Town*, are clearly based on characters and events in St Ives. Francis Bacon, who didn't stay in St Ives for any length of time, appears in fictional form in *From a Seaside Town*.

As for Arthur Caddick, he was, as a poet, not in the same class as W.S. Graham, but he wrote entertainingly about life in Cornwall. I have a copy of his *The Speech of Phantoms*, a very slim volume published by Morris's Latin Press in 1951. The poems are more formal than those Caddick became noted for later, when he had achieved some local notoriety as a bohemian and a boozer, and published a collection of poems called *Broadsides from Bohemia*.

It's also of relevance to refer to *The Cornish Review*, a magazine started by Denys Val Baker in 1949, which went through several issues, died in 1951, and was revived in 1963. He wrote two books about St Ives art, the first appearing in 1950 and the second, better-known one in 1959. And some of his novels and short stories (he was a prolific writer) revolved around Cornish artists and their involvements. The most significant is probably his novel, *A Journey with Love,* which gave Val Baker an opportunity to comment on various styles of painting then current in Cornwall. Another novel, *A Company of Three,* fictionalised a real-life tragedy, the death of the potter Len Missen in a road accident. And a short-story, "Testament of a Green-Eyed Man" focuses on a St Ives sculptress. Anyone wanting to know more about writers and St Ives should refer to Alison Oldham's *Everyone was Working: Writers and Artists in Postwar St Ives.*

One further item worthy of attention is J.P. Hodin's article, "Cornish Renaissance", which was in the penultimate issue of *Penguin New Writing* in 1950. This points to the growing awareness of the importance of St Ives on the British art scene.

The use of the word "community" to describe the artists in St Ives can't hide the fact that clashes of personality were frequent occurrences. Stephens describes how the Penwith Society of Arts in Cornwall was formed, with Hepworth, Nicholson, Bernard Leach and Peter Lanyon as the driving forces behind it. But it was "soon riven with in-fighting and secession", and Lanyon eventually left the Society, as did Sven Berlin.

Berlin, in fact, claimed that by leaving he was ignored by the Arts Council, and that "national, public and corporate galleries left me out of their collections here and in America". His work was dropped by the London galleries and excluded from the 1951 Festival of Britain exhibition. As Stephens says of Berlin, "there are many possible explanations for his exclusion from the artistic mainstream", but it does appear to be the case that questions of patronage were not necessarily improved by the establishment of the Arts Council. Certain people could become too powerful in terms of influencing which forms of art were considered important enough to support. It's what happens with institutions. I do think that Berlin was possibly always something of a maverick, anyway, and he did himself say of his situation with regard to the St Ives artists generally, that he was "with them, but not of them". The exhibition of his work at the Penlee Gallery in Penzance in 2012 demonstrated that he didn't fit into any category that critics tried to establish. He was simply Sven Berlin.

Stephens is informative on the subject of the personalities and in-fighting, but what of the art that was being produced? By the 1950s it was clear that "modern art," especially of the abstract variety, had become the dominant mode. The American Abstract Expressionists (particularly those based in New York) had made their mark with exhibitions of their work in London and elsewhere, and there was sometimes a tendency to suggest that their paintings had a great effect on the St Ives artists. It may have been true in terms of size and aspects of technique, but it has always seemed to me that, if there were influences from America they may have been drawn more from some of the painters not linked to the New York school, like Mark Tobey, Clyfford Still, and Sam Francis.

It's often difficult to know exactly what was seen and by whom, so I'm hazarding a guess based on my own experiences of seeing the work of the artists referred to and that of the St Ives artists. It's a personal opinion, but from the point of view of its quality, I'd place the best of Bryan Wynter's work alongside that of Motherwell, Kline and de Kooning. It's interesting to note that Stephens says that Alan Davie, not a St Ives artist, was probably the British painter of the period who was closest to the Abstract Expressionists.

Patrick Heron always insisted that what happened in St Ives was just as important and original as anything coming from across the Atlantic. The American artist, Mark Rothko, thought it worthwhile to visit St Ives, as did the critic, Clement Greenberg. Heron and Greenberg were friends for a time, though they eventually fell out over the American's boosting of "colour field" painting and Heron's suspicions that Greenberg's links to certain New York commercial art galleries might be shaping his opinions.

Stephens discusses in some detail the work of several individuals, including Nicholson, Hepworth, Wynter, Lanyon (for what it's worth, I've always thought of him and Wynter as the two most interesting artists linked to St Ives) Terry Frost, and Roger Hilton. His comments, which are astute and enlightening without being over-analytical in an academic way, help the reader to understand how and why the artists concerned aimed to achieve what they did. But he doesn't just focus on a few successful painters or sculptors, and is informative about Terry Frost, John Wells, Paul Feiler, Karl Weschke, and others. What it is important to note is that, despite any talk about a "movement", or "school", there was a wide divergence of artistic aims and interests among the St Ives painters. A broad commitment to abstraction may have been the one overall design that could be usefully said about the modernists in Cornwall.

The book is concerned with social as well as art history, and what happened in and around St Ives as the traditional occupations like fishing and mining declined is related to the development of the town as a holiday destination. Day trippers began to flock in, others spent a week or two there. It changed the character of the place and long-term residents were not pleased by it. In the late-1950s, when there was something of a wide revival of the bohemian spirit, St Ives was a Mecca for beatniks. Would-be painters and poets turned up, though few of them ever developed any kind of talent for painting and poetry. I can remember a couple of characters in my own Northern home-town who, inspired by reading the Beats and with aspirations towards creativity, decided around 1960, or so, to hitch-hike to St Ives. They reported that they had got there, but we never heard from them again.

This invasion didn't go down well with the locals, who often blamed the genuine writers and painters for bringing in the great unwashed, as they were seen, and sometimes "corrupting" local people. Norman Levine's novella, *The Playground*, climaxes with the suicide of a garage owner who mixes with the artists, and is based on real events. There were suggestions that he had been drawn into a homosexual circle among the artists and their followers, and Peter Lanyon, one of the few Cornish-born artists, reported that, because of his death, there was an "ugly mood" in the town.

With this in mind there was, perhaps, some irony in the fact that, among the genuine artists, a macho rather than a gay culture was predominant. Stephens refers to "the strongly masculine character" of the social life that largely took place in pubs, which in 1950s Britain, even among supposedly liberated bohemians, were not very welcoming towards women. Alcohol, consumed in liberal quantities, fuelled the conversations and the arguments and physical fights that sometimes resulted from too much to drink. There were talented women in the St Ives community of artists. Barbara Hepworth is a notable example, and Wilhelmina Barns-Graham, Sandra Blow, and Margaret Mellis were also there at one time or another. There was an excellent exhibition, *Wilhelmina Barns-Graham: A Scottish Painter in St Ives,* at the Fleming Collection in London in 2012. There's no doubt, though, that the male artists tended to attract most of the attention.

There were casualties among the artists. Peter Lanyon, whose paintings sometimes reflected his interest in gliding, died in an accident. Roger Hilton, who had established a reputation as a painter and heavy drinker before he settled in Cornwall in 1965, died as a result of his alcoholism. The poet, W.S. Graham, a one-time drinking partner of Hilton's, talked about the "terrible times" they'd had together when he wrote his eulogy for the painter.

The personal stories, the anecdotes, the scandals, are always interesting to read about, and my own feeling is that they can't be divorced from the art that was being created at the same time. It's Chris Stephens' achievement to have written a book that successfully combines analysis of the work of the painters with commentary on the social scene that, in many ways, they helped to create. Their dedication to art, which led to bohemianism, and what seemed to some to be a cultivation of poverty as a way of life, may well have been one of the reasons for the arrival of mostly middle-class young people who wanted to play at being poor. The real artists had been that way out of necessity. But bohemianism, as expressed by the Beat writers, and others like them, was in the air in the late-1950s and early-1960s.

The main question to consider, however, is how worthwhile and lasting was the quality of the work produced in and around St Ives during the period concerned? *St Ives: The Art and the Artists* makes a powerful case for claiming that the best of it made its mark in both national and international contexts at the time, and that a retrospective view adds weight to it still being of value.

ST IVES : THE ART AND THE ARTISTS
By Chris Stephens
Pavilion in conjunction with the Tate. 304 pages. £26. ISBN 978-1-911624-32-5

CREATIVE TENSIONS : THE PENWITH SOCIETY

In 1949 there was an established St Ives Society of Artists, an organisation largely dominated by what can be called "traditional" painters, but with some members drawn from the ranks of the modernists who had begun to make their presence felt in St Ives in the post-war period. Some of the older artists seem to have resented the inclusion of the newcomers, though the fine marine painter, Robert Borlase Smart, thought that they ought to be represented in the Society's exhibitions, as did Leonard Fuller, who ran the School of Painting in St Ives. I would guess that Borlase Smart was a strong enough personality in the community to ensure that a tolerant spirit prevailed, at least while he was still alive. Moderns like Peter Lanyon, Sven Berlin, John Wells, Bryan Wynter, and the printer, Guido Morris exhibited their work in a room under the Society's gallery in the 1940s and were referred to as the Crypt Group.

Smart died in 1947 and by early-1949 it was obvious that matters were about to come to a head. What has been described as a "fractious and insulting" extraordinary general meeting was called by the traditionalists. Chris Stevens, in his *St Ives: The Art and the Artists* (Pavilion Books, London, 2018) suggests that there was some orchestration of events by Peter Lanyon and others. The result was that there was a split in the St Ives Society of Artists and many of the newcomers resigned and formed their own group, to be called the Penwith Society of Arts. I'm deliberately summarising what happened, and a more-detailed account can be found in Chris Stephens's book.

The Penwith group met in the Castle Inn in Fore Street, where the landlord was, at that time, Endell Mitchell, brother of the sculptor, Denis Mitchell, one of the modernists. It was here that the Penwith Society of Arts came into existence. Among its members were Ben Nicholson, Barbara Hepworth, Bernard Leach, Wilhelmina Barns-Graham, and the aforementioned members of the Crypt group. But it wasn't limited to a handful of modernists artists, and included "traditionalist painters and sculptors but also craftspeople".

The driving forces behind the Penwith Society were Nicholson, Hepworth, Leach and Lanyon. However, in many ways, it followed the pattern of similar organisations involving writers and artists, and to quote Chris Stephens, it was quickly "riven with in-fighting and secession, the divisive legacy of which would become a characteristic of the social and professional life of 'St Ives' for another decade or more".

Peter Lanyon and Sven Berlin, for example, soon resigned from the Society. It's probably inevitable that, when strong and determined personalities come together, there is sure to be friction as they attempt to assert their personalities. This can be particularly so when an organisation wants to impose rules on writers and artists, and to make some activities appear more important than others.

The exhibition at the Penlee Gallery in Penzance offers a fairly wide-ranging view of the work of various painters and sculptors associated with the PenwIth Society in the 1950s. Work by many others, besides those named so far, is included, though there's no denying that some of it may be of minor value outside the group context. But it needs to be acknowledged that artists like Marion Grace Hocken, Isobel Heath, Tom Early, and David Houghton, were active around St Ives and helped provide the background against which more-adventurous painters functioned. However, it is the well-known artists, those whose names are often now associated with St Ives, that stand out, and there are good things by Bryan Wynter, Wilhelmina Barns-Graham, Terry Frost, Peter Lanyon, and Barbara Hepworth on display.

If one crosses over from Penzance to St Ives itself, the Penwith Galley in the centre of the town picks up the post-1960 story of the Penwith Society of Artists. Some of the painters already mentioned were active and newcomers like Karl Weschke and Paul Feiler were beginning to be known. And Tate St Ives also looks at the post-war scene in St Ives and places it in a broad context of international influences. For a time, St Ives was seen as having close ties to what was happening elsewhere in abstract art. The influential American art critic, Clement Greenberg, thought it essential to visit the town and meet Patrick Heron and others, and the noted American abstract-expressionist, Mark Rothko, also put in an appearance.

The overall effect of starting off in Penzance with the exhibition devoted to the Penwith Society of Arts, then looking at the work in the Penwith Gallery and Tate St Ives, is to demonstrate how vibrant and important a place St Ives was in the twenty or so years between 1945 and 1965. It wasn't just because artists congregated there during that period. They always had, going back to the turn of the twentieth-century. But there was something about the atmosphere in the years I've referred to that attracted not only forward-looking painters and sculptors, but also poets such as W.S. Graham and Arthur Caddick, novelists and short-story writers like Norman Levine and Denys Val Baker, and the printer Guido Morris, who produced poetry pamphlets, brochures and catalogues for exhibitions, and much more. Baker also edited *The Cor-*

nish Review, which helped highlight the artistic situation in Cornwall, and he wrote a book, *Britain's Art Colony By The Sea,* published in 1959, which was the first to draw attention to the activities and achievements of the artists and sculptors.

It may be a personal obsession, but when there are display cases filled with copies of old posters, novels, collections of poems, letters and postcards, leaflets advertising exhibitions and readings, I'm doubly entranced by the paintings on display. Purists may insist that a work of art ought to stand alone, but I prefer to not only consider it on its own merits, but also see it within a framework of shared activity and creativity.

CREATIVE TENSIONS : THE PENWITH SOCIETY OF ARTS
1949-1960

An exhibition at the Penlee House Gallery & Museum, Penzance, 14th September, 2019 to 16th November, 2019

ARTHUR CADDICK: A POET IN ST IVES

There is a long tradition of British poetry that is used for popular entertainment. It stretches back more years than I want to investigate here,
and I'm just drawing on my own memories of hearing Cyril Fletcher
delivering his odd odes on the radio, Stanley Holloway with "Albert
and the Lion" and similar monologues, and the wonderful Billy Bennett
on records with "Christmas Day in the Cookhouse" and other gems that
kept troops laughing in the trenches during the First World War (Bennett himself was a decorated veteran) and later, audiences in the music
halls. There were many more, such as "Nell" and "Mandalay", and I
suspect that the versions civilian listeners heard may have sometimes
been bowdlerised. And then, in more recent years, there has been the
much-maligned (by snobbish purists), but popular Pam Ayres. Her
work has those literary arbiters, who believe that poets and poems
should always be sober and sombre if they want to be taken seriously,
raising their hands in horror.

Meeting such people always puts me in mind of the amusing passage in
Bulwer-Lytton's *Pelham or Adventures of a Gentleman*(1828) , where
one of the characters reflects on the taste for morbid novels and "dole-
ful ditties", and says: "There seems an unaccountable prepossession
among all persons, to imagine that whatever seems gloomy must be
profound, and whatever is cheerful must be shallow. They have put
poor Philosophy into deep mourning, and given her a coffin for a writing desk, and a skull for an inkstand".

It could be worth having a look at *The Common Muse: Popular British
Ballad Poetry from the 19th to the 20th Century,* edited by V. de Sola
Pinto and A.E. Rodway (Penguin Books, Harmandsworth, 1965),
which, in a particularly good introduction and a fine selection of poems, traces the tradition of popular poetry through the ages. And
demonstrates how humour is a key factor in it. Which isn't to say that
more-serious subjects don't also crop up. They do, but "Then why
should we turmoil in cares and in Fears,/ Turn all our tranquillity to
Sighs and Tears?".

Arthur Caddick was a poet who often worked in what might be called
the "poetry as entertainment" field. He was active in Cornwall when
the St Ives artists of the 1940s and 1950s were at their peak, but the
poet most associated with them is, of course, W.S. Graham. So, let's be
clear from the start that I've no intention of comparing or contrasting
the two poets. I met Graham, heard him read, and much admire the po-

ems he wrote about the artists he associated with, Bryan Wynter, Peter Lanyon, Roger Hilton. I also happen to enjoy Caddick's light-hearted commentaries on his contemporaries and his own follies and foibles. There is no justifiable reason why there shouldn't be a variety of poets and poetry. Graham and Caddick were friends, and there is a record of their times together in Caddick's autobiography, *Laughter from Land's End*, where he recalls also knowing George Barker, David Wright, and John Heath-Stubbs.

I never met Caddick, unfortunately, but I have a recording of him reading, and several of his books. He didn't only write poetry and when he did, it wasn't always just to amuse. He had published a novel in 1940, and before that been at Wadham College, Oxford, where he studied jurisprudence. His legal training may have been one of the reasons why he was among the St Ives residents who took offence at Sven Berlin's satirical novel about the St Ives art colony, *The Dark Monarch*, when it was published in 1962, and threatened to sue for libel. Berlin and Caddick had once been good friends, but some problems arose and the burly Berlin had knocked him out after an argument in one of the local pubs. Berlin's book had left no-one in any doubt as to who the character of the disreputable Eldred Haddock was based on.

I have a small pamphlet, *The Speech of Phantoms*, published in 1951 by Guido Morris's The Latin Press, in St Ives, and the poems in it are conventional in terms of structure and content:

GREEN AFTER RAIN

Green after rain is the hedgerow now,
Sweet with the freshness of leaves,
Cool to the brow
Is the clean, clean air,
Charged with the scent of the shower,
Clean with the sweetness of rain.

It isn't great, or even very good poetry, and I doubt that anyone would remember it after an initial encounter. In some ways, reading Caddick's poems in the pamphlet put me in mind of the old American bohemian poet, Maxwell Bodenheim, and not only because both had a liking for alcohol. It's just the fact that their poems are largely lightweight. They're often not without a relaxed charm, but they seldom progress beyond the ordinary. And they're rarely memorable. It has to be said that the main interest in the pamphlet lies in the fact that it was produced at The Latin Press by Guido Morris. He was something of a character around St Ives, doing the kind of work that enables other people to be remembered. Most printers, publishers, and booksellers get little in the way of attention, but without them poets and others would never have their work published or find an audience for it.

I think it's when Caddick turned to his comic poems that he succeeded in achieving some sort of an individual voice. It may not have been a voice with a wide range, but it was recognisably Caddick's. His collection, *Broadsides from Bohemia*, published in 1973, had poems written, "In Praise of Painters, Publicans, and other Cornish Saints", and it was dedicated to Bryan Wynter, with whom Caddick had shared some "creative carousels". The writer, Denys Val Baker, who edited *The Cornish Review*, and wrote a number of novels and short stories about artists and writers in St Ives and its surroundings, said that Caddick's poems were about "publicans and bohemians and artists and beatniks and Nationalists" and described them as "eminently readable". It's a phrase some writers might shy away from, being seen as dismissing with faint praise, but what's the point of writing if you're not going to be readable?

Caddick had a poor opinion of the beatniks who swarmed into St Ives in the late-1950s and early-1960s, and often made life difficult for the genuine painters and poets who lived there. Their group identity must have seemed strange to a long-time individualist like Caddick, and their anti-social behaviour gave bohemianism a bad name. He wrote more than one satirical poem about the newcomers; "He was a Beat whose horizon/Was bounded by what he could reach./He lived in a length of old drain-pipe/A builder had dumped on the beach". And he mocked abstract painters and sculptors, and some of the poems found a home in *Punch*. Others were about the joys of alcohol and its effects:

NEVER SIT DOWN IN THE DIGEY

Seated alone in the Digey,
Dumb in a doorway at dusk,
My breath full of blessings from Bacchus,
My stomach as empty as husk.

I pondered at peace in the twilight,
But the Vice Squad had sounded alarm,
And a constable marked for promotion
Came up and exerted his charm.

The poem recounts how Caddick, somewhat the worse for wear, was picked up by the police for being drunk and incapable. It was the kind of incident that would quickly go the rounds of the small, regular St Ives community, and they would knowingly recognise the reference to "the Digey", a tiny cobbled street in the town. I acknowledge that it could easily be described as doggerel, but it is entertaining and provides a humorous view of life in St Ives. The fact that a poet like Caddick, with no claims to be writing in a modernist mode, could function alongside someone like W.S. Graham, both responding to what they could see and experience around them, seems to me to be admirable. Any account of the place and the period ought to take notice of both of them.

I've not attempted to do more than give an outline of Caddick's activities, and my intention has been simply to draw a little attention to him. As I've indicated, it is his humorous poems, and their relevance to the story of St Ives, that will ensure his being remembered, if anything does. There is nothing wrong with being a poet who sets out to entertain by being amusing. Caddick worked at it even though he never made much money. He and his family often lived in near-poverty. It would be tempting to laugh at and not with him, but there is a passage in Herman Melville's *Pierre* which seems appropriate:

"Yet let me here offer up three locks of my hair, to the memory of all such glorious paupers who have lived and died in this world. Surely, and truly I honour them – noble men often at bottom – and for that very reason I make bold to be gamesome about them; for where fundamental nobleness is, and fundamental honour is due, merriment is never accounted irreverent. The fools and pretenders of humanity, and the imposters and baboons among the gods, these only are offended with raillery."

Caddick's autobiography, *Laughter from Land's End*, was published by the St Ives Printing and Publishing Company, 2005. *I'll Raise the Wind Tomorrow: A Childhood with Arthur Caddick, Poet of the St Ives Art Colony* by Diana Calvert came from Finishing Publications Ltd., Stevenage, in 2008. It includes a CD of Caddick reading some of his poems. *Under a Cornish Sky: The Poetry of Arthur Caddick* (Scryfa, Cornwall, 2008) offers a wide selection of his work, and has a useful bibliography. *Broadsides From Bohemia* was published in 1973 by Bossiney Books, Tintagel.

Caddick has a place, though a minor one, in Alison Oldham's informative, *Everyone was Working: Writers and Artists in Postwar St Ives* (Tate Publishing, 2003). Sven Berlin's *The Dark Monarch* was originally published in 1962 by the Galley Press, London, but was withdrawn after threats of legal action. A second edition was published by Finishing Publications Ltd, Stevenage, in 2009. The events and personalities surrounding the problems arising from publication of *The Dark Monarch* are explored in Sonia Aarons' *Sven Berlin: Timeless Man* (Millersford Press, Godshill, 2016). Sven Berlin's *The Coat of Many Colours* (Redcliffe Press Ltd., Bristol, 1994) mentions his knocking out Caddick. *The Speech of Phantoms* was published by The Latin Press, St Ives, in 1951. It's of relevance to note that the Winter, 1969, issue of *The Private Library* was devoted to the activities of Guido Morris.

Caddick published a couple of small collections of poetry with the Fortune Press in the 1950s, and a large number of pamphlets and broadsheets with the Phoenix and New Broom small presses in the 1970s and 1980s.

He appeared regularly in Denys Val Baker's *The Cornish Review* with both poetry and prose. The Winter, 1972 issue has an entertaining anecdotal piece, "Marks of Royal Favour" about a visit by John Gawsworth, the so-called King of Redonda. Gawsworth had been a well-known and widely-published poet at one time, often in magazines and anthologies, and editor of *The Poetry Review*, but declined into alcoholism. His visit to the Caddick household was something of a shambles. Caddick, no mean drinker himself, was taken aback by Gawsworth's capacity for alcohol, though he made light of it. The Spanish writer, Javier Marías, wrote about Gawsworth in his novel, *All Souls* (Harvill, London, 1999). Gawsworth was not a supporter of modernism in poetry, and was more concerned with the 1890s and Edwardian poets and the Georgians. There is a well-researched article, "The Lyric Struggles of John Gawsworth" by Steve Eng, on the internet.

It may be of interest to mention one of Caddick's prose works, *One Hundred Doors Are Open: A Guide to 100 Cornish Inns* (Pendragon Publications, Penzance 1956).

For St Ives generally during the period when Caddick was there, see Michael Bird's *The St Ives Artists: A Biography of Place and Time* (Lund Humphries, Aldershot, 2008) and Chris Stephens' *St Ives: The Art and Artists* (Pavilion-Tate, London, 2018). I have a particular fondness for Denys Val Baker's *Britain's Art Colony by the Sea* (George Ronald, London, 1959; second slightly amended edition, Sansom & Co., Bristol, 2000), which seems to me to capture the spirit of the place and period.

IMPRESSIONISM IN THE AGE OF INDUSTRY

In her introduction to this book Caroline Shields refers to "the popular present-day understanding of a movement chiefly concerned with sunny landscapes, bourgeois leisure, and recreation". And it's true that calendars, postcards, prints, and posters often tend to focus primarily on haystacks, fields, gardens, gently-flowing rivers, and generally non-urban scenes. Life is seen as pleasant and unhurried. I often think that Renoir's wonderful *Luncheon of the Boating Party* looms large in many people's imaginations regarding activities among the Impressionists. All those attractive and talented men and women gathered together in a congenial bohemian setting with the sun shining and plenty of food and wine on hand. Who wouldn't want to be part of it?

Life, we know, isn't like that, on the whole. There is a world out there in which most of us have to earn a living, sometimes in not very pleasant situations. And our environment is more often than not one of urban hustle and bustle than of rural relaxation and ease. So, do we blame the artists for selectively portraying a world we'd like to live in but can't, and in doing so ignoring what was really all around them? Shouldn't they have painted pictures of factories and steam trains instead of fields and horse-drawn carriages?

The fact is, of course, that they did turn their attention to the changes that were taking place in towns and cities as industrialisation rolled in. Monet may have produced many paintings which emphasised the countryside, but he also found the steam in the railway sheds fascinating. And Pissarro may have pictured workers on the land, but he also incorporated factory chimneys into his canvases. The artists would have had to be perversely blind to their surroundings to be unaware of the obvious alterations to the appearance of the places where they lived, and the ways in which even rural areas were affected.

Shields, setting out her arguments in favour of Impressionist painters being aware of their rapidly changing circumstances, rightly points to the ways in which French society quickly modernised in the late-nineteenth century. It was especially noticeable in Paris, where Baron Haussmann's developments had transformed how the city functioned and how parts of it looked. The Paris we know today has its basis in what Haussmann did. There were other advances, such as the increased spread of the railway system, as the country recovered from the shock of defeat in the Franco-Prussian War of 1870, and the savage repression of the Paris Commune in 1871.

It seems amazing that just twenty years after these events Paris was becoming known as the City of Light, full of artists and writers and with a vibrant café culture. Life seemed good for the bourgeoisie, and the painters caught it on canvas. It wasn't the whole story, and beneath the glittering surface poverty and prostitution flourished. There were artists who attempted to portray the other side of the picture that showed pretty ladies and top-hatted men strolling along the boulevards. I doubt that they were often noticed then in bourgeois circles, and it's unusual even now for their work to attract attention. People like their Impressionist canvases to be full of light, not social darkness.

This is not the place to provide yet another account of the birth of Impressionism, but it is useful to stress that, as Shields says, "Industrial themes featured in the art of this nascent group from the start". Monet's 1875, *The Coalmen,* "tackles industrial themes more directly than any other Impressionist painting", according to Shields, and it is certainly striking in the way that it captures the repetitive and back-breaking work required to unload coal from a barge. The general industrial setting can be seen in the factory chimneys in the background of this picture.

The full title of the exhibition that this book accompanied was *Impressionism in the Age of Industry: Monet, Pissarro and more*, and in some ways the artists grouped under "more" raise interesting questions about the definition of "Impressionism". It often strikes me that it has become almost a catch-all term that can be used to include any number of late-nineteenth century painters working outside the official guide-lines of the Salon. In some cases they often kept one foot in the Salon.

The changes in the production and marketing of art had led to the rise of dealers who opened their own galleries and promoted the work of new artists. The Salon still had importance in terms of official acknowledgement and possible sales, which is why painters continued to submit their work to it, even if they had claims to be attempting to break new ground. Manet was viewed as a key influence on the Impressionists, but never exhibited with them and was to be seen regularly in the surroundings of the Salon. Monet submitted paintings for consideration by its committee.

I mention these points because, leaving aside Monet and Pissarro, it's often the lesser-known artists who offer an opportunity to see how modern Paris had impinged on their imaginations. Whether or not they were, strictly speaking, Impressionists, I'll leave to the pedants to decide. I'm just happy to be able to see and read about reproductions of paintings by people whose work I admire. I'm thinking of James Tissot, Jean Béraud, and Jean François-Raffaëlli, among others. Tissot and Béraud tended to paint pictures that some would say represented the sunny side of life in Paris. Elegant women, fashionable shops and cafés, and suggestions of consumerism. Raffaëlli did also paint pictures of ragpickers, though they were not products of industrialisation and had been around for years. Daumier had earlier drawn them and Baudelaire written about them.

To be fair, there are meanings that can be read into, for example, Tissot's *The Shop Girl* which, Shields suggests, "portrays a world in which everything – and everyone – can be bought and sold". It was a fact that young women in certain occupations – millinery, shop work, laundering – were sometimes driven to prostitution in order to supplement their low wages. It's implied that the man looking in the window of the shop shown in the painting is weighing up the girls as much as any of the goods on display.

As for laundresses, the nature of their work, hot and repetitious, frequently caused them to discard certain items of clothing. Their bare arms and shoulders could then be seen by male passers-by who were presumably stimulated into thinking that the women might be easily available. Edgar Degas painted more than one picture of laundresses in a state of partial-undress. His *The Laundress* is a good example of what can be taken as evidence of the erotic nature of his portrayal of working-class women. There is an intriguing excerpt from a letter Degas wrote from New Orleans to Tissot: "Everything is beautiful in this world of people. But one Parisian laundry girl, with bare arms, is worth it all for such a pronounced Parisian as I". Was he just expressing a longing to be back on familiar ground, or was there an undercurrent of sexuality in the fact that he specifically referred to a "laundry girl, with bare arms?"

A painter who is now less well-known than others in and around the Impressionist movement was Armand Guillaumin. His *Le Pont-Marie, Quai Sully* neatly mixes elements of a period of transition as modern methods took over. Dredging equipment can clearly be seen, but at the same time the line of horses waiting, presumably, to take away the dirt dug out of the river bed, reminds us that age-old modes of transportation were still in use. Shields thinks that Guillaumin's work, some of which was in the first Impressionist exhibition, "is less recognised today than many of his peers, perhaps because his work was so overwhelmingly devoted to industrial themes during the early years of Impressionism". She adds that he had "working-class origins". Thinking back, it occurs to me that I've seen only a limited number of Guillaumin's paintings during my visits to galleries in France, though I recall an exhibition at the Musée Daubigny in Auvers in 2009 which had him alongside Norbert Goenneutte and Eugène Mürer. A postcard I retained has Guillaumin's *La Seine à Rouen* which has a crane in the foreground and a factory chimney in the background. It looks like a rainy day, but the artist has managed to invest the scene with colour.

It is work by Monet and Pissarro that dominates. Monet's paintings of men unloading coal, and the effects created by clouds of steam in the Gare St Lazare railway station, are highly relevant in the context of the exhibition, the latter in particular. They are recognisably Impressionist pictures. But the style of the coalmen canvas may not be familiar to viewers with a notion of Monet as a creator of pleasant pictures of water lilies, haystacks, and fields of flowers. It's perhaps too stark to be considered for a poster or postcard.

As for Pissarro, I wonder how much of his work is known to viewers in Britain? Again, it may be that his paintings of peasants in fields, or of a woman selling chestnuts, of *Poplars, Grey Weather, Éragny*, and another of the river near Pontoise, may be thought of as typical. But look closely at the latter and notice the factory chimneys. And pay prolonged attention to *The Pont Boieldieu, Rouen*, and observe the crane and what looks like a small steamer moored alongside the quay, the activity on the bridge, and several factory chimneys in the distance. Pissarro, rather than railing against the spread of industrialisation, appeared to welcome it. His canvases absorbed the factories into the landscapes. They were, possibly, relatively small scale operations and might offer steady jobs to low-paid rural workers who were often affected by the ups and downs of seasonal employment.

There are welcome surprises in the works displayed. Maximilien Luce's *Man Washing* shows a sparsely furnished room in a house that clearly lacks a bathroom. His *The Steelworks,* and a painting of men mending a road in Paris, plus another of a gang of pile-drivers, are direct representations of working-class life. And there's the striking *Factory in the Moonlight*, which is evocative of an almost-eerie atmosphere, and nears photography in its overall effect. The same can be said, though even more so, of Henri Riviére's illustrations of men working on the Eiffel Tower. It looks horribly dangerous and probably was. There would be few concerns about health and safety.

There are photographs, some of railway trains and stations, of crowds clustered around the Eiffel Tower, of Parisian street scenes, and of workers (mainly women) leaving the Lumière Brothers factory. You can see that they're anxious to get out even before the doorman has managed to open the large doors properly. I was amused and it reminded me of similar scenes almost seventy years ago when I was a young boy in a cotton mill (another female-intensive occupation) and joined in the rush for the doors when the end-of-the-day hooter sounded.

Who bought the pictures which showed factories as well as fields? It's perhaps difficult to pin down exactly who purchased what unless one spends time exploring the provenances of paintings. Shields names various individuals, and goes on to add that "several other major Impressionist collectors acquired work with industrial themes". She then concludes, "the people who supported the Impressionists were members of the bourgeoisie, wealthy industrialists, entrepeneurs, and professionals", who had prospered under the Third Republic and had different interests and tastes than the aristocracy. The buying power of the aristocrats had declined as the *nouveau riche* entered the art market. They "had no reason to avoid scenes of modernity. They took equal interest in scenes of bourgeois leisure and of industry; they were not instinctively resistant to smokestacks poking into their landscapes, or railroad tracks slicing across it".

I have to say that I have doubts about this. I suspect that the collectors of new work were in a minority and many bourgeois gentlemen and their ladies would prefer a comfortable rural scene, preferably without hungry workers, to one showing barges and smoky chimneys, or stripped-to-the-waist labourers digging up a road. I could be wrong, and perhaps I'm taking Britain as a guide to the tastes of the bourgeoisie. They mostly evinced little interest in Impressionism, at least until much later, and largely favoured Pre-Raphaelite paintings or historical scenes. Galleries in industrial centres such as Birmingham and Manchester have large collections of Rossetti, Burne-Jones, and the like, which were often donated by the wealthy merchants and factory-owners who had originally bought them.

Impressionism in the Age of Industry has much to recommend it and raises some interesting questions about how art captured the changes in French society in the late-nineteenth century. I don't think it matters too much that the definition of Impressionism has been stretched a little, and easily takes in Neo-Impressionism and more, because whatever the group relationship, if any, of the artists concerned, their work has been judiciously chosen to represent a theme, not a movement, and is always worthy of attention. The book was published in conjunction with the exhibition, *Impressionism in the Age of Industry: Monet, Pis-*

sarro and more at the Art Gallery of Ontario, February 16, 2019, to May 5, 2019.

IMPRESSIONISM IN THE AGE OF INDUSTRY
Edited by Caroline Shields
Delmonico Books/Prestel. 243 pages. £39.99.
ISBN 978-3-7913-5845-1

PIN-UPS: TOULOUSE-LAUTREC AND THE ART OF CELEBRITY

As the introduction to the excellent catalogue for this exhibition points out, a "culture of celebrity" is not something that suddenly appeared around the mid to late-twentieth century when the world of pop began to demonstrate how important publicity was to the success of many musicians and singers. Back in the Paris of the 1880s and 1890s a variety of entertainers thrived on the attention focused on them. There was a difference, of course. Contemporary celebrities can depend on all the technological devices available to disseminate their photos, actions, pronouncements, no matter how banal, on a world-wide basis. Even the least talented among them, including those who are simply celebrated for being seen in the right company, often have their moments of fame or notoriety.

In Paris, however, it was largely the poster that provided a basis for circulating the names of the performers, and the places where they appeared. This may have been a limiting factor in some ways in that it may have led to the awareness of a performer's skills being known to only Parisians and some foreign visitors to the city. It's true that some of the better artists from the Moulin Rouge, the Chat Noir, and elsewhere, did perform outside Paris and even travelled abroad to appear in theatres in London, New York, and other cities. But it's hard to dispel the idea that the kind of performances, and those who gave them, referred to in the posters included in the exhibition, were largely a Parisian phenomenon. It may even raise the question that, had it not been for a major talent like that possessed by Lautrec, would we now be looking back to the late days of the 19th century with a kind of nostalgia (it is possible to be nostalgic for something one didn't directly experience) or at least with a romanticised notion of what went on in Montmartre?

The fact is that faded photographs, scratchy recordings, and a few similar mementos apart, little exists of the work of most of the performers to persuade us that they were as good as contemporaries claimed them to be. We rely on the posters to recreate what we imagine they were like. Interestingly, the value of many of the posters as art, and not merely as advertisement, seems to have been recognised almost from the start as technical innovations, and a loosening of licensing laws, caused them to proliferate. People went out and stripped them from walls and hoardings almost as soon as they were put up. Exhibitions of poster art were organised, dealers began to specialise in them. The first poster exhibition took place in Paris in 1884, and a major one in London in 1894/95. I don't think we ever had any poster artists in this country to compare with Lautrec, Jules Chéret, and Théophile-Alexandre Steinlen. They were among the leading names, along with Alphonse Mucha, who largely specialised in advertising Sarah Bernhardt, but many other artists produced posters, if not to the same degree as Lautrec. Pierre Bonnard is an example. Designing posters presumably paid reasonably well and could help support struggling younger artists.

It is Lautrec who occupies the key role in the exhibition, and more than a few of his best-known posters can be seen on its walls. Aristide Bruant, Yvette Guilbert, La Goulue, and Jane Avril. They're all there. He also portrayed some lesser-known performers, such as May Milton and May Belfort. The latter had a brief success with the song, "Daddy Wouldn't Buy me a Bow-Wow", though her career failed to develop after that. If the song is ever heard now I doubt that many people will know who first sang it. As for May Milton, she soon disappeared from the stage and would be completely forgotten were it not for Lautrec's poster.

There are other posters and paintings in the exhibition that are well worth mentioning. Jules Chéret's design for Loïs Fuller's appearance at the Folies Bergère is eye-catching. Fuller, an American, specialised in dancing while "dressed in reams of white silk, with wands sewn inside the sleeves, she would swirl the fabric to create spectacular sculptural forms". Henri-Gabriel Ibels' poster for "the popular entertainer Jane Debary" is less colourful than Lautrec and Chéret, but is still striking. And Steinlen's brilliant poster, "Cabaret of the Chat Noir with Rudolph Salis", is a stand-out item. He amusingly mocked Alphonse Mucha's liking for the halos he often placed around the heads of his females by showing his cat with one.

Two small, but typical Daumier lithographs, a 1930s painting by Sickert of high-stepping chorus girls, and his early 1900s, "The Old Bedford", a music-hall he frequented, and several works by the Scottish colourist, John Duncan Ferguson are bonus items. I was particularly taken by Ferguson's, "The Terrace at the Café d'Harcourt", which is described as "a fashionable meeting place for writers, artists and intellectuals".

Pin-Ups: Toulouse-Lautrec & the Art of Celebrity doesn't break any new ground, but it is a thoroughly entertaining and in some ways instructive exhibition. The emphasis is obviously on personalities, but posters also played a key role in advertising products. Bonnard's poster promoting a brand of champagne is a notable example.

PIN-UPS: TOULOUSE-LAUTREC AND THE ART OF CELEBRITY
An exhibition at the Scottish National Gallery, Edinburgh, 6th October, 2018 to 20th January, 2019

PIN-UPS: TOULOUSE-LAUTREC AND THE ART OF CELEBRITY
Edited by Hannah Brocklehurst and Frances Fowle

National Galleries of Scotland. 120 pages. £19.95. ISBN 978-1-911054-21-4

VAN GOGH IN 50 WORKS

It's common knowledge that Vincent Van Gogh sold only one painting in his lifetime. He lived frugally for the most part, supported by his brother, Theo, and with his work appreciated by a few fellow-painters and a handful of others who could see that the turbulent Dutch artist was producing art that would later be critically acclaimed, hung in galleries around the world, and coveted by collectors.

The intriguing thing about Vincent, as John Cauman's stimulating book aptly demonstrates, is that his life can be followed through his paintings. He didn't only paint what he saw, he also painted what he felt. His physical location at a certain period can be identified through the paintings, and so can his mental condition at the time. It's no secret that Vincent had a troubled life, with frequent breakdowns. These were no doubt exacerbated by his heavy drinking, irregular eating habits, and financial pressures. He was usually short of money for food, rent, and supplies of art materials.

He was born in 1853 in Zundert, a small rural town in Holland. There were some links to the arts in the family. His mother sketched, and several of his uncles were art dealers, a trade that Vincent's younger brother, Theo, would eventually take up. When Vincent himself was sixteen he was employed by Groupil, "a leading French art dealership". This led to him working for seven years at their premises in The Hague, London, and Paris. Cauman says : "The art education he acquired in the process was rooted in conventional naturalistic painting, rather than in the avant-garde". At the same time he became proficient "in the English and French languages, and educated himself in art history, and in English and French literature".

It may have been a sign of Vincent's emotional instability that he was eventually dismissed by Groupil because, Cauman suggests, he was spending so much time "reading the Bible, to the detriment of his gallery work". His father was a pastor of the Protestant Dutch Reformed Church, and Vincent always had a deep religious sensibility as part of his character. For several years he drifted between jobs, at one point teaching in English boarding-schools and working in a Dutch bookshop. He also tried to qualify for the church, but failed to pass the necessary examinations. He did work for six months as a lay preacher in the Borinage region in Belgium, attempting to share in the poverty-stricken lives of the coal miners.

Although he had no formal training as an artist, he decided in 1880, at the relatively late age of twenty-seven, that it was what he would now devote his life to. As mentioned earlier, his time with Groupil had given him an insight into the history of art, but he knew little or nothing about the innovations introduced by the Impressionists and others. He did have some skills as a draughtsman, and one of the earliest illustrations in Cauman's book is the 1882 pencil on paper, "Worn Out", which shows an elderly man, head in hands, and obviously in a state of despair. It was during this period that Vincent received some tuition from his cousin, Anton Mauve, a member of the Hague School of Dutch artists who were realist painters of peasants, rural landscapes, and coastal scenes. Among earlier artists that Vincent admired were the Frenchmen, Daumier, Delacroix, and Millet, all of them having a strong social element in their work.

On a personal level, his emotional problems surfaced again when his approaches to a widowed cousin were rejected. He next had a relationship with an artists' model and prostitute which ultimately failed when he was unable to financially support her and her child. A move to Drenthe, a rural province, followed, and then he returned to live with his parents. While he was in Nuenen, where his parents were now domiciled, he produced what may be one of his most easily-identifiable paintings, the 1885 oil on canvas, "The Potato Eaters". Depicting a poor family clustered around a table for what is clearly a basic meal, it at first sight seems dark and grotesque, the faces exaggerated to emphasise their "homeliness". But, as Cauman points out, in refusing to idealise them, "He sought to convey his empathy with poor and oppressed people, an impulse that was manifest in his previous vocation as a lay minister".

It was obvious that Vincent would have to move to Paris if he wanted to develop as an artist and familiarise himself with new ideas. He had previously written to Theo to say that he was not at all clear about what Impressionism was. He arrived in 1886 and began to study at the atelier of the academic painter Fernand Cormon. But probably of more importance was the fact that he got to know young painters, such as Émile Bernard and Henri de Toulouse-Lautrec, and saw work by, among others, Paul Gauguin, Edgar Degas, Georges Seurat, Berthe Morisot, and Mary Cassatt.

Cauman draws attention to two paintings of "La Butte Montmartre", the first dating from 1886 (mistakenly shown as 1866 in both the caption and the accompanying text), the second from 1887. The earlier is traditional in style, and bears resemblance to the work of The Hague and Barbizon schools of painting, having a "solidity of form". The second is much more modern. Cauman comments that, "The artist has freely adapted Impressionist and Neo-Impressionist brushstrokes to suit his own needs.......In the course of one year, Vincent had transformed himself into an avant-garde painter".

He eventually tired of Paris and decided to move south, staying for over a year in Arles where many of his most significant works were produced. It was also where some of the events that have gone towards constructing the legend of the chaotic but creative painter took place. Vincent had an idea of forming an artists' colony in Arles, and to this end rented The Yellow House and began to make preparations for it to become the centre of activity. As it happened, the only artist to spend any time with him was Gauguin, and he eventually left when he could no longer cope with Vincent's bouts of manic behaviour. This was, of course, when the Dutchman sliced off at least part of one ear and tried to present it to a girl in a local brothel. All sorts of stories have accumulated around this episode in Vincent's life. He did paint a self-portrait which shows him with his ear tightly bandaged.

It needs to be said that several paintings from his early days in Arles do show him in a positive frame of mind. "The Langlois Bridge at Arles with Women Washing" is alive with colour, and there is an attractive "Still Life : Blue Enamel Coffeepot, Earthenware and Fruit", which Cauman describes as of "great importance" for the painter. The items on the table were to "consecrate the Yellow House", the focal point for the projected artists' colony. There is also the panoramic "The Harvest", which Vincent acknowledged as showing some influence from Cezanne.

Of the other canvases from the time spent in Arles, "The Yellow House" naturally stands out: "For Vincent, the Yellow House holds a significance beyond its role as his personal home and studio......yellow and its juxtaposition with blue was replete with spiritual meaning: blue is the colour of the sky: yellow, of the sun". And, as Cauman emphasises, "Yellow and blue would dominate not only Vincent's diurnal paintings such as this one, but also nocturnal canvases such as "Café Terrace at Night". Cauman describes this painting as "benign" when compared to "The Night Café", which shows the interior of the Café de la Gare", an all-night establishment with a clientele of "pimps, prostitutes, drunkards, the poor and the homeless". In a letter to his brother, Vincent wrote: "I have tried to express the terrible passions of humanity by means of red and green........the café is a place where one can ruin oneself, go mad, or commit a crime". The much quieter, "Bedroom in Arles" might well relate to Vincent's need for somewhere that could offer "a reassuring sense of shelter and protection from the exterior world".

Going mad was what was happening to Vincent, and he became a voluntary patient in a psychiatric asylum. Paintings from this period, such as "The Starry Night" and "The Olive Trees", offer evidence of his increasing agitation, the swirling colours having more to do with his disordered and feverish state of mind than with a direct representation of what he saw. It's difficult to accept that the same person painted the beautifully simple "Almond Blossom", a work influenced by his long-standing interest in Japanese art. It's of interest to note that Van Gogh went back to "Worn Out". his earlier drawing of an old man, this time painting the same picture in oils. He had written that he was "sadder and more wretched than I can say". Caumer thinks that it "may be regarded as a spiritual self-portrait".

In May, 1890, Vincent moved to Auvers-sur-Oise to be supervised by Dr Paul Gachet, a physician with a deep interest in art and the problems of those who created it. Initially, he appeared to be in a calmer frame of mind, and paintings such as "The Church at Auvers", "Stairway at Auvers", and "Farms near Auvers", do appear to point to this. Cauman, in fact, says of "Farms near Auvers": "It is as if the artist is presenting a Utopian vision of country life as shelter from the storm that he fears is approaching". That "storm" may well have been forecast in the more-ominous, "Wheatfield with Crows", where a threatening sky and the flock of crows indicate that all is not well.

Vincent shot himself on the 27th July, 1890, and died two days later. There have been speculations that he didn't, in fact, carry out the act himself, and that he may have been shot accidentally by some boys who were killing crows in the vicinity. But I think there is good reason to believe he had reached the point where he wanted to end his suffering by committing suicide.

His reputation began to grow after his death, with exhibitions here and there, critical and popular acclaim, and the beginning of a legend. There is irony in all this. He had been the recipient of only one critical study (by Albert Aurier, who himself died in 1892) while he was alive. His brother, Theo, who had been Vincent's main supporter, died just a few months after Vincent. It was largely due to Theo's widow, Johanna Van Gogh-Bonger, that Vincent's work was kept in the public eye, and his standing in the world of modern art began to grow. Soon there would be major exhibitions, books, essays, academic conferences, even whole museums devoted to the paintings. And they would sell for pric-es that the artist would have found impossible to comprehend. With an art market these days that has little to do with an appreciation of artistic qualities and more to do with investments and other forms of making money, it's wise to remember how Vincent struggled and suffered to create art.

The well-illustrated *Van Gogh in 50 Works* could make an excellent introduction to the artist's work for anyone not too familiar with it. By relating Vincent's movements, and his erratic mental condition, to the paintings, John Cauman throws light on his development as an artist, and the way in which the work reflects what was going on in his mind. The critical comments on the individual canvases are informative and to the point, and Cauman avoids art jargon. There are useful notes and a short bibliography. He has clearly aimed his book at a general audi-ence without in any way trivialising the tragedy of Van Gogh's life or treating the paintings as little better than subject-matter for postcards and posters. There was much more to the work that Vincent Van Gogh created, even if most people at the time failed to appreciate it.

VAN GOGH IN 50 WORKS
By John Cauman
Pavilion Books. 144 pages. £20. ISBN 978-1-911624-43-1

COLOR AND LIGHT: THE NEO-IMPRESSIONIST HENRI-EDMOND CROSS

I'm not sure if the name of Henri-Edmond Cross is known to visitors to exhibitions in Britain? I suspect that, a few specialists apart, it would not arouse a positive response. But that could be because little of his work has been shown here. A quick check suggests that it may only be represented in one public collection, that of Walsall Art Gallery.

With this in mind, it's a great pity that the exhibition this splendid book accompanies isn't crossing the Channel. It goes a long way towards explaining why he's considered important enough to warrant the attention he's now receiving. To be fair, the introduction does acknowledge that, even on the Continent, he has been overlooked in some ways: "In recent years, no major retrospective has been devoted to the work of the neo-impressionist artist Henri-Edmond Cross, either in France or abroad". It's suggested that his "relatively meagre output and the fragility of his canvases" may have been among the reasons why would-be exhibitors have been reluctant to undertake large exhibitions of his work. It's interesting to look at the list of lenders. France is naturally the main one, with the United States coming second, and then a scattering of items from Spain, Belgium, Germany, and a few other countries.

Cross was born in 1856 in Douai, France. His father was French and his mother English, and the family name was actually Delacroix. The reason why he changed it to Cross when he was a young artist is immediately obvious; he didn't want to be confused with the older, famous French painter Eugène Delacroix, or with an academic artist called Henri-Eugène Delacroix.

Cross spent some time in England, having been sent there when he was eleven, and if the later example of him translating Ruskin's *The Elements of Drawing,* a work he admired, into French is anything to go by, he presumably had a good command of English. It's difficult to know exactly how long he spent in England. He didn't visit the country again, though there was a planned trip with the painter Paul Signac which Cross pulled out of, according to Signac, because of objections from his wife. Not too much appears to be known about her, or at least little information is provided in *Color and Light.* Cross married her when persuaded by his parents that it was the proper thing to do, rather than living with her as his mistress.

Cross was recognised as having talent by his father's cousin who arranged for him to have a few lessons with the noted artist, Carolus-Duran. His main artistic training appears to have started in 1878 when he joined the studio of Alphonse Colas. He was also learning a great deal through regular visits to the Musée des Beaux Arts in Lille where he could study paintings by Corot, Courbet, Rubens, Van Dyck, and Delacroix. In 1881 he made the move to Paris that was necessary for any ambitious young artist.

It is important to note that Cross didn't just suddenly appear as a neo-impressionist. His early work shows him to be talented and a good draughtsman, but working within what might be called a conventional framework. A fine self-portrait, *Convalescent*, from 1882-5, demonstrates how skilled he was (its title might also refer to the health problems that marred much of his life), and portraits of his mother, and Doctor Soins, who had initially encouraged the young Cross, further pointed to his craftsmanship. A garden scene in Monaco, and another of a village by the Mediterranean, along with an attractive canvas called *Women Tying the Vine,* indicate that Cross could easily have been succesful as a painter functioning within established boundaries had he chosen to do so. They also help us to appreciate his parents lack of understanding when he switched to working in a neo-impressionist manner once he encountered artists like Seurat and Signac. The family financing of his training simply didn't envisage him throwing in his lot with the avant-garde. Cross was exhibiting here and there, and he had also discovered the attractions of the Mediterranean and would make regular visits to the region. In 1884 he met Signac, Georges Seurat, Albert Dubois-Pillet, and Charles Angrand, and joined them in forming the Société des Artistes Indépendants, with whom he was to exhibit regularly until the end of his life. In 1885 Seurat's *A Sunday on La Grande Jatte*, was exhibited, and the critic Félix Fénéon coined the term "neo-impressionism" to describe what Seurat and his associates were doing. But Cross, while knowing Seurat, Signac, and others of a similar inclination, had not yet become completely identified with them

In 1891 Cross decided to move permanently to the Midi, partly because he thought the climate might help alleviate some of the problems caused by the chronic rheumatism he suffered from. It is from around this time that his work begins to show definite signs of a neo-impressionist style, with pointillist applications of paint and heightened colours. It's said of his work that it becomes more lyrical and points to a "pagan sensibility". Maurice Denis said that Cross was "increasingly replacing the play of light with the play of colour". And Cross himself said that he wanted to "paint happiness".

COLOR AND LIGHT: THE NEO-IMPRESSIONIST
HENRI-EDMOND CROSS

One of the fascinating aspects of Cross's approach to what his work represents is his interest in anarchism and in Nietzsche's writings. The 1890s were a time of anarchist activity in Paris and elsewhere, with various strains in the movement, ranging from philosophical anarchism to the more violent anarchism of the deed. The latter led to bombings and assassinations, and was not what Cross and his friends like Signac ever had in mind.

They envisaged a utopian future in which men and women would commune peacefully with each other and the natural world. Nature was thought to be "a source of individual and social renewal". To most people, especially those living in industrial towns and large cities, it would probably have seemed hopelessly naïve and idealistic. For an artist like Cross it provided much of the stimulus for his work. Many of his paintings represent his vision of such a society. They are focused on rural settings or on coastal scenes that look idyllic. The harsh lives of those labouring in the fields, or in fishing villages, are nowhere to be seen. As Daniel Zamani remarks when writing about Cross's landscapes: "Works such as these ultimately reflect a romanticised view of provincial life that may have had little in common with the social reality of the figures depicted".

And Cross rarely, if ever, looked at the urban environment in his work. There is one notable exception, and it's quite a good painting. *Quai de Passy*, dating from 1899, shows a barge and a small steamship on the river, with buildings in the background. It's colourful, and well in the neo-impressionist style, and is striking, perhaps because it is so different from many of his other canvases.

Marina Ferretti Bocquillon, in her essay on "Henri-Edmond Cross and Germany", says that the First World War rendered "the hedonistic credo of Cross's generation obsolete". The advent of dada, surrealism, and overtly-political art seemed to suggest that painting pictures of idealised nudes in imaginary situations was a way of hiding from reality. Cross's belief in anarchism was genuine enough in its way, even if it was largely passive. He did help anarchist publications, such as the newspaper, *Les Temps Nouveaux,* sometimes with money and occasionally with drawings, though he elected not to sign them so that his parents wouldn't be upset by his political leanings. He was, after all, supported by capitalist money for much of his life.

There is truth in the suggestion that Cross essentially lived a life apart from the wider society, but he wasn't a hermit, hiding away from anything new and modern. The development of the rail network along the

Mediterranean Coast had opened up the region and did lead to more tourists arriving. But it also enabled Cross to travel to see friends like Henri Matisse and Pierre Bonnard, and for friends from Paris to visit him. And he went to Paris fairly often, sometimes for health reasons and also to see exhibitions and meet his dealer.

It's unfair to criticise Cross too much for what he didn't do in relation to reacting to the wider world and its realities. I have to admit that, in terms of its subject-matter, I tend to find a painting like the 1906-07 *The Clearing* somewhat risible. With its bevy of naked women gaily holding hands and dancing in a clearing in the woods, while others drape themselves languidly in a nearby tree, it could be designed to titillate the bourgeoisie likely to buy such a painting or view it in a gallery. I accept that this probably wasn't what Cross intended. I think he genuinely imagined that he was creating a picture of an idealised society and that others would view it in the same spirit. Nietzsche talked of a "new symbiosis of man and nature in a state of Dionysian *ekstasis*", which might be what Cross had in mind?

On the other hand, looking at the picture for its painterly qualities does bring out its attractiveness. And it shows how Cross can be said to have influenced Matisse and the Fauves. There is a riot of colour to be seen in *The Clearing*, and in *The Forest*, where again Cross places his female nudes in a setting where the colours of their bodies, reflecting the play of light, blend with the bushes and trees to create that harmony with nature that he proposed could exist in an ideal world. Some observers might argue that Cross's landscapes lack realism from the colour aspect, but the Belgian poet Émile Verhaeren got it right when he said that the painter was no longer concerned with the "glorification of nature", but rather with the "glorification of an inner vision". In any case, the sheer delight when looking at *Underneath the Cork Oaks, Toulon, Winter Morning,* and *Cap Layer* more than outweighs the irregularities with something like *The Flight of the Nymphs*, where the nudes seem clumsily executed and the colours of little interest. Not every Cross canvas is a masterpiece.

I mentioned earlier that Cross suffered from health problems. His rheumatism got worse, and he had difficulties with his eyes. Despite these drawbacks he continued to travel and paint until it became too onerous to carry on. What finally put paid to his career was when he was diagnosed with cancer. He died in May, 1910, just short of his fifty-fourth birthday.

Color and Light is a superbly-produced book which pays tribute to an artist who seems to have been unfairly overlooked in many ways. It could be that his contemporaries like Seurat and Signac have tended to attract the attention of art historians, and that the advent of Matisse and the Fauves while Cross was still alive drew attention away from his use of colour as a basis for his paintings, though he may have some claims as an originator in this respect. And his intentions relating to the anarchist ideology represented in his work may have deterred some viewers, especially those with a commitment to more direct social commentary. Whatever the reason for his being sometimes overlooked, *Color and Light* may help to restore his reputation.

The catalogue, was published in conjunction with the exhibition, *Color and Light: The Neo-Impressionist Henri-Edmond Cross* at the Musée des impressionnismes, Giverny, July 27th, 2018 to November 4th, 2018, and the Museum Barberini, Potsdam, November 17th, 2018 to February 17th, 2019. It has several well-written, informative essays, including one which looks at Cross's works on paper (he sometimes used watercolours, as well as working with chalk, crayons, and charcoal), and another which describes his life in Le Lavandou, the area where he lived and which he said was "The most beautiful region in the world". There is a lengthy bibliography, and a detailed chronology.

COLOR AND LIGHT: THE NEO-IMPRESSIONIST HENRI-
EDMOND CROSS
Edited by Frédéric Frank, Marina Ferretti Bocquillon, Ortrud Westheider, and Michael Philipp

Prestel Publishing. 272 pages. £39.99. ISBN 978-3-7913-5773-7

Does anyone really remember the models who posed for the famous, and not so famous, paintings and sculptures we come across in galleries? It may depend, of course, on how you define "model". We know the names of the often-titled ladies and gentlemen who commissioned portraits from fashionable artists of the period concerned. The viewer was meant to know who the person portrayed was. The walls of town halls and other civic buildings are lined with pictures of one-time Lord Mayors and other worthies. We know their names, and perhaps those of the painters, but does it matter? A dullness has descended on the portraits that is almost impossible to remove.

There were many other models, of course, and some are remembered because they were the wives and mistresses of the artists. It was cheaper to use them than pay for professional models to turn up at the studios. But I must admit that often, when I think of a model, it tends to be the fairly anonymous hired-by-the-hour females ranging in ages from fourteen to forty and beyond, who stood for hours in sometimes cold and draughty rooms while earnest students and accomplished artists drew inspiration from their bodies.

I referred to females, and there were male models, though on the whole it is the women who are written about. In many cases, however, even they lack any real identity. No-one remembers the names of most of the models who posed in provincial art schools, or even in those in major cities like Paris and London. They arrived, did what they were paid to do, and departed. One or two may have left behind a name because they got involved with an artist or sculptor. When the young Spanish artist, Carles Casagemas committed suicide in a Montmartre restaurant in 1901 it was because his advances had been spurned by a model named Germaine Gargallo (some accounts say her name was Laure Gargallo, others that it was Laure Florentin, or Germaine Pichot). Would we now know her name, or anything else about her, had it not been for the tragedy surrounding Casagemas? And the fact that she later had an affair with Picasso and was portrayed by him in some of his early paintings?

Lucy Merello Peterson takes a broad view of what "model" means, but there is, possibly, something of a parallel to be drawn between the case of Germaine Gargallo and that of Cecilia Dennis, who had modelled for Mark Gertler. He committed suicide, but had claimed that the portrait he was working on would be his "finest picture yet". Peterson says that it "seems unlikely, given his body of work, but it was a story told by the sitter many times over". What later happened to Dennis isn't documented by Peterson, but she does add: "As for public recognition, she was yet another artists' model known almost solely through misfortune".

Using Peterson's wide-ranging definition of "model" it's easy to see that many of them can be identified and named. After all, as mentioned earlier, they were often the wives and mistresses of the artists. Gwen John really doesn't need her associations with other artists to justify her existence. She was a talented painter in her own right, though it has taken time for her quiet canvases to be given their due recognition. But it's a fact that she had an ill-fated affair with the sculptor, Rodin.

Nina Hamnett, who showed great promise in her early days but later declined into alcoholism and a role in the Fitzrovia and Soho bohemias of the 1930s and 1940s, acted as a model for Gaudier-Brzeska who famously sculpted her torso. She was also a model for Walter Sickert and Roger Fry and both painted portraits of her. It would be a pity, however, if she was only remembered for these links. Denise Hooker's splendid biography, *Nina Hamnett: Queen of Bohemia,* (Constable, 1986) has numerous reproductions of her paintings and drawings and demonstrates how talented she was.

There is information about the dreadful Patricia Preece who posed seductively for Stanley Spencer, led him a merry dance which caused him to divorce his wife and marry Preece, and then deprived him of his house and money while she continued her lesbian relationship with Dorothy Hepworth. Peterson suggests that the paintings Preece exhibited under her own name may have been created by Hepworth. They had met while students at the Slade, and had received encouragement from members of the Bloomsbury Group. According to Peterson, Preece and Hepworth "spent four years studying in Paris at Roger Fry's urging, where they found an acceptance of lesbianism that was lacking in Britain".

Peterson inevitably writes about the Bloomsbury set, and Lady Ottoline Morrell, who was portrayed by Augustus John, among others. As she says, "The group's members often rivalled professional models for sheer amount of posing.........The ubiquitous Morrell is represented in almost 600 portraits (art and photography) at the National Portrait Gallery and is associated with a staggering 1,700 others. Vanessa Bell, Clive Bell, Duncan Grant, Dora Carrington, John Maynard Keynes, Mark Gertler, Lytton Strachey, Virginia Woolf, Roger Fry, Wyndham Lewis, Bertrand Russell and E.M. Forster are each represented by eighteen or more portraits, some exceeding fifty".

Following these familiar (too familiar, some might say) names, it's a relief to turn to the Avico sisters, Marietta, Leopoldine, and Gilda, who figure prominently on the cover of the book, but are dealt with in a chapter at the end of it. All three worked as models, in one way or another. Marietta posed for John William Godward's striking, "Contemplation", which is reproduced on page 132. The relationship between artist and model was perfectly proper, but Marietta was called on to testify about Godward's state of mind when he committed suicide in 1922. He was depressed because he thought that his kind of painting was becoming outdated. She did continue to pose for other painters, but later moved to the United States and seems to have given up modelling.

Gilda modelled for Ivon Hitchens and C.R.W. Nevinson, as well as for life classes, and she was also involved with commercial photography. The photograph on page 132 might well be classified as a "glamour girl" pose and shows off her long legs. Leopoldine "earned a reputation for absolute professionalism at the Slade School, where she enjoyed a long tenure". She was also the model for Gilbert Bayes's sculpture, "The Queen of Time", which was placed over the entrance to Selfridge's department store in London.

The Women Who Inspired London Art is lively and packs in a lot of information about artists and their models. It's not surprising that Lucy Merello Peterson largely relies on fairly well-known names. The information about the no-doubt many obscure models who posed for life classes or for individual artists, themselves now often forgotten, simply doesn't exist. Even if a name or two can be found in an old notebook or other document, it won't tell us much, if anything, about the person concerned, and where they came from and what happened to them later.

With regard to the young girl who was the model for the famous Degas sculpture, "Little Dancer Aged Fourteen," we do have a name, though not much else. She was Marie Geneviéve Van Goethem. Her parents were Belgian, but Marie was born in Paris on the 7th June, 1865. She had two sisters. According to Camille Laurens, the oldest of the sisters, Antoinette, had modelled for Degas when she was twelve, but became a prostitute, and "driven by hunger, a petty thief" eventually serving time in prison. She then seems to have disappeared into anonymity. The youngest sister, Louise Joséphine, did achieve some success. She joined the Paris Opera as a "little rat", the name given to the young (often very young) would-be dancers who hoped to become famous one day. Laurens says that of the three, "she had the least tragic life: she was selected for the corps de ballet and later became a successful dance teacher – one of her pupils was the great Yvette Chauviré".

Marie also joined the Paris Opera as a "little rat", though her career never took off and she was eventually dismissed because of her poor attendance record at rehearsals. Laurens is quite clear about the reason for her mother enrolling her at the Paris Opera: "An auxiliary source of income was therefore available to the little Opera rat", in the form of what could be earned by catering to the tastes of the often-wealthy men who hung around the Paris Opera: "Backstage, procurement was the quasi-official function of a mother, who was expected to 'present' her daughter to male admirers". Nobody, including the police, seemed concerned about paedophilia.

Degas could be observed backstage, though in his case his concern was to sketch the dancers as they practised their steps and poses. He didn't glamorise what they did. It was hard, tiring work and the weariness it brought on in its young practitioners can be seen in his drawings and paintings.

Maria had modelled for Degas before "The Little Dancer" and has been identified in some of his other works. And he made a number of preparatory sketches for his sculpture. Did he portray Marie as she really was, or was the sculpted figure deliberately given a certain kind of facial appearance? It certainly aroused some strong reactions when it was displayed. Laurens writes about nineteenth century notions of the way in which physical appearance could be related to class, and to propensities for crime and violence. And she adds: "The face of the *Little Dancer* undeniably has some of the features identified by the phrenologists and medical anatomists of the day as typically criminal: a sloping forehead, a protruding jaw, prominent cheekbones, thick hair". It was not a face likely to match up to bourgeois ideas of beauty.

The general response to Degas's sculpture when it was on display in 1881 was largely hostile, and he then kept it in his studio and refused to sell it. It was only after his death that twenty-two bronze casts (the original was wax) were manufactured and circulated to various museums and private collections. Laurens refers to this action as "a quick and dirty decision by Degas's heirs, which showed little respect for the artist's personality and wishes". There was money to be made.

Laurens charts the history of *The Little Dancer* and informs us about nineteenth-century Paris, Degas's personality, some of his contemporaries, and similar matters. What she can't do, of course, is tell us a great deal about Marie. Nor what went on in the studio as she posed and he worked. "Did Degas talk to Marie during the first modelling sessions", Laurens asks, and the simple answer is that we don't know. He presumably had to give her some basic instructions about how to pose, but as he was famously less than sociable he may not have gone any further than that. Laurens is a novelist and likes to suggest what could have taken place.

There were reports that Marie was sometimes seen in the Chat Noir and other Montmartre hang-outs, and she may have been in Belgium at some point in the early 1890s. After that, she disappears, to be remembered only because she was the model for Degas's sculpture.

THE WOMEN WHO INSPIRED LONDON ART: THE AVICO SISTERS AND OTHER MODELS OF THE EARLY 20th CENTURY
By Lucy Merello Peterson
Pen & Sword Books. 180 pages. £25. ISBN 978-1-52672-525-7

LITTLE DANCER AGED FOURTEEN: THE TRUE STORY BEHIND DEGAS'S MASTERPIECE By Camille Laurens
Other Press. 166 pages. $33.95. ISBN 978-1-158051-858-5

LOTTE LASERSTEIN : FACE TO FACE

I'm not sure if Lotte Laserstein's name will bring any nods of recognition from regular visitors to British art galleries. Little of her work appears to be available in this country, apart from some items in the fine collection of German art at Leicester's New Walk Museum and Art Gallery. There may be a variety of reasons for this, but the main one could well be that Laserstein spent the greater part of her adult life in Sweden. She had gone to live there in 1937 when it became obvious that she would be unable to continue functioning as an artist after the Nazis came to power. She didn't stop painting when she settled in Sweden, but her work was little-known outside that country, even after the war ended. One of the essays in this catalogue puts it more bluntly: "Laserstein's name fell into oblivion beyond the borders of Sweden".

Laserstein was born in 1898. Her father died in 1902, and the family eventually moved to Danzig to be near her grandmother. Her aunt, who ran a small drawing and painting school, recognised that the young Lotte had some talents in that line and gave her lessons. In 1912 the family moved to Berlin. In 1918 she graduated from a grammar school for girls, but was unable to enrol at art academies because women were barred from entry. She then enrolled at the university to study philosophy and art history.

The art academies were finally opened to women, and by 1925, Laserstein had become a "master student of Erich Wolfsfeld". His work "bore the strong stamp of nineteenth century realism", and was to have a major influence on her. Some charcoal drawings of male nudes, dating from the mid-1920s, demonstrate how confident and skilled she was with human anatomy. Her ambition was to achieve success as a portraitist, and she frequently used people she knew as models. The oil painting, *My Grandmother*, from 1924 is revealing and effective, as is *Self-Portrait before a Red Curtain* from around the same period.

The 1920s were years when the so-called "New Objectivity" was in vogue, though the term could cover a number of current styles, "encompassing such reticent, austere and rigorously classical pictorial language found in the compositions of Christian Schad and Alexander Kanoldt; the magical realism championed by Franz Radziwill and Georg Schrimpf; but also a kind of exaggerated, caricature-like style that decried the social hardships of the time, as seen in the works of Otto Dix, Jeanne Mammen and Elfriede Lohse-Wächtler".

Did Laserstein's work fit into any of the above-mentioned categories? It doesn't seem so, judging from what is to be seen in the catalogue. It is true that she did sometimes picture aspects of the contemporary world, as in her 1929, *The Motorcycle Driver*, and also *Tennis Player* from the same year. She additionally captured something of the Weimar years when she used Traute Rose as her model: "Her phrenotype corresponded to the ideal of the time. An athletic, androgynous, emancipated young woman with short hair and loose-fitting clothes. Traute embodied the New Woman type propagated in the magazines, films and advertising of the interwar period".

Traute Rose continued to be portrayed in many of Laserstein's works until 1937. The relationship between the artist and the model is largely a matter for speculation. That a degree of intimacy existed between them seems to be evident in certain paintings. Some viewers might want to read a sexual meaning into an exceptionally-fine painting, *In My Studio*, which shows Laserstein at her easel and, in the forefront of the canvas, a naked, provocatively-posed Rose. But a perhaps deeper relationship is caught in the less-dramatic, *I and My Model*, which has Rose looking over Laserstein's shoulder at what she is doing. The hand resting lightly on the painter's shoulder, and the closeness of the two women, gives me a greater sense of their involvement with each other.

There is little doubt that Laserstein was ambitious. She entered competitions, had her work published in magazines, and joined various art associations, though the associations were usually what might be called conventional organisations and not directed towards any kind of radicalism. It's not easy to imagine her associating with the painters who so graphically portrayed the prostitutes, fat businessmen, disabled soldiers, hustlers, and hungry workers, any more than it is to imagine her prowling the night-clubs, bars, and ill-lit back streets in search of subject-matter. There is a painting called *In the Tavern*, which shows a lone, thoughtful-looking woman sitting at a table, though there is nothing to suggest that either her, or her surroundings, are anything less than respectable. But, according to Anne Carola A. Krausse, it was still looked on as "degenerate" by National Socialists because the woman represented "an emancipated, composed and confident New Woman from the public spaces of the Weimar Republic".

Did Laserstein ever reflect the social or political situation in the Germany of the 1920s and 1930s? She must have been well-aware of the rising political tensions, the turmoil on the streets, and other similar factors. What has been described as her "masterpiece", the 1930 group-portrait, *Evening over Potsdam*, might be read as a kind of oblique comment on the generally worsening atmosphere as the effects of the 1929 Wall Street Crash began to be felt world-wide, and the Nazis were increasingly making their presence felt. There is something of a sombre tone pervading the picture. The five people in it do not appear to be in a happy frame of mind. The catalogue refers to "a general disillusion-ment and lack of orientation", and also describes "uncertainty drenched with melancholy". A "pervasive melancholy" may have been a La-serstein characteristic.

A later painting, the 1934 *The Discussion*, might also be interpreted as making a social comment, even if indirectly. Its date could be signifi-cant. By 1934 Hitler was well-entrenched and any form of dissent was being silenced. Are the three men in the picture discussing politics? The painting is dark in tone and the men seem to be in a small room. It's not exactly conspiratorial in its inferences, but it does tend to sug-gest that they've gathered somewhere where they're not likely to be overheard by anyone unsympathetic to what they're talking about. La-serstein, when asked in later years, insisted that the obviously animated discussion was about art, not politics. But it's difficult not to think oth-erwise. Even a discussion about art could have been dangerous as the authorities increasingly denied many painters the right to exhibit or teach, and drew up guidelines covering what could be portrayed and in which manner.

There may be an interesting comparison to be made between *The Dis-cussion* and the 1948 *Evening Conversation*, which has a much more relaxed feeling about it. It's perhaps not surprising when one considers the difference suggested in the two words, "discussion" and "conversa-tion".

Laserstein was affected by the rulings of the new regime. In addition to her activities as an artist she had run a small painting school, but was forced to close it down. She had been baptised as a Christian, but be-cause "both her paternal grandparents and her maternal grandfather" were Jewish, she was categorised as Jewish under the Nazi race laws. By 1937 it was obvious to her that she would no longer be able to func-tion as an artist in Germany and she moved to Sweden. A marriage of convenience to a Swedish citizen was arranged for her so that she ac-quired the right to stay in the country permanently. She made attempts to get her mother and sister out of Germany, but failed. Her mother died in Ravensbrück concentration camp. Her sister survived in hiding throughout the war, often in squalid conditions.

In Sweden Laserstein continued to paint, producing portraits of people in the upper ranks of Swedish society. It is suggested that her work lost something of its "edge" when she left Germany: "Many of the works she created in the Swedish countryside lack the captivating intensity and psychological depth that characterised the personal artistic style of the portraits she painted in Berlin". There are also references to the "increasingly commercial character of her art". Necessity forced her to produce paintings to order. It is noted that in two 1939 paintings, *Woman in a Café* and *Woman in Blue with Veiled Hat,* "her palette lightened, sometimes even to the point of watercolour-like daintiness, presumably in deference to the tastes of her new patrons". One item from her Swedish years that I do like is the 1938 *Self-Portrait at the Easel* in which, as the accompanying caption says, "Laserstein pictures herself proudly at work, firmly determined to continue her interrupted career in new surroundings".

Maureen Ogrocki says that : "So far, 43 solo and 33 group exhibitions by the artist have been documented during her 55 years of emigration". And furthermore, "it is estimated that the artist created 10,000 works during this period, 1,000 of which were probably commissioned portraits". It's impossible to comment on their overall quality as there are only a few examples in the catalogue.

I indicated earlier that one of the reasons for Laserstein being neglected for so many years was the fact that she lived for such a long time in Sweden. There are other possible reasons. When there have been re-evaluations of the work of German artists, often male, active during the years between 1918 and 1933 the emphasis has often been on those who were frequently politically involved, and whose work was included in the infamous "Degenerate Art" exhibition in 1937. Some, at least, of Laserstein's work was condemned by the Nazis, but it wasn't used in the exhibition. This may have inclined researchers in later years to overlook her.

There is, also, the question of her essentially formal, almost traditional methods of composition. She wasn't an experimenter and that, coupled with the fact that her work didn't, on the whole, portray the social and political controversies and concerns of the Weimar years, or incorporate avant-garde ideas about representation, may have limited interest in it. There are a few hints here and there, perhaps, of the role of the New Woman, but even those are restricted to straightforward portraits of her independence and physical appearance rather than her political involvements and activities.

When critics and academics write books, and curators mount exhibitions, they often like to select artists who will illustrate a thesis they have already formulated. Alexander Eiling makes a good point when he says: "Retrospective views of art history all too often mislead us into reading history as a succession of avant-gardes and, in the process, underestimating the art that corresponds more closely to the aesthetic norms of a given era". And so, talented artists like Lotte Laserstein can too easily be written out of history, and their work, with all its virtues, seen as unimportant or minor, at best. We lose a lot when it is.

Lotte Laserstein died in 1993. She once remarked that, despite living in Sweden for so many years, the kindness of the people, and having a successful career there, she never really felt at home in that country.

Lotte Laserstein: Face to Face has been published in conjunction with the exhibition of the same name at the Städel Museum, Frankfurt am Main, 19 September, 2018 to 17 March, 2019, and the Berlinische Galerie, Berlin 5 April, 2019 to 12 August, 2019.

LOTTE LASERSTEIN : FACE TO FACE
Edited by Alexander Eiling and Elena Schroll
Prestel. 192 pages. £45. ISBN 978-3-7913-5823-9

SOPHIE TAEUBER-ARP : TODAY IS TOMORROW

It could be that the name of Sophie Taeuber-Arp will, for most people, immediately bring to mind the antics of the Dadaists at the Cabaret Voltaire in Zurich while much of the rest of Europe involved itself in the madness of the First World War. She had a key role in many of the performances that were staged in the Swiss capital. As Hans Richter put it in his engaging memoir, *Dada: Art and Anti-Art:* "There were abstract drawings, extraordinary Dada heads of painted wood, and tapestries, all of which could hold their own alongside the work of her male colleagues. She was Arp's discovery, just as he was hers, and in their unassuming way they played a part in every Dada event".

There was far more to Sophie Taeuber-Arp than the contributions she made to the Dadaist revolt. Born in 1889 in Davos-Platz, Switzerland, she was already established as an artist and designer in 1916, and was a teacher of textile design at the Trade School in Zurich. Prior to that she had studied in Munich and Hamburg. Her training was mostly in the applied arts, and when she returned to Switzerland in 1914 she worked as a "free artisan". The fact that so much of her work was in the field of the applied arts probably led to her being neglected by critics and art historians. It is pointed out that: "Men were celebrated as avant-garde and pioneers of abstraction in the high arts, while the women were ascribed a supporting role and their occupation with arts-and-crafts was presented as 'traditionally 'feminine' production in most cases".

The largely male-dominated avant-garde was not a place to look for enlightened views about the role of women generally. And the Dada movement was noted for its liking for manifestos, which Taeurber-Arp thought were essentially "a means of self-aggrandisement". She said: "If I were an artist and my name were constantly made to look foolish by such shouting, squealing, howling, scrawling, and printing, then I would stuff mud in the author's mouth and bite his finger so that he couldn't do it anymore. All that matters is the work. Making manifestos like that is more than idiotic". She didn't need to add that manifestos were often mainly a male prerogative.

The evidence offered in *Today is Tomorrow* seems to refute the suggestion that Sophie Taeuber-Arp was, in any way, lacking when it came to being seen as avant-garde and a pioneer in the high arts. Richter said that "she was above all a painter of modern abstracts at a time when abstract painting was still in its infancy". Her contribution to the activities of the Dadaists appears to have been quite significant. With regard to the masks she designed, Hugo Ball said that they "dictated utterly specific, lofty, even nearly mad gestures". She herself took part as a dancer in some of the Dada performances.

The Dada movement eventually and inevitably petered out, with individuals moving into different areas of activity in the 1920s. Taeuber-Arp had continued to earn a living by being steadily employed in aspects of the applied arts. But after 1926 she gave up "making small-format wood objects and beadwork.........She continued to design textile wall hangings, but at the same time, became more occupied with large-format murals and colourful window designs".

It was around this time that the Arps decided to move to France, her earnings from interior design and decorating for private houses probably providing the means to do so.They eventually settled in Meudon, and Taeuber-Arp "concentrated on painting and sculpture, which she shaped abstractly, for the most part". It's said that she "constantly varied new constellations of different basic forms of the circle, square, and rectangle, and experimented with colour". Their home became a centre for gatherings of avant-garde artists and writers. There is an interesting comment by Hans Richter regarding Taeuber-Arp's character: "Sophie was as quiet as we were garrulous, boastful, rowdy and provocative. Even later, when she and Arp were living in their little house in Meudon, her voice was scarcely ever heard. It was Arp who asked their guests to 'come upstairs` and see Sophie's work. Left to herself, she would never have shown it to anyone". Other visitors to Meudon are quoted as saying that they "recalled her more as a host and housewife and less as an artist".

Despite the suggestion of a reluctance to promote herself, there is plenty of evidence to show that Taeuber-Arp was "internationally well-known, that she corresponded in several languages without any difficulty, held the reins and ignited the spark for quite a few projects, whether her own or those of others, and accompanied them persistently. She was a networker and a doer, not primarily a dreamer – or at least one who was quite capable of differentiating between dream and reality".

She became active in avant-garde groups in France and joined the Cercle et Carré, which focused on non-figurative art, and the Abstraction Création movement. Among her friends were Sonia and Robert Delaunay, Jean Miró, and Wassily Kandinsky. She also helped found, and became editor of, the Constructivist review, *Plastique,* described as "an international forum for abstract-concrete art". Any publication of this kind requires a benefactor to give it some financial security, and the American collector and painter, A.E. Gallatin, provided the necessary support in this case.

A reproduction of the front cover of the fifth issue lists Hans Arp, Leonora Carrington, Marcel Duchamp, Paul Eluard, and Max Ernst as among the contributors. Earlier issues had illustrations by Malevich, El Lissitzky, and others. As it happened, the fifth issue, published in 1939, was the last one. Taeuber-Arp had wanted it to continue, but with the situation in Europe it became impractical. The Arps soon had to abandon their house in Meudon and flee into Vichy France as the Nazis occupied the rest of the country. A little later they moved to Switzerland, and it was while they were living there that Taeuber-Arp died in a tragic accident in 1943. She was asleep in a room which had a faulty stove and was poisoned by carbon monoxide fumes.

It's obvious from this profusely illustrated book that Taeuber-Arp was a multi-talented artist. While allowing for the fact of the prejudice that existed, and perhaps still does, against applied art when compared to so-called fine art, it may have been that not enough serious consideration was given to her work because she functioned in so many different fields. It seems to be true, too, that Hans Arp was less than positive in his later appreciations of the work she did: "Hans Arp, in poems and everyday statements, presents Taeuber-Arp to posterity as a dreamer and an artist who primarily works intuitively". With regard to her activities in the applied arts, he additionally appeared to be concerned "that the inclusion of these practical activities would lead to a devaluation of Sophie Taeuber's artistic achievement, placing it on a par with arts and crafts".

It's also worth noting that: "The authors of the first and to-date only catalogue raisonné on Sophie Taeuber's oeuvre, although well-intentioned and based on decisions made in a particular era, already deliberately ignored works and work genres, or did not recognise them as part of a body of work".

Sophie Taeuber-Arp: Today is Tomorrow is a splendidly informative book in that it illustrates the full range of her activities. The arguments about the supposed differences between applied and fine arts will no doubt continue. And some people will always look at a lot of geometric abstraction paintings and see them as having more to do with design and decoration than with "pure" art. Their opinions might be reinforced by a casual comparison of certain of her paintings and some of her textile designs. It could also be true that the old cliché about someone being a "Jack of all trades, but master of none" might be called into play when Taeuber-Arp's work is discussed. She involved herself "in the areas of design, painting, textiles, drawing, sculpture, clothing, architecture, theatre, and dance". Can anyone be so equally talented in such a wide range of activities? She may well have excelled more in one or other of her involvements, but the evidence provided by the book seems to show that she maintained a high standard in all of them.

This is a second, revised edition of a publication originally designed to accompany the exhibition, *Sophie Taeuber-Arp: Today is Tomorrow* at the Aargauer Kunsthaus Aarau, 23rd August, 2014, to 16th November, 2014, and Kunsthalle Bielefeld 12th December, 2014 to 15th March, 2015.

SOPHIE TAEUBER-ARP : TODAY IS TOMORROW
Edited by Thomas Schmutz, Scheidegger and Spiess (distributed by the University of Chicago Press). 288 pages. $65.
ISBN 978-3-85881-757-0

INTO THE NIGHT: CABARETS AND CLUBS IN MODERN ART

There is something enticing about the idea of cabarets, clubs, and cafés where writers, artists, musicians, comedians, and a variety of entertainers got together in Paris, Berlin, New York, and various cities to perform, talk, drink, and meet others with similar tastes and interests. Cities is the key word, perhaps, because it needs a concentration of the people concerned in sufficient numbers to make up a regular clientele with enough money to enable the cabaret or whatever to survive. It has to be said that many clubs, cafés and cabarets didn't survive on a permanent basis. If they did it was sometimes at the expense of losing their original character and becoming merely fashionable places where the well-to-do gathered to see and be seen.

It is a fact that, in any case, most cabarets and clubs weren't opened with the intention of providing homes where groups of impoverished bohemians could congregate, keep warm, and while away the day for the price, if they had it, of a single coffee. There are stories of legendary café owners who had a fondness for struggling painters and poets and would accept a painting or a poem as payment for a drink or even a meal, but they were few and far between, and most preferred people who settled their bills with cash.

The strictures about attracting people who had money can be particularly applied to cabarets. Some clubs and cafés could, perhaps, get by with a lesser income, and cafés could pick up passing trade. But a cabaret often had to hire performers, unless it could draw on the voluntary talents of some of its customers, and also needed to provide suitable decorations and fittings. Again, these might well have been designed by artists and architects who were commissioned to carry out the necessary work, or were known to the owners of the cabarets involved.

There is an informative chapter on the Cave of the Golden Calf (also known as the Cabaret Theatre Club) which operated in London between 1912 and 1914. The iconoclastic artist and writer, Wyndham Lewis, was involved in decorating the premises, as were painters like Spencer Gore and Charles Ginner, then active as members of the Camden Town Group. Some of the murals appear to have depicted "exotic landscapes and frenzied dance". The term "Futurist" was often used to refer to them, but as Jo Cottrell's excellent essay points out, it was, for the press, a "catch-all label for artists experimenting with the avant-garde". A real Futurist, the redoubtable Filippo Tommaso Marinetti, did perform at the Cabaret. The person behind the establishment was

Frida Strindberg, one-time wife of the playwright August Strindberg, and the woman "once described as one of the inspirations behind Strindberg's tirades against women in general".

The problems of establishing any kind of unusual activity in Britain, especially in the wake of the scandal surrounding Oscar Wilde, when "outside influences" were detected at work, were highlighted by newspaper reports "revealing an underlying English reticence towards the foreign". These reports attracted the wrong kind of attention, with the result that "there was soon a notable shift in the make-up of the club's clientele". Those "it was intended to attract could no longer afford to keep it up. The vulgar stockbroking element soon preponderated". There were police raids. ostensibly connected with the licensing laws, and financial problems, and the club closed in 1914. Frida Strindberg disappeared to America, and it's said that "many of the artists were never paid".

Financial problems also brought an end to the Cabaret Fledermaus in Vienna, though it did stay in business from 1907 to 1913. Lavishly decorated, it was created by a group of artists and designers, and set out "to stimulate the senses through a synthesis of modern architecture, painting, poetry, music and dance". It had a "spectacular bar" and "meticulous attention was paid to everything from the ashtrays and stationery to the silver pins worn by the waiting staff". It's obvious that, whatever ideals there were about providing space for "ease, art and culture", it would be necessary to draw in a well-heeled clientele. But it did also employ the talents of a wide range of writers, musicians, and artists, including Klimt and Kokoschka. It is suggested that some of the performances had aspects that were akin to what was known as Dada a few years later.

The ambitions of those who opened a club or cabaret often did outstrip the realities of making it pay. L'Aubette in Strasbourg was designed to incorporate "a cinema-cum-dancehall, a tea-room, a cabaret and a billiards room, as well as bars, restaurants and ballrooms". Sophie Taueber-Arp, Hans Arp, and Theo van Doesburg (from the Dutch De Stijl movement) were all involved with creating what is described as "a dynamic and interdisciplinary experience under one roof", which sounds horribly like the kind of description used to extol the virtues of contemporary shopping centres incorporating cinemas, shops, bars, restaurants and anything else designed to pull in crowds. It's interesting to note that the public did not appear to take kindly to the interior decorating: "Although a landmark in architectural history, the radical designs of L'Aubette were not well received by its local public. After less than a decade, the interiors were altered".

Despite the involvement of Sophie Taueber-Arp, Theo van Doesburg, and Hans Arp, it could be that the L'Aubette project was never going to be suited to a link between artistic invention and creation, and popular appeal. I always nurse an underlying notion that all such experiments are more likely to take place in smaller locations and will incorporate fewer people than are likely to be found in a large complex. The fascinating (because it largely charts unknown territory for most people in Britain) look at the activities of writers and artists in Mexico City in the Twenties and Thirties seems more relevant. And it's interesting to note that they clustered around cafés and not cabarets. A café suggests a more-open area (the description of a painting reproduced in the catalogue mentions the café requisites – "coffee cups, a book, and the smoke that emanates from the pipe in the artist's self-portrait"), whereas cabarets and clubs seem to imply membership, or at least entrance limited by money, dress, or other signs of affluence, and often class.

The Café de Nadie "provided a gathering place for the writers and artists central to the avant-garde movement Estridentismo (Stridentism)" which "set out to overturn artistic conventions, developing forms rooted in popular tradition as well as the modern industrial city". They had a slogan – "Chopin to the electric chair", which was in the same spirit as the Italian Futurists who made loud pronouncements about rejecting the past and burning down libraries and museums. Mexico had undergone an extremely violent revolution between 1910 and 1920, and the mood of young writers and artists reflected this fact. A later, more socialist-inclined group, called itself ¡30-30! (a "popular rifle cartridge") and carried out its events in a large tent named The Carpa Amaro, "a travelling tent used for low-cost popular entertainment". In this way they could take their exhibitions and performances to working-class and peasant audiences outside Mexico City. Their activities were frowned on by conservative elements in the government, and they were harassed by the authorities, and their publications censored.

I mentioned the Futurists earlier, and their presence in Rome in 1921 and 1922 centred around the Bal Tic Tac and the Cabaret del Diavolo. The artist Giacomo Balla was the designer for the Bal Tic Tac and his intention was to "reflect the speed of the machine age". It was "one of the earliest places in Rome to champion jazz music and became a hit with fashionable society". Another Futurist, Fortunato Depero, designed the Cabaret del Diavolo, and used Dante's poem, *The Divine Comedy*, as his inspiration. It's easy to see how it would appeal to the wealthy and those who wanted to appear up-to-date and be seen in the right places: "The night-club was constantly packed with members of the Roman and international nobility, as confirmed by reports and reviews".

If this was the case, why did both establishments have only a limited lifespan? It would appear that the Cabaret del Diavolo lost its impetus when its initial aim to function primarily as a cabaret was changed. But I wonder if the rise of Fascism in Italy in the 1920s may have had an effect? Revolutionary movements, whether of the Left or the Right, tend to take exception to anything they can't easily control. It's true that some artists and writers among the Futurists did ally themselves with Fascism, at least in its early days, but even so, art which challenged Mussolini's taste for classical sculpture, and poems which didn't exalt the glory that was Rome, would not have been popular. And policemen are always suspicious of places where people get together to be entertained in unorthodox ways or take an interest in anything outside a clearly-defined and widely-understood framework.

This was certainly true of post-revolutionary Russia as the Bolsheviks tightened their grip on power, and began to impose controls on the subjects writers could write about and painters paint. The early days of the 1917 Revolution had seemed to promise opportunities for freedom and experimentation. but those hopes would soon be shattered as Civil War and shortages descended on the country. The poets and painters, and their audiences, who met at the Café Pittoresque in Moscow in 1918/19, huddled in their hats and coats in the unheated premises and dined on "sour milk and little pies of frost-damaged potatoes".

Despite the adverse conditions, poets like Vladimir Mayakovsky (active at the Stray Dog Cabaret in St. Petersburg before the First World War), Vasily Kamensky, and David Burliuk performed their Futurist-influenced works ("Futurism was the aesthetic equivalent of social-anarchism", according to them), and a multitude of artists, including Aleksandr Rodchenko, Vladimir Tatlin, and Alexey Rybnikov, participated in providing lighting effects, interior decorations, paintings, and sculptures. For a time, at least, it must have seemed that some of the dreams about what a revolution would bring might be changing to reality.

The writing was on the wall, however, and "the café's private ownership – and its genteel Francophile name – evidently no longer seemed appropriate for the fervid post-revolutionary climate". The People's Commissariat for Enlightenment took control of the Café Pittoresque, renamed it The Red Cockerel, and gave its programme a more-revolutionary flavour. It closed in 1919, "perhaps due to ongoing polit-ical and economic instability". I have a feeling that the Bolsheviks simply didn't want something that they couldn't strictly control to con-tinue to exist. The focus on Futurism and its relation to "social-anarchism" might have had a role to play in the decision to close The Red Cockerel. Communists had always hated anarchists even more than they despised the bourgeoisie.

Harlem, New York, in the 1920s and 1930s, was a mecca for white people wanting to slum it, and establishments like the famous Cotton Club and Connie's Inn didn't even allow blacks in, other than as enter-tainers. Duke Ellington's orchestra was a fixture at the Cotton Club and his appearances there, and on live radio broadcasts from the club, helped establish his reputation. The performances at the Cotton Club were designed to highlight the exotic and erotic nature of black music and dancing, and so titillate the affluent white audience. But as Amy Helen Kirschke's essay about Harlem makes clear, a lot of the more-adventurous activity could be found in small clubs and at rent parties, those gatherings in private houses and apartments where the entrance fee went towards helping the tenants pay their rent.

There is a useful map showing all or most of the cabarets and clubs in Harlem, but it's dated 1934. It would have been useful to push the nar-rative into the early-1940s and include Minton's Playhouse and Clark Monroe's Uptown House, both of which provided space for young black musicians, who saw themselves as innovators and not entertain-ers, to experiment and develop a form of jazz, bebop, which influenced many black and white jazzmen. Artists and writers also fell under its spell in the 1940s. The painter Larry Rivers played saxophone with big-bands before turning to art. The Beat novelist, Jack Kerouac, wrote en-thusiastically about bop, as did his fellow-novelist, John Clellon Holmes. A poet like Robert Creeley picked up on the rhythms of bebop and the language of its practitioners and their followers. The black po-ets, Leroi Jones and Ted Joans, grew up with bebop and later wrote extensively about the new jazz.

I suppose that, in wide terms, the cabarets and clubs that may be best-known to non-specialists were those in Paris during the Belle Époque, and in Berlin during the Weimar years. It might be possible to also in-clude the Cabaret Voltaire in Zurich in 1916 where the Dadaists cavort-ed as the "civilised" nations of Europe competed in seeing how many people they could kill in various ways.

The story of how Tristan Tzara, Marcel Janco (both with a background in the cafés and cabarets of Bucharest), Hugo Ball, Emmy Hennings, and some others, came together in the neutral city of Zurich and opened the now-legendary Cabaret Voltaire is so well known that it raises the question of whether or not there really is anything new to add to it? However, Raimund Meyer does a first-rate job in summarising the birth, life, and death of the original Cabaret Voltaire, and in describing how it operated and the poets and artists performed. It isn't easy to rec-reate live performances from the past, and it's sometimes best left to the imagination rather than try to. What is clear is that Dada quickly spread to other countries, especially Germany, where it became more politically militant, and France, where it later vied with surrealism for the attention of would-be radical artists and writers.

The cabaret tradition in Berlin has some popular appeal, largely thanks to the novels of Christopher Isherwood, and the film, *Cabaret*, adapted from his *Goodbye to Berlin*. I've never been able to shrug off the feel-ing that, in some ways, both book and especially the film give a some-what misleading picture of what it was like to be in Berlin in the Wei-mar period, 1918-1933. Certainly, a thoroughly-realistic picture might have to show a more-balanced account of the times, and take in the hunger and unemployment, the violence, the way in which ordinary people lived their lives and what they thought about the general situa-tion. Not every Berliner frequented the cabarets and clubs. They per-haps seem attractive to audiences now, who imagine an openness about sexuality and personal inclinations that was widespread. But on the streets there were battles between left and right forces, and only one could eventually come to power. The Nazis did and quickly clamped down on anyone not fitting to their ideas of clean living and conformity to recognised social norms. No doubt the communists would have done exactly the same if they had seized control of the country.

But what I've said doesn't alter the fact that, for a time, the cabarets and clubs and cafés did exist, and reading about them, and looking at the paintings by artists like Otto Dix and George Grosz, has its values. Both Dix and Grosz portrayed the syphilitic prostitutes, the maimed and disabled soldiers, the greedy businessmen, and the Nazis who, in the early-1920s, could still be mocked and caricatured. But they would exact their revenge in due course.

Probably even more than Weimar Germany, the Paris cabarets, clubs, and cafés of the Belle Époque, the period between 1871 and the start of the First World War in 1914, might be the most familiar on a popular level. Books, posters, postcards, calendars, and films celebrate its fa-bled celebrities, like Toulouse-Lautrec, and the places where they congregated. Who hasn't seen the 1953 film, *Moulin Rouge*, with its flamboyant Can-Can dancers?

The Chat Noir in Montmartre was the most famous of the Parisian cabarets and offered a programme of "poetry performances, improvised monologues, satirical songs and debates on contemporary politics". There were others, frequented by painters like Monet, Degas, Renoir, and Manet. It wasn't that cafés attracting bohemians were anything new in Paris. The poets and painters immortalised in Henry Murger's *Scènes de la vie de Bohème* patronised the Café Momus back in the 1840s.

But it was only later in the century that the cabaret really took off in terms of appealing to a wide audience, albeit that its members tended to be from the middle and upper-classes. There is a story about Rodolphe Salis, founder of the Chat Noir, being approached by the actress Louise France, who at the time was struggling to earn a living. Her hair was dishevelled, she wasn't wearing a hat (women were usually expected to when out-of-doors), and her clothes were shabby. She asked if she could read something at the evening poetry recital, but Salis responded negatively: "I don't know you, go sing in the street if that pleases you, but not here". Luckily, someone interceded on her behalf, and she later regularly led the poetry recitals, and helped out with the "shadow theatre shows". It could be that Salis was simply behaving in a dismissive way towards yet another unknown wanting to perform. But the tone of his response seems to indicate that he was concerned to maintain a certain standard with regard to dress and appearance, which might suggest how he viewed the performers and their respectable audience.

Does a cabaret and club culture still exist in the way that it did in those locations and times I've referred to? There are chapters on the 1960s Mbari Artists and Writers Club in Ibadan, Nigeria, and the Rasht 29 private members' club in Tehran which ran from 1966 to 1969. It's unlikely that anything similar to the latter now exists in Iran. Like Russia in the 1920s and Germany in the 1930s, an authoritarian regime has clamped down on freedom of expression and the open exchange of ideas.

This splendid book, well-written, packed with information, and with dozens of illustrations that include paintings, photos, posters, leaflets, poems, and many other items, accompanies an exhibition at the Barbican. As well as the individual sections where the paintings are displayed, there are a number of rooms where recreations of some parts of specific locations have been created. Do they work? I'm not sure, and I found that I got more from looking at what was on the walls, or in the display cases, in the main part of the exhibition. A leap of the imagination may be all that is required to give one an impression of what it was like being present in Paris or Berlin or Zurich. But it isn't truly possible to recreate the atmosphere of the past, no matter how much we try to physically re-enact it. But this is a minor criticism and the exhibition, taken as a whole, is visually exciting and intellectually stimulating.

INTO THE NIGHT: CABARETS AND CLUBS IN MODERN ART
Edited by Florence Ostende with Lotte Johnson. Prestel & Barbican Art Gallery. 344 pages. £45. ISBN 978-3-7913-5888-8

INTO THE NIGHT: CABARETS AND CLUBS IN MODERN ART
An exhibition at The Barbican, London, 4th October, 2019 to 19th January, 2020

CREATIVE GATHERINGS : MEETING PLACES OF MODERNISM

There is the idea of the lone genius, the writer or painter shut away some-where creating masterpieces. And it's true that the actual job of creation can be a lonely process. The creator is on his or her own as they write the poem or paint the picture. But before that something has fed into their need to put the words on paper and the paint on canvas, and it might well have come from having met with others who have stimulated their imaginations sufficiently for them to want to create a work of art. Poets and painters often like to exchange ideas, argue about them, and even fall out. They also like to gossip and compete. Or, perhaps, just live it up a little with like-minded people.

There probably are, and always have been, little gatherings of writers and artists in all kinds of places, sometimes on a temporary basis, sometimes more permanently. As anyone who has done the poetry-reading circuit will know, most towns and cities have their local groups who get together on a formal or informal basis to listen to each other's poems and pass on infor-mation about possible outlets for their work. And sometimes these groups will start a magazine or compile an anthology. Such publications may not circulate much beyond the locality of their contributors, but they are, none-theless, a contribution to the creative spirit. They often provide a beginning for someone who may well move on to bigger things. And if they don't, people enjoy themselves, anyway, and do sometimes produce minor works of art that can entertain and educate in their own manner. "O, little lost bohemias of the suburbs", says a line in a poem by Donald Justice.

It would be easy, but wrong, to dismiss many of these small groups as largely irrelevant in the larger scheme of things, and they can occasionally have an exaggerated idea of their own importance. They perhaps pale into insignificance in comparison with more-celebrated collections of creative types encountering each other in more-famous locales. The cafés of Paris, the pubs of Soho, bars and bookshops in numerous cities, private houses where patrons held soirées. They're too numerous to list. And then there are artists' colonies and the like where sometimes-clashing egos are thrown together.

Mary Ann Caws doesn't claim to be presenting a survey of all the places where "creative gatherings" happened. Her selection of cafés and other favoured spots where icons of modernism were to be found at one time or another largely focuses on a few well-known areas, often those which

Caws herself has visited. It's worth mentioning at this point that she was lucky enough to have had a grandmother, Margaret Walthour Lippitt, who was an artist and had visited or stayed in artists' colonies in the United States and Germany. As a little girl, Caws listened to her grandmother reminiscing about the places she'd been and the talented people she'd met. It's easy to see that an interest in them rubbed off on Caws.

Paris, and France generally, inevitably play a large part in *Creative Gatherings*. Barbizon, south of Paris, was the first artists' colony, attracting painters and others because of its surroundings, which could still seem quite wild and even dangerous, and the availability of cheap lodgings. The invention of paint tubes around 1840 had made it easier for painters to work *en plein air* as it did away with the need to carry paint in bottles and animal bladders. It was also around this time that artists were rebelling against academic restrictions on subject-matter. It's worth noting, as Caws does, that four key painters linked to Barbizon – Rousseau, Millet, Daubigny, Corot – had either failed their Académie des Beaux Arts exams or not bothered to take them. And they had all been impressed with work by Constable, Bonington, and Turner that was exhibited at the Paris Salon.

If painters congregated in Barbizon early in the nineteenth century (Caws says its importance had lessened considerably by 1875), they came together, at least as young students, at the Académie Julian in Paris later in that era. The list of artists linked to it is extensive and includes Maurice Denis, Pierre Bonnard, Henri Matisse, and André Derain, to mention just a few of the better-known names. I think anyone familiar with histories of Parisian bohemia, or memoirs of time spent in the City of Light, will have come across references to the Académie Julian more than once. Recent encounters for me were when reading William Dean Howells' *The Coast of Bohemia,* and Robert W. Chambers *In the Quarter,* in which some of the characters, American artists, have been to Paris. Caws mentions that her grandmother studied at the Académie Julian. It's obvious that throwing students of varying backgrounds and temperaments together can result in exchanges of ideas which are sometimes useful and sometimes simply aggressive. Whatever, the point is that places like the Académie Julian brought artists into contact and probably led to the development of not just individual careers but also the founding of art movements like the Nabis and the Fauves.

Outside Paris, Pont-Aven and Le Pouldu attracted painters from several countries. Gauguin played a significant part in activities there before he decided to move to Tahiti. Caws says that it was a group of American art students arriving in 1866 that got the idea of an artists' colony going in

Pont-Aven. They were soon joined by more Americans, a couple of Englishmen and two Frenchmen. By 1880 or so its fame had spread "far and wide" and many other painters poured in. There is a photo (undated but presumably from the late-1880s or thereabouts) which shows Gauguin and a group of fellow-artists in Pont Aven, all of them looking suitably bohemian. Ideas and opinions were undoubtedly thrown around, though it wasn't all work and intense conversation, and people had fun, probably drank too much on occasions, and when they could, paid their bills with a painting or two. What is noticeable in the photo is the lack of women, other than what are obviously some locals standing in the background. But where were the women painters?

Women perhaps felt more secure in the cities, at least in certain parts of them, though they were not necessarily always to the fore when the surrealists were being photographed. Caws' engaging chapters on "Surrealist Cafés in Paris" and "The rue Blomet, Paris and Surrealism" do draw attention to Paul Éluard's unnamed wife, Simone Collinet, Joyce Mansour, Méret Oppenheim, and a couple more. There is a photo of half-a-dozen male surrealists listening to a reading by the poet, Giséle Prassinos. And another of Pablo and Magali Gargallo in their room in rue Blomet. It and they made for a seductive picture of a contemporary bohemian couple.

Still, there are no women mentioned when Caws passes through the small coastal town of Collioure in the south of France. Matisse, Signac, Derain, Henri-Edmond Cross, Albert Marquet, they're all there, but no women painters. The Fauves do seem to have been heavily male-oriented. And only a few women occur in the chapter on Mallarmé's soirées in Paris and Valvins. Saint-Pol-Roux, Verlaine, Auguste Villiers de l'Isle-Adam, whose 1890 novel, *Axel,* set the style for literary symbolism, take precedence in the list of notables present.

I don't want to limit Caws to Paris, or France in general, and she pays a visit to Barcelona, where Picasso frequented Els Quatre Gats and associated with Spanish artists such as Ramon Casas and Santiago Rusinol. They, like Picasso, had lived in Montmartre, and Casas produced what is one of my favourite paintings, "Madeleine", or as it's sometimes called "Au de la Galette", which shows a young woman seated at a table in the establishment concerned (a favoured spot for painters and their friends), a glass of wine on the table in front of her, and her gaze directed somewhere beyond the viewer. It seems to me to be a wonderful visual expression of bohemia, and I was thrilled when I saw the original in the large exhibition about bohemianism at the Grand Palais in Paris in 2012.

England gets a look in when Caws goes to Charleston Farmhouse in East Sussex, and St Ives in Cornwall. It may be because I live in England that I sometimes think there is far too much written about the Bloomsbury crowd and their various bed-hopping arrangements. But I know that many people find them fascinating, and I can see how they fit into Caws' choice of "creative gatherings". On the whole, though, I prefer to read about St Ives and the artists who resided there. She focuses on the period associated with modernism, which essentially got underway with Ben Nicholson and Barbara Hepworth moving there when the Second World War started. The town became renowned in the 1950s for its concentration of painters like Terry Frost, Bryan Wynter, Patrick Heron, Peter Lanyon, and others. But it had long been an artists' colony, with roots stretching back to the late-nineteenth century. A now-forgotten 1904 novel, *Portalone* by Ranger Gull, offers a picture of St Ives in the early days, and a later novel, *The Dark Monarch* by Sven Berlin, looks at the 1950s, though it had to be withdrawn when it was originally published in the early-1960s because of threatened libel action by several residents of St Ives. It has been safely published in more-recent years. It perhaps illustrates that "creative gatherings" often have their frictions and fallings-out.

St Ives by the sea had its equivalents in the United States, especially at Provincetown and Old Lyme in Connecticut. Caws focuses mostly on Hans Hofmann in Provincetown, though the town was notable for attracting artists generally. But Hofmann's classes were popular, and Caws lists Helen Frankenthaler, Allan Kaprow, Lee Krasner, Larry Rivers, Milton Resnick, and Louise Nevelson as among his students at one time or another. Seeing Resnick's name reminded me that I have a curious little book, *Up and Down: poems by Milton Resnick*, published in New York in 1961 (though printed in Paris), and inside which someone had slipped a cutting showing a meeting of The Club, the gathering of abstract expressionists where they tossed around arguments and ideas. Resnick can be seen in the photo. They also met up with each other in the Cedar Tavern.

As for Old Lyme, Caws says: "At Florence Griswold House, in Old Lyme, Connecticut, and dating from 1900, the origins of America's first art colony are clearly in evidence". The Cos Cob art colony was nearby, and "in 1892 John Henry Twachtman and J.Alden Weir taught summer classes for their students from the Arts Student League in New York". Other painters, like Theodore Robinson and Childe Hassam, soon followed, and Holley House in Cos Cob was a meeting place for them, along with the Florence Griswold House in Old Lyme. Impressionism was a major factor among the artists, and it's significant that several of them had spent time in France, and especially Giverny, where Monet lived. Until a few years ago, the gallery in Giverny was run by the Terra Foundation and had regular exhibitions of American artists who had lived and painted in France. I was fortunate enough to have seen several of them, and so become familiar with painters who, when they returned to their home country, were often involved with artists' colonies.

France, England, America, and there is Germany, where Worpswede, in-land from Bremerhaven, "was both modern enough and conventional enough to be included in the movement of the Secession, from the Munich Secession in 1892, the Vienna Secession in 1897, and Berlin subsequent-ly". If a name is known in connection with Worpswede, it's probably the painter Paula Modersohn-Becker, interest in whom "has blossomed into a full-fledged cottage industry", according to Caws. The poet, Rainer Maria Rilke also had links to Worpswede, though his "not drinking and his sort of prudery" didn't go down well with local artists. It might be of interest to have a look at Sue Hubbard's novel, *Girl in White*, which is about an "intense relationship" between Modersohn-Becker and Rilke.

Florence (Henry James, Edith Wharton, Thomas Mann, John Singer Sargent) and Venice (John Ruskin, James Abbott McNeill Whistler, Robert Browning, Edgar Degas) are visited by Caws. What I like about her writing is that she has asides offering useful information about novels and other material of relevance. In connection with Degas, she mentions B.A. Shapiro's *Art Forger: A Novel*, which touches on Degas and the 1990 theft of works of art from the Isabella Stewart Gardner Museum in Boston. And William Dean Howells' *Indian Summer* for its fictional portraits of Frank Duveneck and Elizabeth Boott, and the American artists, John Henry Twachtman and Julius Rolshoven. I find myself keen to read the books she recommends.

Prague (Kafka, but also some Czech Surrealist poets and painters) is a fascinating city in many ways, though it seemed somewhat grey and dull when I visited it. But the communists were still in control, goods of most kinds were clearly in short supply, and I doubt that the Party would have approved of revivals of surrealism, or most other deviations from social realism. I haven't been back since, but I know from the publications of Twisted Spoon Press that many "forgotten" Czech writers are being rediscovered and translated into English. Paul Leppin's *Blaugast* and *Severin's Journey into the Dark,* and Vitězslav Nezval's *Valerie and Her Week of Wonders,* deserve to be better-known in Britain.

Zurich seemed livelier when I went there, and I was invited to give a couple of readings in the city, as well as associate with some German and

Swiss poets and artists. I have to admit that my knowledge of it as a centre for modernism was largely limited to what the Dadaists had got up to at the Cabaret Voltaire around 1916 and thereafter. Tristan Tzara, Marcel Janko, Emmy Hennings, Hugo Ball, were present, bouncing ideas off each other. It's of value to note that Tzara and Janko had arrived in Zurich from Bucharest, and that there was a tradition of provocative cabaret performances in that city (see Tom Sandqvist's *Dada East: The Romanians of Cabaret Voltaire*, MIT Press, 2006). Dada didn't just spring from nowhere. Zurich had also seen James Joyce in residence. My own experiences didn't involve any Dadaistic acts. I saw an Andy Warhol exhibition, and another smaller one of the work of Carl Meffert/Clément Moreau, a German artist and book illustrator who had left when the Nazis came to power. I also sat in a bar with the artist, Berndt Hoppner, and talked and joked about little magazines and their peculiarities. He sketched out a cover for a publication we would edit and call *The Procrastinator*. It would, of course, always be promised but never appear.

A publication that did appear was the *Black Mountain Review,* seven issues in all, in which, according to Caws, "only some of the contributors had any connection with the college". I've only got one issue, the seventh, and it was published in 1957, the year when the college closed. It reflected the arrival of the Beats on the American literary scene, with poems and prose from Kerouac, Ginsberg, Burroughs, Gary Snyder, and Michael McClure, none of them ever students at Black Mountain. But, interestingly, there were contributions from Alfred Kreymborg, whose autobiography, *Troubadour*, is a mine of information about previous bohemias and their meeting places, and Sherry Mangan, a poet, journalist, and political activist with Trotskyist connections. His poems appeared in avant-garde magazines like *larus* and *Pagany*. In the 1950s he was investigated by the House Un-American Activities Committee. He died in Rome in 1961 "in penurious conditions and almost unsung". There was a kind of continuity with earlier aspects of modernism implied by the inclusion of work by Kreymborg and Mangan.

The college had been stumbling towards closure all through the 1950s, but it's more than likely that it's this period it is often remembered for, despite having been open since 1936 with quite a distinguished cast of staff and students. Josef Albers, Ben Shahn, Robert Motherwell, Elaine de Kooning, and Buckminster Fuller are just a few names pulled from a long list that Caws provides. In the 1950s, with Charles Olson in charge, the emphasis was often on poetry, and Paul Blackburn, Robert Creeley, Robert Duncan, Denise Levertov, and Louis Zukofsky put in appearances. The main point to remember is that Black Mountain was a place for modernists of every persuasion (art, dance, music) to come together and compare notes about their respective activities. They didn't always get on and, among others, the novelist Edward Dahlberg and the critic Alfred Kazin tended towards negative views of the place and its people.

When Caws closes her brisk survey in Saint Germain-des-Prés and Montparnasse the names roll off the pages in profusion. There were, and are, so many meeting places – the Café de Flore, Les Deux Magots, the Café Cyrano, La Rotonde, Le Dome, La Coupole – each with its cluster of poets, painters, models, journalists, and others, and with famous names tied to them. Sartre, Beauvoir, Breton, Soupault, Cendrars, Reverdy – there are just too many to catalogue, and we haven't even returned to the 1920s when Hemingway, Robert McAlmon and a whole gang of American expatriates made Montparnasse their home, at least until the money began to dry up, and they drifted back to the United States and, in some cases, joined the Communist Party. Which makes me wonder where the left-wing writers and painters met in New York? Something like Jerre Mangione's *An Ethnics at Large* paints a lively picture of struggling writers meeting up here and there during the Depression. The WPA (Works Progress Administration) became something of a focal point for dissident painters and poets to compare notes. They also met at the John Reed clubs, at least until the Communist Party dissolved them in 1936.

It would be possible to expand Caws' selection of "Meeting Places of Modernism" to take in many more artists' colonies, bars, specific areas of cities, and private houses. During the late nineteenth century artists' colonies could be found almost everywhere. Staithes on the east coast of England, where Laura Knight and her husband, Harold, lived for a time. The Hague in Holland which gave its name to a whole school of Dutch painting. Concarneau in Brittany where the American artist, Edward Simmons, painted during his expatriate days, and Blanche Willis Howard used it as the location for her 1884 novel, *Guenn; A Wave on the Breton Coast*, about the supposed relationship between a painter and the local girl he hires as a model. And many others scattered around Scandinavia. As for the watering holes favoured by writers and artists, London's Soho saw Francis Bacon, Lucien Freud, John Minton, and the "Two Roberts," Colquhoun and MacBryde, falling into pubs like "The French" and the famous (infamous?) Colony Club, and falling out with each other. The fine short-story writer and memoirist, Julian Maclaren-Ross, was often around to observe the goings-on among the poets and painters.

It's an almost-endless subject. What about bookshops? Shakespeare and Company in Paris in the 1920s, and in its later version when George

Whitman was there. City Lights in San Francisco, the Gotham Book Mart in New York, Indica and Compendium in London in the 1960s and 1970s when there was a boom in little magazine and small-press publishing. I can recall bumping into poets and editors in bookshops and adjourning to a nearby pub where the talk was lively and sometimes resulted in my being invited to contribute poems or a review or article to a new magazine, or give a reading at some future date.

None of that in any way detracts from my appreciation of Caws' informative and easy-to-read account. She has produced a well-written (and well-illustrated) book which neatly combines the histories of the meeting places with comments on many of the characters to be found there, and reflections on her own more-recent visits to them. She's not just an acknowledged authority on various aspects of the modernist movement, she's also someone who likes good food (see her *The Modern Art Cookbook)* and wine. With the Barbican in London about to mount an exhibition called *Into the Night: Cabarets and Clubs in Modern Art* later this year, her book has arrived at an opportune moment.

CREATIVE GATHERINGS : MEETING PLACES OF MODERNISM
By Mary Ann Caws
Reaktion Books. 352 pages. £25. ISBN 978-1-78914-055-2

ARTIST QUARTER: MODIGLIANI, MONTMARTRE & MONTPARNASSE

It's useful to spend a little time looking at the origins of this book. It was first published by Faber in 1941, and the author's name, Charles Douglas, was made up from the names of the two writers involved, Charles Beadle and Douglas Goldring. The latter may be reasonably-familiar to anyone interested in English literature in the period between the two World Wars. He was a prolific novelist, poet, and critic, and his memoir, *The Nineteen Twenties*, is still worth reading.

But who was Charles Beadle? There isn't a lot of easily-available information about him, and I'm indebted to Neil Pearson's scholarly *Obelisk: Jack Kahane and the Obelisk Press* (Liverpool University Press, 2007) for the details I'm listing here. Beadle was born "around 1880" and had led an active and varied life in different parts of Africa and elsewhere, which included participating in the Boer War. He published several adventure novels, some of which are still in print, and short stories in pulp magazines. He had lived in Paris before the First World War, spent some time in the United States, and returned to Paris in the mid-Twenties. A couple of his novels from the 1920s are set among the expatriate community in the French capital.

A third, *Dark Refuge* (1938), could only have come from the Obelisk Press. Pearson says: "In earlier books Beadle denounced the Paris-based expatriates for a bohemianism he deemed so insipid as to scarcely merit the name. In *Dark Refuge* he spells out how it should be done properly, and does so without paying any heed to what was considered publishable at the time. Beadle's ticket to the dark side is opium, and in his world 'dark' has no negative connotations, but refers instead to the side of the self that sees too little light". Mix that with what appears to be an open approach to matters of sex, and the language to describe it, and no publisher in America or Britain would have dared to put *Dark Refuge* into print. It's a pity that no-one has seen fit to re-print it in recent years.

It is difficult to work out exactly who wrote what in *Artist Quarter*. Goldring had lived in Paris and knew artists there, but I would guess that most of the reminiscences and anecdotes relating to Modigliani and others, as opposed to the historical information about the development of Montmartre and Montparnasse as centres of artistic ferment, were probably supplied by Beadle.

Anecdotes are at the core of *Artist Quarter*, many of them about Modigliani, but most of them generally highlighting the activities of the artistically inclined but often impecunious. Utrillo is seen in his usual alcoholic haze, avoided by others in the bohemian community because of his behaviour when drunk. He wasn't a happy drunk, likely to lapse into silence or even sleep, but instead tended to shout, break glasses, and generally misbehave. Utrillo's paintings of Montmartre became popular, though the increased income they brought only enabled him to drink more. His work did have a certain charm, the kind that would appeal to tourists, though I recall seeing an exhibition in Paris some years ago which had his paintings alongside those by his mother, Suzanne Valadon, and thinking she was the more-talented and interesting artist. It was most likely Beadle's opinion that Utrillo "talks and sees like a child and therefore paints like one".

Picasso was, of course, very much a notable figure in Montmartrc in the pre-1914 period, living at the Bateau-Lavoir, a tumble-down building which served as a gathering-place for painters and poets, such as André Salmon, Kees Van Dongen, Vlaminck, Derain, Max Jacob, Apollinaire, and associated models and mistresses. Fernande Olivier was with Picasso in those days, and "he was so jealous of her that he would not let her go out, but trotted out himself with the market bag every morning to the rue de Abbesses, just below the studio, to buy the day's supplies". A view of Picasso's studio refers to it as "dirty, curtainless, and in disorder. Unfinished canvases are propped against the dusty walls……..A towel and a bit of yellow soap lie on a table among tubes of paint, brushes, and a dirty plate containing remnants of a hasty meal……On the floor there is another litter of paints, brushes, bottles of paraffin". It's a colourful description and perhaps intended to confirm everyone's suspicions regarding how bohemians lived.

It was during this period of Picasso's career that he painted a portrait of one of the Montmartre bohemians, an oddball called Bibi-La-Purée, a one-time drinking companion of the poet, Verlaine: "Bibi was an authentic relic of the period of *Trilby* and Henry Murger, true to type in every particular". He knew all the tricks of surviving with a little dishonesty and deviance, but came to a sad end when, having obtained some money, "he killed himself by an excess of alcohol". I recall that the painting of Bibi was in an exhibition about Picasso's early days in Paris at the Courtauld in 2013. It conferred a kind of immortality on someone who might otherwise have been forgotten as those who knew him left their bohemian days behind or died off.

I was intrigued to see that, on the opposite page to the notes about Picasso's studio, there is an illustration of the Passage Cottin in Mont-martre taken from a lithograph by Rowley Smart. He is an artist I've long been curious about. Born in Manchester he served in the First World War and afterwards gravitated to Paris, where he was said to have enjoyed the bohemian life. It probably didn't do him any good as he suffered from tuberculosis which eventually killed him in 1934. Did Beadle or Goldring know him? Or is it just a coincidence that one of his illustrations is in their book? I don't suppose that Smart's name means much to many art-lovers these days, but I have seen some of his small, but pleasant Paris scenes in galleries in Manchester and Roch-dale.

According to the account in *Artist Quarter*, the poet and painter Max Jacob lived by a form of voluntary poverty. Beadle, or was it Goldring, once told a gallery owner that Jacob, then domiciled in the provinces, was still poor, to which she replied, "Oh, that's only because he wants to be". When he lived in the Bateau-Lavoir, Jacob got high on ether, as did others, including Modigliani, at least until opium became easily available. Jacob, a Jew, was arrested in 1944 and died in the Drancy transit camp.

Bohemia had its characters, some talented, others simply remembered for their eccentricities and sometimes their bad behaviour. Modigliani had skills as a sculptor and painter, but was also noted for his tendency to become noisy, angry, and disruptive when under the influence of drugs and alcohol. There are numerous anecdotes and observations in *Artist Quarter* about his escapades and occasionally destructive actions. Interestingly, when he first arrived in Paris, he was quiet, shy, and so-berly dressed and well-behaved. After a time, the bohemian life appears to have exerted its influence on him and that, together with his failure to sell his work to any great degree, no doubt caused him to feel bitter and neglected, and to turn to stimulants of one kind or another to com-pensate for the lack of success he thought he deserved. His resultant life-style, with its emphasis on alcohol and hashish, and a lack of regu-lar meals, exacerbated his tubercular condition.

The Polish poet, Leopold Zborowski, sacrificed a great deal of his time, energy, and money, trying to help Modigliani, though he was often abused and exploited by the artist, and when Modiglani died he was accused of profiting from the sale of some of his paintings that he had. But it's documented how dealers descended on anyone who had a Mo-digliani work in their possession and bought and resold them for ever-increasing prices. It took Modigliani's death, and that of his last female companion, the ill-fated Jeanne Hébuterne, to bring him the fame he never had in his lifetime. Their story became the basis for novels and films, and any number of supposedly-factual accounts.

Modigliani had several affairs, one of them with a woman the book refers to as "The English Poetess", presumably because the person concerned was still alive in 1941 and wouldn't have wanted her name made public. It's now known that she was Beatrice Hastings. Their intense but tumultuous relationship lasted for around two years before she brought it to an end. She eventually returned to England, but doesn't seem to have made an impact on the literary scene. It's difficult to know what her poetry was like, very little of it being available, though there have been attempts in recent years to acclaim her as "a lost modern master". Hastings, suffering from cancer, committed suicide in 1943.

The English artist Nina Hamnett also knew Modigliani in the years before the First World War and seems to have liked him. Reminiscing about her time in Paris, she thought that some of the accounts of his misbehaviour may have been exaggerated, though it's hard to accept that was the case when reading the parade of anecdotes about his escapades. But there may be something in her suggestion that "A man may live quietly for months without anyone noticing it; but if he breaks out and gets roaring drunk, as of course Modi often did, then everyone remembers it and records it". Hamnett herself can be said to be a victim of that sort of treatment. She's probably best-known now for stories about her days around Soho and Fitzrovia in the 1930s to the 1950s when, alcoholic and short of money, she could be seen in the pubs and clubs of the area, often the worse for wear and cadging drinks. But her paintings are rarely discussed or seen anymore.

Artist Quarter is full of the names of painters and poets who failed to survive the bohemian scene. The artist Jules Pascin "destroyed himself at the height of his fame, when his work was in great demand and he had no financial worries. Perhaps that was a reason for his suicide: he was surfeited with success, physically worn out with years of riotous living, and life had nothing more to offer him". And there was the poet, Ralph Cheever Dunning, who was published in expatriate magazines like Ford Madox Ford's *The Transatlantic Review* and Ezra Pound's *The Exile*. Pound was an advocate for his poetry, though it's difficult now to know why. It must have seemed old-fashioned even then, especially when Pound's clarion call, "Make it New", could still be heard. Dunning was an opium addict and died of tuberculosis and starvation in Paris in 1930. Curiously, a short story, "Tony", that he had published in *The Exile*, did seem quite modern as it told, in near-monologue form,

MILITANTS, ARTISTS, POETS

about a young lesbian's unrequited love for another girl.

Beadle and Goldring don't have much to say about the influx of Americans in the 1920s, though they do mention Harold Stearns, an intellectual who wrote a book called *America and the Young Intellectuals* and edited another called *Civilisation in the United States*, and then went to Paris, where in "Montparnasse the 'antilectual' toxin took so well that he became 'Peter Pickem' for the *Chicago Tribune* – and afterwards the Paris *Daily Mail* – and for years, from the top of a stool in The Select, picked winners with uncanny accuracy". Kay Boyle's 1938 novel, *Monday Night*, features a character closely based on Stearns.

There is so much packed into the pages of *Artist Quarter* that it's impossible to mention all the painters, writers, and others who were around Montmartre or Montparnasse at one time or another. The anecdotes come thick and fast, some funny, some sad, but all helping to present a vivid picture of bohemian Paris in its heyday. It's gratifying to know that someone thought it worth reprinting. There are numerous books dealing with aspects of artists in Paris, and some undeniably analyse the art more closely than Beadle and Goldring did. They make a few references to Cubism and not much else. But their book can't be beaten for its evocation of the spirit of a time and place.

ARTIST QUARTER: MODIGLIANI, MONTMARTRE & MONT-PARNASSE By Charles Douglas
Pallas Athene (Publishers) Ltd. 353 pages. £14.99. ISBN 978-1-84368-153-3

PROVISIONAL AVANT-GARDES: LITTLE MAGAZINE COMMUNITIES FROM DADA TO DIGITAL

There is a problem here in that we are faced with the difficulty of defining the avant-garde. Sophie Seita offers the following suggestion: "The word *avant-garde* is popularly understood to refer to an individual or group with an anti-establishment attitude, producing stylistically innovative work, often with political aims in mind, sometimes articulated aggressively against previous generations or against tradition more broadly".

She further says that, if this is the definition most people are likely to accept, it has "led to a seemingly coherent set of now-canonical and historical avant-garde movements with key players, clear manifestos, and an identifiable style". Which seems to be true enough. There are books providing detailed accounts of all the "isms" that are an essential part of any history of the avant-garde. And there is what some might see as the irony of those anti-tradition individuals and groups now being part of the canon and often almost-revered by would-be experimentalists.

Seita quotes Ben Hickman, who stated "an avant-garde in a university is a contradiction in terms", though it's not something that she herself would agree with. And the subversive thought occurs to me that what we find in universities is not so much an avant-garde, but often a mannered mode of writing (I'm thinking of poetry, in particular) that seeks to separate itself from the kind of work that most people prefer to read. Seita asserts: "Thanks also to the New Critics' appraisal of difficult modernist poetry, and its incorporation into university syllabi, our own appreciation of the 'difficult' as critics and poets has reinforced a striking difference from so-called mainstream and more-accessible writing". I think it was Norman Holmes Pearson who claimed that an academic career studying and teaching modernist poetry had equipped him for work as a cryptoanalyst when he was recruited for the OSS during World War Two.

There are some other anti-avant-garde comments from a poet and publisher, Richard Owens, who declares that "what publicly announces itself as avant-garde through market and state-funded megaphones scarcely ever is. Their daring lies in doing what others have done with the blessings of the market" and "any identification with an avant-garde or commitment to innovation paves the way to a promising career in the culture industry".

The literary avant-garde often made its first claims to originality in the pages of little magazines. Seita says that "Definitions of the little magazine have been debated as hotly as those of the avant-garde, and these definitions resemble one another in telling ways". She quotes Elliott Anderson and Mary Kinzle as asserting in their *The Little Magazine in America: A Modern Documentary History* (Pushcart Press, 1978) that little magazines "generally put experiment before ease". I'm not sure that this is always the case, though looking at Anderson and Kinzle's selection of magazines they deal with, it might appear that way. But there have been hundreds of little magazines, most of which were fairly conventional in their choice of the work they published. It may be that such magazines are not seen as worthy of consideration (Ezra Pound said, "a review that can't announce a programme probably doesn't know what it thinks or where it is going"), but not everyone feels the need to "make it new" or concoct a manifesto. I'm put in mind of Sophie Taeuber-Arp, (very much a member of the avant-garde of her day) who thought that manifestos were largely a male-prerogative and "a means of self-aggrandisement".

However, leaving aside the question of the general run of little magazines, we can discern that Seita's main concern is fixedly with what she sees as the current avant-garde. I'm tempted to play devil's advocate and wonder whether or not there is an avant-garde anymore? Some people would incline to the view that there isn't. And it's often hard to single out what is avant-garde about much of the work that lays claim to being in that category. Most conceptual art simply stems from a few provocative acts many years ago. Marcel Duchamp has a lot to answer for. Before him, they were painting copies of the *Mona Lisa,* with a pipe in her mouth, back in Montmartre in the 1880s, but it was looked on merely as a joke. I doubt that anyone at that time thought it was much more than a cheeky send-up of the artistic establishment's worship of the painting's supposed value.

There are some interesting comments relating to conceptual art: "Lucy Lippard, one of the earliest scholars and curators of conceptual art, defined it as 'work in which the idea is paramount and the material form is secondary, lightweight, ephemeral, cheap, unpretentious, and or 'dematerialised'. The dematerialised art object was often supplemented or replaced by a text that outlined the purpose of the object, or, in the absence of an object, of the project, and labelled it as art". I'm slightly puzzled by the purpose of such an exercise which seems to relieve the artist of having to actually create anything worthwhile in terms of an art object.

Talking about art thus takes the place of producing it, which some might say makes it ideal for a university. Others might want to see it as a recipe for pretentiousness, and a refuge for those lacking the skills to paint a picture or shape a sculpture. Conceptual is usually a term applied to the visual arts, but if extended to poetry or the novel could eliminate the need to write anything once the thought about it has occurred. Félix Fénéon may have got it right in the early-1900s with his novels in three lines, though an extremist might want to dispense of the three lines as well.

Seita does appear to accept that from around the 1970s, "you notice a distinct trend: the little magazine has become a critical-theoretical apparatus". She discusses the "Language Poets" and their magazine L=A=N=G=U=A=G=E, and states that: "Although the definition of Language writing continues to be disputed, the group's early critics generally agreed that it rejected the 'expressive self' of the so-called romantic lyric and marked a 'shift of emphasis away from subjectivity' ". There was no longer "the cry of the heart" but instead "the play of the mind". It's frankly not easy to get away from the "academicisation" of Language writing as critics applied theory to it. And the question might arise, was it almost a creation of academic critics who ensured its success with reviews in influential magazines and newspapers, and publication in trend-setting anthologies? In fact, it could be suggested that Sophie Seita is contributing to the "academicisation" with her book, which it can't be denied has been written for specialists in the universities and colleges. A general reader who likes to read poetry for pleasure ("How quaint", the professors and poets may say, as they play with their minds, though that can also be a pleasure) will find it sometimes hard to get to grips with the academic nature of the prose.

It's difficult to know how much of the poetry that seemed to come under the term, "Language writing", if only because of where it was published, did actually meet the criteria that was established for it. Seita points out that there was a "more-divided and diverse network than is acknowledged in canonical accounts". She is of the opinion that "Most critical studies of Language writing tend to focus on a narrow range of authors", and a limited number of magazines. In contrast to this, Seita ranges around the avant-garde little magazine network, and while doing so concludes that the work in them can include poems that don't necessarily conform if strict guidelines are applied. I suspect it has always been the same for any movement that, in retrospect, is seen as avant-garde. A glance at the 1932 *Objectivist Anthology* will come up with a few names that no longer find a place in later accounts of the group.

Robert McAlmon is one example I can immediately bring to mind.

As the title of Seita'a book indicates, the emphasis in publishing by so-called avant-garde poets has moved away from print to the Internet. There are now numerous publications which exist solely on-line. But Seita's concerns rest with what she considers represent an avant-garde. And it's true that Internet outlets provide places to experiment with typography and the like to usefully supplement the texts of the poems. Publishing in this way also emphasises what became obvious during the so-called "mimeograph revolution" of the 1960s - it's possible to produce a magazine without having to conform to commercial require-ments. In addition, being on-line can help to avoid the distribution problems faced by little print magazines. Gone are the days of weary editors calling at scattered bookshops with copies of their magazines, an experience I encountered when editing a couple of little magazines in the 1960s and 1970s. I hasten to add that I never thought of myself as avant-garde, either as editor or poet, though as a critic I don't think I was unsympathetic when I wrote about poets who were seen as practi-tioners of what was then often referred to as avant-garde work. I did object to what I felt was almost-wilful obscurity.

I suppose the only difficulty is that, as happened in the 1960s when everyone and his brother who had access to a mimeograph machine (duplicators, as they were referred to in Britain) became editor of a magazine, there were wide variations in what developed. Some of the results were excellent as the imaginative combined good taste in the poets they published with a concern for the appearance of their publica-tion, whereas others were often scrappy sheets of self-indulgence. I'm not sure what standards are like on the Internet. Possibly not much dif-ferent, and in any case, most poetry at most times is mostly quickly forgettable. And it has often occurred to me over the years, as I've col-lected and written about a range of little magazines, that nothing looks so dated as the minor work of yesterday's avant-gardes. As for avant-garde ideas, does anyone apart from a number of academics still bother to read Charles Olson's long-winded theories of "Projective Verse"?

Provisional Avant-Gardes is a stimulating book in some ways, despite its insistence that an avant-garde of major significance still exists. And there is the worrying evidence that its academicisation has led to a situ-ation where so many poets are located in universities and other places of higher education, and as a consequence feel the need to accord to the ideas and opinions of those establishments. One has the impression that if a poet who favoured the "cry of the heart", as opposed to the "play of the mind", turned up on campus he or she might well have a hard time of it, and almost certainly wouldn't be taken seriously.

I could be wrong, and it needs to be noted that Seita is largely writing about the situation in the United States. There are only a few, scattered references to British publications and poets. However, she has obviously done a great deal of research into the magazines and their contributors, and provides a lot of useful information about both print and on-line outlets for the poets she favours. I still can't be sure if an avant-garde does continue to exist. Perhaps the answer lies in the words of Gabriel Josipovici in "Off the Grid: Thoughts on the avant-garde" (TLS, 9th August, 2019) when he suggested that the test shouldn't be whether or not a work of art is "experimental" or "avant-garde", but is it good or bad?

PROVISIONAL AVANT-GARDES: LITTLE MAGAZINE COM-
MUNITIES FROM DADA TO DIGITAL
By Sophie Seita
Stanford University Press. 256 pages. £24.99.
ISBN 978-1-5036-0957-0

THE INSTITUTIONS OF RUSSIAN MODERNISM: CONCEPTUALISING, PUBLISHING, AND READING SYMBOLISM

Symbolism was among the first literary expressions of modernism in Russia. Arriving on the scene in the 1890s, it was designed by its practitioners and promoters to offer an alternative to the nineteenth century tradition of realism. As Jonathan Stone puts it: "Little could be farther from the weighty and detailed prose works of Realism than Symbolist poetry". The influences came from elsewhere, most notably France. It was, in a way, presaged by Decadence, a description certain writers liked to function under, and it was initially sometimes hard to decide where Decadence ended and Symbolism began. Stone says that they "frequently overlapped with one another and could even become interchangeable". Movements in literature do not run on roads that are neat and tidy and easy to negotiate. Decadence had, perhaps, alerted some critics, readers, and others, to changes in the possibilities of poetry.

It had also alerted them to the possibilities of satire. The initial critical response to Symbolism was often hostile. People will take pleasure in ridiculing what they don't understand. And the appearance of a single-line poem, "Oh, cover your pale legs", in the 1895 issue of *Russian Symbolists*, was an open invitation to mockery. It also didn't help that a plethora of publications purporting to represent Symbolist poetry started to become available in 1895, a year that Stone describes as "remarkable". Among the leading lights of the new movement were Aleksandr Dobroliubov, Aleksandr Emel'ianov-Kokhanskii, and Valerii Briusov, all of whom, according to a critic in one newspaper, were "literary posers" and given to "Poprishchin's literature", a phrase derived from the ramblings in Gogol's *Diary of a Madman*. Time may have been relatively kind to the three poets referred to, but Stone admits that most of the poems published as by Symbolists were not guaranteed to survive for very long : "Very few of the works published by the 'Russian Symbolists' in 1894 and 1895 would make a lasting impact or warrant consideration solely for their poetic quality". They were in print notably because they pointed to the existence of "an active community of poets".

The reception of Symbolist poetry in Russia was coloured by the fact that Alexsandr Dobroliubov was a noted eccentric and Aleksandr Emel'ianov-Kokhanski a joker: "Dobroliubov's notoriety as a Russian Decadent was a prominent part of the early image of Symbolism in

Russia". According to Stone, he had a "thorough knowledge of French literature", was odd in both "appearance and behaviour", and had a taste for opium. He left the literary world to "lead the life of a religious pilgrim". He was only "vaguely aware" that a collection of his poems was published in 1900.

As for Aleksandr Emil'ianov-Kokhanski, he seems to have had some importance during the early days of Russian Symbolism, but his penchant for playing the jester didn't endear him to Valerii Briusov who referred to his collection, *Bared Nerves* as "charlatanism", perhaps because he "understood the impact that he could make by flaunting the extremes of his Decadent persona". Briusov, as Stone makes clear throughout his book, was determined to give Symbolism an appearance of seriousness that would make it acceptable to both critics and committed readers. This is not to say that he was averse to publicising the work of the poets he favoured. He simply didn't want acknowledgement of their poems to rest on a notoriety resulting from bizarre personal behaviour and outlandish extremes of verse making. Briusov was soon to become a major force in Russian Symbolism, shaping the direction it took and cultivating its image in the eyes of the public.

Any new literary movement needs outlets in the form of magazines and books. An individual, or a small group of friends, can start a magazine, but establishing a publishing house is often a more daunting prospect. Briusov was lucky in that he established a rapport with Skorpion, a press that soon became, under Briusov's tutelage, the major publisher of the Russian Symbolists. Because he almost dictated what Skorpion published, he could determine who was to be regarded as a Symbolist. If a reader wasn't sure what Symbolism represented he or she could safely look to the Skorpion list for guidance. It's perhaps almost impossible to know how many of the people reading the Symbolist poets truly knew what the term meant. Throughout his book Stone carefully notes that, as with many avant-garde groups, there was a feeling that they were essentially writing for each other and a few informed readers. A limited circulation could thus be seen as representing quality. If the mass of people were indifferent then that just proved how ignorant they were. Only the initiated and discerning could properly understand what Symbolism was.

Which brings us to an interesting question. What was it? I'm not sure that Stone provides a satisfactory answer in terms of explaining its basic methods and aims. It sometimes seems that he's accepted Briusov's definitions, possibly in the same way that Russian readers accepted them. If Briusov included a poem in a Symbolist publication then it must surely be Symbolist. But did those readers truly know what Symbolism meant? Or was it just a term that was, in Stone's words, "an effective shorthand for all that was new" and which "gave writers and readers easy access to a host of ideas associated with modernism".

Stone does, at various points, provide limited definitions of Symbolism. It's a "poetics that relies on symbols in the generation of meaning" and it generates "meaning from nuance or obscurity". And elsewhere, "Symbolism is an orchestrated set of interactions motivated by the reciprocal nature of the symbol". Stone says that theoretical overviews of Symbolism were not a prominent part of the early days of the movement. The reader had to accept that "Russian Symbolism was that which was published by the Russian Symbolists in books titled *Russian Symbolists*". Which possibly caused Nikolai Mikhailovskii to comment: "It may be asked what ties together all of these people into a single, albeit blurry and motley, whole? Or is there no general bracket into which we can place them all – the talented and the hapless, the believers and the tricksters?"

Reading Stone I was reminded of the situation in the United States when the Beat movement began to emerge in print in the 1950s. There was no real agreement amongst the writers about what Beat meant, and the term was often used to describe writers who weren't Beat, however one defined it. There were certainly plenty of tricksters around and more than a few of the hapless. Stone's comments about very few of the works published by so-called Symbolists making a lasting impact, or warranting consideration for their poetic qualities, could certainly apply to most of the minor Beat poets, as could his observation that they were in print to demonstrate the existence of a poetic community. Independent publishers sprang up, and magazines were started. And, for many readers, I would guess that the fact of inclusion in an anthology or magazine that was believed to represent Beat meant that the writer was Beat. Other factors may also have been similar. Stone refers to the Symbolists as a coterie, an in-group who would attract readers who, perhaps, saw themselves as sharing the values of the coterie. The same could have been said of the Beats. I'm talking about the Beat literary movement and not the social aspects of it that were exploited by the mass media. It's also worth noting that there was the same sort of a largely hostile reaction to the Beats, both as poets and people, and the same sort of ridiculing of their work.

But I'm straying from the subject of Stone's book. It's difficult to know how many readers the Symbolists had, and who they were. Stone has some interesting things to say about the number of copies of Symbolist books that were produced. He points out that Skorpion print runs were modest, ranging from 300 to 600 copies. Most of its catalogue was still available four years after the company started in 1900. An exception was Dobroliubov's *Collected Verses*, the last copy of which was sold in 1903. But it had only been published in an edition of 300 copies. As Stone says: "Not many people were noticing or reading these books, a situation exacerbated by the rudimentary dissemination and advertising structures of the small press".

Briusov carried on as an advocate for Symbolism, though by 1910 it was evident that, as a movement, it had lost its momentum and cohesion. Other groups had come to the forefront in the modernist camp in Russia. The Acmeists and the Futurists were attracting the attention of critics and readers. Both were opposed to Symbolism, and it needs to be said that, on the whole, they involved poets who will probably be better-known outside Russia than most of those mentioned by Stone in his survey of Symbolism. The Acmeists, preferring "direct expression through images" to "intimations through symbols", attracted Osip Mandelstam and Anna Akhmatova to their ranks.

There is a fascinating anthology, *The Stray Dog Cabaret* (New York Review of Books, New York, 2007), which has poems by Mandelstam and Akhmatova, alongside some by, among others, Vladimir Mayakovsky, Alexander Blok, and Velimir Khlebnikov, who might all be classified as Futurists. Their manifesto, *A Slap in the Face of Public Taste*, summed up their determinedly confrontational stance when compared to the Symbolists. It's interesting to note that Blok ("arguably the most significant and successful poet of Russian Symbolism") had earlier been published by Skorpion, and that, as Stone describes it, his book was among the "indisputable milestones of Russian Symbolism". He also says that Briusov was largely responsible for shaping it "for Skorpion's particular exposition of Symbolism". He also did the same for Andrei Bely's work that Skorpion published.

It's sobering to recall how many of the poets linked to the Stray Dog Cabaret in St. Petersburg came to what might be called sad endings. Mayakovsky, Sergei Esenin, and Marina Tsvetaeva all committed suicide, Blok died in 1921, "possibly of venereal disease", and Khlebnikov of "disease and malnutrition" in 1922. Mandelstam, a victim of Stalin's purges, died in a camp in 1938. Others, such as Boris Pasternak and Anna Akhmatova, survived but were persecuted, in one way or another. Stone has little to say about the later years of most of the Symbolist poets, though he does mention that Dobroliubov re-surfaced in the 1930s "in the guise of a thoroughly Soviet writer interested in reinventing his literary career". It may have been a useful way of escaping the attentions of the secret police. Or maybe just another expression of his eccentricity. He also asserts that Emel'ianov-Kokhanskii ended his life "in the literary world of Stalinism", though he does add that he was in a "declining mental state" at the time.

The Institutions of Russian Modernism is a complex book and frankly not always easy to follow if one is not well-read in Russian literature. Many of the poets and critics named by Stone have probably never been translated into English, or if they have it has likely been on a limited basis. Stone's research into Russian Symbolism has clearly been deep, and he is to be admired for that. His book will no doubt prove invaluable to anyone wanting to look further into aspects of Russian poetry in the late 19th and early 20th centuries.

THE INSTITUTIONS OF RUSSIAN MODERNISM: CONCEPTU-
ALISING, PUBLISHING, AND READING SYMBOLISM
By Jonathan Stone
Northwestern University Press. 304 pages. $39.95.
ISBN 978-0-8101-3572-7

DARKNESS: A CULTURAL HISTORY

Darkness. We talk about dark thoughts, dark deeds, the dark at the top of the stairs which might hide someone or something frightening. "Dark shadows everywhere/misery and despair", sang vocalist Earl Coleman on a 1947 recording by Charlie Parker. There it is, the association of "misery and despair" with the dark and the shadowy side of our lives. There are songs and poems which extol the virtues of the night, though I'm hard pressed to think of too many of them. References to the dark seem to inevitably invoke unease and uncertainty: "When the sun goes down and it gets dark/I saw an animal in a park" wrote Robert Creeley, and for me it implies a possibility of danger from the animal. "A dark bell brings the dark down" is a line in a poem by Roy Fisher and there is something ominous in its tone. The title of the poem is "The Hospital in Winter". We don't usually associate winter and hospitals with light and well-being.

Nina Edwards points out that "the language of dark and light is so familiar a feature of our manner of speaking that it is easy to overlook its significance". And she adds that "we are primed to look to the association of light for understanding and joy". But darkness "feeds the imagination", and it can have a special visual beauty all of its own. Think of paintings by the wonderful Atkinson Grimshaw. True, some of them do hint at mysteries when they portray lonely roads at night, or darkened houses half-hidden behind trees. But others, especially those of scenes in Leeds and Liverpool, with street lamps and the light cast from shop windows and restaurants creating their own kind of pictorial magic, can be immensely attractive. They can still point to hidden dangers in dark corners and areas where the light can't penetrate with any great effectiveness. But the paintings largely present scenes that might not raise any doubts in most of our eyes.

This may be because what we see isn't real darkness, the kind where it's difficult to know where we are and what's directly in front of us. Most of us live in towns and cities, and it's unlikely that we've ever had any direct experience of perfect darkness, even within the safety of our own bedrooms. There is almost always light of some sort from one source or another. Moonlight penetrating a thin curtain, street lights. When I was a child growing up in a house without lighting in any of the bedrooms, I'd sit near the window and read by the light of a street lamp directly outside the window. When I closed my book I easily fell asleep in the half-light of the bedroom.

Darkness doesn't necessarily hold any terrors for many people. It can be quite comforting in some ways. There is a fine short-story by Jerome Weidman called "My Father Sits in the Dark" in which the narrator, coming down to the darkened kitchen for a drink, finds his father sitting there. "Why do you sit in the dark"? the boy asks, and his father says that it's "restful" and he doesn't think about anything special, he just likes to sit in the dark. We could also suggest that sleep is a kind of retreat into darkness that provides us with relief from the worries of the everyday world. Freud gets a look in here with his idea that "sleep is a narcissistic regression into the mother's womb". And dreams are discussed. As someone who can never remember what his dreams were about, I'm in no position to offer any useful comments on the subject. Freud would have found me a profound disappointment in more ways than one.

Still, for a lot of the time we do tend to think of darkness as representing something inherent with danger. Crimes, particularly those, like mugging or burglary, which may affect us on a personal level, usually take place when it is dark. We know that we're not necessarily always safe during daylight, but when we go to bed we carefully lock our doors at night and check that the burglar alarm is on. There is a suspicion that anyone who is out at night without a good reason might be up to no-good. When I was young and walking back from a party or seeing a girl home it never surprised me when I was stopped and questioned by the police. What was I doing hurrying down darkened streets?

It may be that our inclination to associate darkness, shadows, night-time, with the negative stems from cultural influences we grow up with. As mentioned earlier, terms such as dark thoughts and dark deeds are in common use. Books, plays, poems, all use the idea of the dark to suggest the morbid, the threatening, and the mysterious. Conrad wrote *The Heart of Darkness*, and Shakespeare has Macbeth saying, "Stars, hide your fires;/Let not light see my black and deep desires". Dirty deeds need to be carried out in the dark by "night's black agents".

There is a whole genre of Hollywood films under the title, *Film Noir*. The classic images coming from them are of night-time, dark streets, albeit illuminated by street lighting, headlights from cars, and the flickering lights from cheap hotels and bars. The effect is to immediately plant a feeling of tension and something about to happen in the viewer's mind. The *Film Noir* category has expanded to include films in which the action takes place in daylight, with little reference to the visual impact of lighting or lack of it, but the themes continue to focus on the dark in terms of the intentions of the characters. Women plot to murder their husbands, husbands to murder their wives. The shadowy corners where evil lurks are in the mind.

But is darkness, with all its associations of night and shadows, necessarily always to be suspected? Edwards asserts that "Darkness can be thrilling. It can seem like everything is latent, without borders, without limitations, and the entire universe thrown in. It is full of scintillating potential for poets and playwrights, musicians and visual artists. The dark has always been able to entertain us". I suppose obvious examples would be ghost stories, which inevitably take place at night, often in buildings which are badly-lit and full of shadows, and if there is a moon, it is likely to be obscured by clouds at strategic moments. A sudden plunge into near-total darkness is enough to un-nerve even the most courageous of people. And send a shiver down the spine of the reader, even though he or she may be sitting in a warm, well-lit room at the time. As an avid reader of ghostly tales (*The Supernatural Omnibus,* a classic collection edited by Montague Summers, has been in my possession for many years) I still ensure that the landing light is on before I venture upstairs. My imagination, and whatever primeval fears have been aroused, combine to make me wary of the dark.

Edwards observes that "In the nineteenth century The Gothic Revival created an enthusiasm for an imagined dark medieval period, which was cast as a time of thrilling ghostly excitement". Jane Austen nicely lampooned the taste for Gothic novels in *Northanger Abbey,* where the heroine, Catherine, her mind awash with *The Mysteries of Udolpho*, imagines all kinds of hidden passages and dark secrets when she is invited to stay with a family who live in an abbey. Personally, I always rather liked Bulwer-Lytton's comment on the cult of the Gothic in his *Pelham or Adventures of a Gentleman* (1828): "There seems", said I, "an unaccountable prepossession among all persons, to imagine that whatever seems gloomy must be profound, and whatever is cheerful must be shallow. They have put poor philosophy into deep mourning, and given her a coffin for a writing desk, and a skull for an inkstand".

We go out at night to have a good time. Edwards discusses Vauxhall Gardens which, in its heyday, was a popular place for entertainment of various sorts. It was there that meetings were arranged between lovers, and places could be found where they might engage in whatever activities they had a taste for. Night-time lends itself to furtive fumbllngs in the bushes, whereas day-time would hardly provide the cover needed. Prostitutes plied their trade in Vauxhall Gardens, needless to say, which gave moralists the opportunity to condemn the area as encouraging vice and debauchery. The same condemnations cropped up in wartime when street lighting was switched off and no-one quite knew what was taking place in back-alleys and darkened corners.

Leaving aside the sexual aspect, there is a practical reason why Vauxhall didn't flourish in the day-time. Fireworks displays were a feature of the entertainment, but when they were put on during the daytime they were a flop. Obviously, fireworks needed the contrast between their light and the night-time sky to bring out their full effect.

Edwards ranges far and wide in all aspects of darkness. She writes about how dress code over the years has dictated that men, if they want to be taken seriously, inevitably wear dark suits: "Darkness somehow lends a garment intrinsic *gravitas*". There are, perhaps, valid reasons for suggesting that "In the recent past, as now, dark clothing was often preferred because it was easier to maintain". But modern cleaning methods make it easier to get rid of most stains. And yet, dark suits continue to be the standard garb of many leading businessmen and politicians. Is it that if they wore something lighter they might be viewed as frivolous, and it would be supposed that their clothing reflected their character? And why should it be seen as disrespectful if one wears light, even colourful, clothing at a funeral? It's surely the quality of the emotion that counts, not the colour of one's shirt? Many funerals are attended by men in dark suits who cared little for the deceased. They're simply conforming to a convention by being there and dressing appropriately.

A friend of mine used to walk dogs that were being trained to accompany blind persons. Labradors are a favourite breed for this work, and she recalled that, wherever she went, on trains, buses, in the streets, people would make a fuss of the light-coloured dogs but would be noticeably less enthusiastic about the black ones. There was, of course, no difference in the temperaments of the dogs or their ability to learn quickly and adapt to their circumstances. It was the colour that determined the responses to them. It raises interesting questions about colour and how black people have been viewed over the years. I'm old enough to remember a time when "black man" was sometimes used in working-class circles, at least, in the same way as "bogie man" as a means of frightening children. Those days have happily gone, or at least I hope so. Edwards doesn't explore the racial angle too far in relation to reactions to blackness, though she does note that Othello is "damned for his colour".

Darkness: A Cultural History is a stimulating book with a wide range of examples drawn from literature, art, music, philosophy, and other sources. Darkness is an integral part of our lives in every sense of the word. Would we like to live in a world of permanent light or of endless darkness? It's unlikely. We need the contrast to help us sleep, add variety to our lives, and carry out all kinds of functions. Think of the ways in which people could be exploited in permanent light. Factory owners were quick to extend the working day once artificial lighting was installed in their premises. And now certain locations, such as airports, can operate around the clock, thanks to artificial lighting. Not everyone finds this beneficial. The book has ample notes and a good bibliography.

DARKNESS: A CULTURAL HISTORY
By Nina Edwards
Reaktion Books. 288 pages. £25. ISBN 978-1-78023-982-8

WHITECHAPEL NOISE: JEWISH IMMIGRANT LIFE IN YIDDISH SONG AND VERSE, LONDON 1884-1914

"Between 1881 and 1914, 100,000 to 120,000 Yiddish-speaking Jews settled in London, mostly in the East End". Quoting these statistics, Vivi Lachs points out that they do not include those people who were temporarily in the city while they were on their way to the United States. And she says that "at any one time, numbers were up to three times higher than official figures".

Most of the Jews who arrived in the period concerned were from Eastern Europe, and were not wealthy. They came from The Pale of Settlement, the designated area for Jews in Russia, and from shtetls in Poland, and elsewhere, and their presence was seen as something of a threat by English trade-unionists who thought that they undercut wages and consequently took jobs away from local workers. They were also resented in many ways by middle-class Jews (Anglo-Jewry) who had been in Britain longer and had attempted to assimilate by toning down obvious signs of Jewishness. The concentration of large numbers of poor Jews in one area, and their speaking Yiddish and bringing the manners and habits of the shtetls with them, led to tensions between the established Jews and the newcomers. As Lachs puts it, the culture of the immigrants "was deeply strange to the established Anglo-Jewish community".

The fact of Yiddish being the common parlance among the East End Jews meant that there was a market for songs and poems in that language. Once they were written, outlets for them to be printed and performed soon sprang up in the shape of Yiddish music-halls, and a variety of publications, including newspapers. Lachs has calculated that "Over 400 Yiddish poems, songs and verses, which I call `London's Yiddish lyrics'," were written between 1884 and 1914 and published in local Yiddish newspapers, pamphlets, magazines, penny song-sheets, and songbooks". I doubt that much, if any, of this material ever came to the attention of anyone outside the East End of London, apart from perhaps among Jews who had moved to other cities, like Leeds and Manchester, where there were sizeable Jewish communities. It wouldn't have attracted the attention of metropolitan literary critics. Even some Yiddish-speaking commentators and critics were inclined to the view that it lacked sophistication and literary merit.

It wasn't only the middle-class Jews who were opposed to shtetl culture: "Socialists and anarchists saw immigrant workers as clinging to

outmoded ideas that they needed to reject in order to embrace modernity and fight for a socialist future". They were internationalists and
thought that Jewish workers ought to be involved in radical politics
generally, and not just in local matters, and that they should take an
interest in the work of British trade-unions. There was a noticeable reluctance on the part of many Jewish workers to join a union.

It was a fact, however, that in order to get through to the mass of Jews
in the East End it was necessary to use Yiddish. This applied as much
to entertainment as to social and political concerns, and the line between the two was often blurred. Lachs devotes a fair amount of space
to Morris Winchevsky, a poet who, for a time when he lived in London,
became almost the voice of the East End Jews, telling of their problems
and the struggle to overcome them. There was little finesse about
Winchevsky's poems. It was the content he cared about, and he had
what Lachs describes as an "activist and anti-aesthetic stance" when it
came to constructing a poem. She notes that: "The poems by Winchevsky that stood the test of time were those put to music and sung on union demonstrations". There is one Winchevsky poem that was immediately popular when it was first published, was set to music, and is still
sung today by performers specialising in Yiddish songs. Called "Dray
shvester," it tells the story of three sisters who can be seen regularly
plying their wares in Leicester Square:

> The youngest sells flowers there,
> The middle one – shoelaces
> And late at night you can see approaching
> The oldest, who sells herself.

Lachs comments that Bertold Brecht "loved the song for being so
strong with the social idea – because the sisters blame the circumstances and society for being a prostitute, not their sister herself".

"Tired immigrant workers were not paying their hard-earned money to
be given lectures or analysis", says Lachs, when she turns to the subject
of the Yiddish music-halls: "Over eighty songs were written by and for
local performers. And over half of them have verses that relate in some
way to sex and sexual relationships". I can't quote figures for the number of songs sung in music-halls that catered for English-speaking audiences, but it's a fair guess that many of them followed the same pattern in utilising sex, if mostly by innuendo, as their basis. Audiences
would have been well aware what Marie Lloyd was referring to when
she sang, "A little of what you fancy does you good".

Needless to say, both Yiddish and English music-halls were subject to adverse comments and even censorship, partly because of their use of sexually-suggestive songs, but also because the halls were looked on as places where people would fritter away their earnings. And where sexual liaisons could take place. Or, in the views of socialists, where the workers would be distracted from their true purpose, i.e planning for the next strike, if not the revolution.

There is a song by Arn Nagel about Victoria Park, a popular meeting place for East End Jews, that Lachs analyses to show how certain Yiddish words had dual-meanings that could be employed to exploit the sexual implications of the lyrics. "There goes Mr Itzik, scraping his bow/His nose is pointed, because he's called Itzik" seems innocuous enough when translated into English, but *shmitsik* (Yiddish for bow) is close to the slang word, *smitshik,* which means penis. The Yiddish *rayhn* refers to using the bow on the fiddle, but is also slang for "sexual intercourse, equivalent to 'screw,' and *rahyn zikh* is to masturbate. The use of the word *noz* in the next line makes connection to the expression, meaning 'to give it to a person'." Lachs suggests that the word "it" would have added emphasis, supplemented with gestures on the part of the performer.

Because of the compactness of the East End Jewish community it could be that audiences might recognise references to known individuals. But if not to individuals then certainly to easily identifiable types and situations. The influx of hundreds of young, single men into the East End, where there was already a shortage of accommodation, meant that many of them had to seek lodgings with families that needed to bring in some extra money. What was likely to happen in some cases was, as Lachs mentions, a fairly common theme in English music-hall songs. She quotes Vesta Tilley's "Our Lodger's Such a Nice Young Man" as an example, where Tilley, playing the part of the daughter, tells how the lodger "helps everyone out, but in particular her mother". I don't like to quibble, but I think it was actually Vesta Victoria, not Tilley, who popularised this song.

Lachs lists a selection of similar Yiddish music-hall songs, including "Fri ov Tshrdzh" (Free of Charge) where, when the husband leaves the house, "the wife gets her 'tiddle idl lomtom/totally free of charge". There were also songs which made fun of newly-arrived immigrants who naively attempted to maintain orthodox standards. "Freg keyn katshanes es is England" (Don't ask silly questions, this is England) places an orthodox Jew in a room alone with his landlady, who seduces him. In songs like this, "sexual behaviour becomes an exemplification of the freedom of England", though the orthodox establishment no doubt saw that "freedom" as leading to moral downfall.

It may have been that a lot of non-Jewish people would have looked on the Jews in Whitchapel and thought of them as a unified body with similar tastes and interests. It was far from the truth. Leaving aside the separation between the more orthodox Jews whose appearance (clothes, ringlets, etc.) would have made them stand out from the less-religious Jews, there were differences in what might be called everyday practices that marked where an individual came from. Yiddish may have been the standard form of communication, but there were variations according to a person's origins. As for religion, Lachs stresses that "observance, however, was not homogenous in practice. Orthodoxy from the old country had a range of religious expressions, and the East End became a microcosm of Eastern European sects and factions, each with its own specific codes and styles".

Lithuanians, Poles, Russians, Romanians. They could be placed by other Jews through their speech and habits, in the same way that English people could be identified by their accents and other factors. But to the anti-Semitic element among the population, all Jews were the same. There was a body of opinion in Britain, and perhaps especially so among the English, which actively called for strict limits on the number of immigrants allowed in. The British Brothers' League campaigned for restrictions. The 1905 Aliens Act was a step towards them. Some incidents, which were blamed on Jews, reinforced stereotypical ideas about unrestricted immigration allowing criminals to freely enter Britain. Lachs lists several violent episodes, including the famous Siege of Sidney Street, and indicates how they could easily persuade the general public that there were connections to be made between violence and anarchists and then from anarchists to Jews.There was an active group of anarchists in the East End, though they didn't necessarily indulge in criminal activities.

Increasing assimilation, particularly after the First World War, and the movement of some Jews out of the East End, inevitably led to a decline in the use of Yiddish. The closure of the Yiddish music halls meant that many performers simply disappeared, though a strong Jewish presence made itself felt in mainstream entertainment and the arts. But the singers, musicians, and others were not using specifically Jewish material. I do recall one singer, Issy Bonn, with a song called "My Yiddishe Momme" as being a favourite on the radio in the 1940s. His style, both as a singer and comedian, was clearly based on performing in music-halls. From references in the lyrics of "My Yiddishe Momme", it was obviously American in origin.

Whitechapel Noise is a valuable book, particularly so because it deals with Jewish life in the East End of London. There have been quite a few publications looking at Yiddish poetry and music in New York, where there was a much bigger concentration of Jews. And it's worth noting that Vivi Lachs points to the exchange of material between London and New York. Morris Winchevsky, in fact, moved to America and was prominent in Yiddish poetry circles. There have been one or two books dealing with specific aspects of the London Jewish community. William Fishman's *East End Jewish Radicals 1875-1914* (Duckworth, London, 1975) comes to mind immediately. But Vivi Lachs with *Whitechapel Noise* has opened up some new ground by looking in detail at the poems and songs that dealt with Jewish life in the East End of London in the years between 1884 and 1914.

Lachs states that her book had its origins in her Ph.D, but it is, I'm happy to say, thankfully free of the academic jargon that mars so many publications. She writes good, clear prose, and offers ideas for consideration instead of theories. *Whitechapel Noise* has extensive notes and a good bibliography.

WHITECHAPEL NOISE: JEWISH IMMIGRANT LIFE IN YIDDISH SONG AND VERSE, LONDON 1884-1914
By Vivi Lachs
Wayne State University Press. 331 pages. £25.95/$36.
ISBN 978-0-8143-4355-5

STAGING LIFE: THE STORY OF THE MANCHESTER PLAYWRIGHTS

There is a scene from a British film of the 1950s that has stayed in my mind since I watched it in an army camp in Germany in, if memory serves me right, 1955. It's of Charles Laughton drunkenly peering at the reflection of the moon in a puddle and trying to work out what it is. The film was *Hobson's Choice,* and it was based on a play of the same name by Harold Brighouse which was first performed in London in 1916 after opening in America the year before. It was a Manchester play, despite it not appearing there until after its New York and London successes.

Hobson's Choice and *Hindle Wakes* are the two plays that are most identified with a period when there appeared to be something of a boom in the writing and performance of plays by playwrights from in and around Manchester and, with one or two exceptions like *Hobson's Choice*, initially staged there. And it's largely due to one person that the impetus to write many of the plays came about. Annie Horniman established the theatre that was prepared to provide an opening for new plays by writers who didn't have national or sometimes even regional reputations.

She arrived in Manchester in 1907, having previously been involved with the Abbey Theatre in Dublin. She was not a playwright, actress, or director, but she had a deep interest in the theatre, and the money to indulge that interest to the extent of financing the production of plays. Her first activities in Manchester were centred on a small theatre in the Midland Hotel, and the aim was to establish "A Repertoire Theatre with regular changes of programme no matter how successful the play".

Horniman purchased the Gaiety Theatre, an existing building on the corner of Peter Street and Mount Street in Manchester, and had it extensively refurbished. Ben Iden Payne was appointed as producer and director, and it was made known in the local press that both he and Horniman were keen to be offered work by writers from the North West. They were both also determined to form a company of reliable actors: "The selection of a suitable company was thus extremely important as the bulk of the proposed repertoire of the theatre comprised new and recently written plays. The kind of actor needed for these plays was one who would act well in an ensemble and who would work for the sake of the play".

The Gaiety Theatre opened its doors in September, 1908, which was a time when trade depression, strikes, and a lock-out were affecting the city and its surrounding areas. According to John Harding, "many of the actors in AH's company were socialists or so inclined.........while the Gaiety itself would become a focus for left-wing-leaning individuals". But he also records that the opening night saw the theatre "filled with a fashionable audience, the beautiful dresses and jewels being shown to great advantage against the artistic decoration". There was still money in Manchester despite the unemployed demonstrating on the streets.

The first item to be performed in the new theatre was a one-act play by Basil Dean, who was also an actor with the company. Harding is interesting on the nature of one-act plays and the number of them performed at the Gaiety. There were over fifty in its first three seasons. As Harding says, "A one-act play is, in fact, a separate literary form by itself", and he adds that "It is far easier to write at length than to compress", and writing one-act plays helps a writer hone his craft: "That some of the best of the longer plays written by the Manchester playwrights were the work of men who achieved distinction in the one-act form is no coincidence".

It needs to be understood that the Gaiety was in no way an experimental theatre, other than in its desire to establish a regular repertory programme. The actual plays themselves were conventional in structure and content. Nor was it political in an overt way, despite the affiliations some of the actors, authors, and members of the audience may have had. On the other hand, there was what might be called a strong social sense running through much of the material. Harding provides an analysis of several plays and it's plain to see that when they succeeded they did so because they dealt with situations audiences could quickly identify with. True, Ernest Hutchinson's *The Right to Strike* touched on a serious subject, but it came at the very end of the Gaiety Theatre's existence. His earlier one-act, *Complaints*, is set in a cotton-mill context, but was described as a "clever little comedy", something which might have appealed to any working-class members of the audience more than didactics about industrial relations.

The three main playwrights that Harding deals with are Allan Monkhouse, Stanley Houghton, and Harold Brighouse, all of whom were successful, in one way or another, though Houghton sadly died young so never fulfilled the promise that others saw in him. He's now mainly remembered for *Hindle Wakes*, a play which combined humour with some quite hard-hitting social comment about the hypocrisy surround-

100

ing what was expected of young women and what was accepted from young men.

The confident mill-girl, Fanny, who has a fling with the boss's son and then refuses to marry him disconcerted some people, especially in London when the play was performed there. But it's a mistake to assume that her character was looked on favourably by any working-class audiences who encountered the play. Then, as now, they could be as narrow-minded as anyone else. Fanny telling the man that her night in bed with him was "an amusement – a lark", shocked people. And her statement that, as a skilled worker in a mill, she could be financially independent probably didn't go down well with many men.

Allan Monkhouse had a much longer career than Stanley Houghton, and was successful as a playwright, novelist, and critic. He was older than most of the others who contributed plays to the Gaiety, and in 1908 was an established theatre critic for the *Manchester Guardian*. He had already published novels and a collection of literary essays and had worked for twenty years as a yarn agent on the floor of Manchester's Royal Exchange. Harding says that all his novels and short stories "were situated in Manchester and its surroundings and drew their characters from the life that Monkhouse knew best, that of newspaper offices and of business, the theatre, the profession of letters, and the social contacts and humour and aspirations of the suburbs".

Monkhouse had contributed a couple of one-act plays to the Gaiety's repertoire, but it was his three-act *Mary Broome* which gave him some stature as a playwright. It dealt with a fairly well-worn theme – the seduction of a maid by the irresponsible son of a wealthy family. Unlike the girl in *Hindle Wakes,* Mary doesn't seem as independent, no doubt because she's pregnant, so she marries the man, but eventually leaves him when his selfishness leads to the death of their child. It's doubtful if it could be revived now with any chance of great success. It seems to lack the humour and warmth that can still give performances of *Hindle Wakes* and *Hobson's Choice* a great deal of appeal. The strong female characters in both plays cut across the years and have relevance. Another Monkhouse play, *The Conquering Hero*, has been revived in recent times, albeit not on a national scale.

Harold Brighouse, like Monkhouse, carried on writing and, like Houghton and Monkhouse, he had experience of the cotton trade, working as a salesman in a shipping merchant's warehouse while immersing himself in the theatre in his spare time. He was sent to London by his firm to run a small office, which gave him the opportunity to visit the theatres. When he returned to Manchester he had several plays which he submitted to the Gaiety, though only one of them was initially staged there. The plays all showed an awareness of social and economic circumstances affecting people and society. As Harding puts it: "All three of Brighouse's first plays were set in bleak, industrial situations". One called *The Doorway*, premiered at The Gaiety, focused on a couple finding shelter in a factory doorway until a policeman moves them on. The others, *Dealing in Futures* and *The Price of Coal*, got their first airings at the Glasgow Repertory Company. The latter play had been set in the Lancashire coalfields, but was adapted for its Scottish location.

Brighouse's *Lonesome-like*, described by Ben Iden Payne as "a masterpiece in miniature" also opened in Glasgow, and in some ways anticipated *Hobson's Choice* in that the central male character is shy and diffident, and nervous with women, where the female one seems much more forceful and determined. Brighouse was also the first British playwright to write a play about football. His *The Game* wasn't too well-received on stage, but it was turned into a film called *The Winning Goal*, which Harding says was successful. It's impossible to know how good it was, though, because no print of it now exists.

It's most likely the films that were made of *Hindle Wakes* and *Hobson's Choice* that partly enabled them to survive and to be occasionally revived on stage. As I noted earlier, I saw *Hobson's Choice* in the 1950s, and I have a memory of seeing the 1952 film of *Hindle Wakes* around the same time, possibly at the Plaza Cinema in Preston, which was not far from Horrockses Mill, where my mother was employed and I started work when I left school in 1952 at the age of sixteen. I have to admit that there always seemed to be an incongruity about British films of this period in that most of the actors and actresses had little or no conception of what Northern accents sounded like. And dialect would have totally defeated them. Their well-mannered pronunciations seemed odd to me. No-one I knew talked like that. But the shots of the factories, and of crowds leaving town for the seaside as the Wakes Weeks started, seemed real enough.

The Gaiety Theatre closed its doors in 1920, and it was converted into a cinema, something that probably attracted more working-class audiences than ever went to the Gaiety. I don't doubt that some working-class people did attend performances at the theatre – there are memoirs which mention it – and others may have seen some of the plays when they toured to other towns and cities. There's a reproduction of a poster advertising "Miss Horniman's Company" at the Theatre Royal in Preston in 1909, where they presented George Bernard Shaw's *Candida,* supported by J. Sackville Martin's *Cupid and the Styx,* which Harding refers to as "a decidedly comic piece" and "a favourite with the Gaiety audience". Martin drew on his experiences as a doctor for this play.

I suspect, however, that it was the middle-classes that mostly patronised the Gaiety, though it doesn't seem that there were enough of them to keep it financially viable at the end. There's a lot more in *Staging Life* than I've been able to refer to in this review. I've not mentioned the actors and actresses, some of whom moved on to greater acclaim in the London theatres. Sybil Thorndike is an outstanding example. And the directors – Ben Iden Payne was succeeded by Lewis Casson, who when he resigned in 1914 expressed a somewhat dim view of Manchester's hostility to "any new experiment". Looking back some years later, Allan Monkhouse thought that the Gaiety went into decline after Casson's departure. Its productive life had been short-lived, but it had at least provided opportunities for new writers, even if it was within a relatively orthodox framework. I doubt that any of the Manchester writers broke new ground, unless it was in terms of using their region as a basis for drama. There were, as far as I can tell, no working-class writers involved. Manchester Grammar School was in the background of more than one of the playwrights.

There is one point I'd like to mention, and not in the spirit of nit-picking. Harding refers to Jack Kahane, who had a play, *The Manor,* performed at the Gaiety. He later lived in Paris and founded the Obelisk Press which published Henry Miller and others, including any number of books banned in Britain because they were said to be pornographic. Harding says that he also published William Burroughs, but he only came along years after Kahane died in 1939. It was Kahane's son, Maurice Girodias who published Burroughs' *Naked Lunch* in his Olympia Press series in 1959. There is a lot of information about Kahane, including his time in Manchester, his involvement in the founding of the Swan Club, and his friendships with Harold Brighouse and others, in Neil Pearson's *Obelisk: A History of Jack Kahane and the Obelisk Press,* published by Liverpool University Press, 2007.

Staging Life is a fascinating book which throws light on a mostly-forgotten period in the history of theatre in Britain. It's clearly written, has extensive notes and a useful bibliography. It's too much to expect that many of the plays John Harding mentions will ever be performed again, but he at least provides a good account of their existence.

STAGING LIFE: THE STORY OF THE MANCHESTER PLAY-
WRIGHTS
By John Harding
Greenwich Exchange. 280 pages. £18.99. ISBN 978-1-910996-17-1

STREET SONGS: WRITERS AND URBAN SONGS AND CRIES, 1800-1925

Are there any street singers now? Some people will say "Yes", and point to the young men in town centres who strum a guitar and try to imitate Bob Dylan and other popular entertainers. Others will dismiss this suggestion, and say that such people are hardly original in terms of them using mostly well-known songs, but how original were earlier street singers? Still, the contemporary singers certainly seem a long way from the man I remember walking down the middle of a street in a working-class area of a Northern industrial town, singing loudly. That would have been in the mid-1940s and I can't remember what song he was singing, though I doubt it was one he'd composed himself or even an old folk song. He clearly wasn't a local drunk on his way home from the pub, and I can only assume that he was something of an elderly leftover from the 1930s and the dark days of the Depression. Around the same time, I also still heard the voice of the rag-and-bone man calling out as his horse-and-cart trundled along the street.

Daniel Karlin surveys how some writers incorporated references to, and sometimes quotes from songs and street cries of a (mostly) 19th century provenance, into their work. His study largely focuses on Robert and Elizabeth Barrett Browning, William Wordsworth, James Joyce, Virginia Woolf, Walt Whitman, and Marcel Proust, with numerous additional acknowledgements to a wide range of novelists, essayists, and poets. There were no doubt plenty of other writers, including minor and now-forgotten figures, whose work could be usefully explored for traces of old songs and vanished street cries, even if they were used only for local colour. Clarence Rook's 1898 detective story, "The Stir Outside the Café Royal", contains the following line: "flower girls were selling 'nice vi'lets, sweet vi'lets, penny a bunch' ".

Writers, on the whole, appear to have delighted in the noises that could be encountered in the streets, to the extent that some thought that it wasn't just the songs to be heard, and the voices of traders advertising their wares, but all the additional sounds (carriages, conversations, etc.), that added up to what might be called the symphony of the streets. But not everyone shared this view, and Karlin uses Hogarth's illustration, "The Enrag'd Musician", to demonstrate how a man practising with his violin has found it impossible to concentrate because of the noises from the street. A child beats a drum, a baby wails, a knife-grinder is busy at his trade, a milkmaid is passing by, and the musician despairs. What one person finds appealing another dislikes. There is often an assumption that everyone will enjoy the cacophony of contemporary life. Take a walk down Market Street in Manchester any Saturday afternoon but leave your sensitivities behind as guitarists, singers, saxophonists, religious speakers, and more, not to mention the crowds of shoppers, set up a constant barrage of noise.

Karlin, in fact, refers to people who complained about the noise from the street, and wanted street singers and traders shouting out what was on offer, actually banned. The mathematician Charles Babbage, who "waged a vigorous campaign against all forms of street music in the 1860s", included 'The human voice in its various forms' in his pamphlet, *A Chapter on Street Nuisances* (1864)". He was, of course, unsuccessful, it being a fact of life that urban living inevitably brings one into close contact with other people's noise. And some people enjoy the familiarity and the noise of urban life.

It's perhaps only marginally relevant, but there was a popular song, "Tenement Symphony", sung by Tony Martin in an early-1940s Marx Brothers movie, *The Big Store*, which was built around the various sounds – a child crying, someone practising on a musical instrument, a gramophone blaring out, kids running down the stairs, etc. – to be heard when living in a tenement. It had a romantic feeling to it, perhaps almost influenced by a Popular Front ideology, which may not have been shared by anyone experiencing on a daily basis the realities of life in a tenement.

Karlin mentions a letter that Charles Lamb wrote to William Wordsworth in which he declined "to join the nature-worshipping choir", giving a Whitmanesque catalogue on the sights and sounds of Fleet Street and Covent Garden, and declaring that he 'often shed tears in the motley Strand from fullness of joy at so much life' ". Karlin will perhaps forgive me if I say that this reminds me of the poet Frank O'Hara's response when asked if he'd like to live in the country. He wouldn't mind, he said, provided there were bookshops and bars, theatres and cinemas, galleries and other signs that people hadn't given up on life.

I've talked a little about the general outline of *Street Songs*, but Karlin is, of course, concerned to deal with specifics in terms of pointing out where examples of a song or street cry can be discerned in a piece of literature. It should also be noted that his book "is about what street songs are doing in works of literature, not about the songs themselves........I am not "a musicologist or a historian or a social geographer; street song has found its way into works of literature.......what interests me is something that goes beyond mere reference, or that adds local colour to a realist fiction: something that plays a specific part in an artistic design".

A good idea of what Karlin is aiming for can be seen in his chapters on the work of Elizabeth Barrett Browning (EBB) and Robert Browning (RB). Living in Italy, they were sympathetic to efforts to bring about the unification of the country. Discussing EBB's poem, "Casa Guidi Windows", with its opening lines where the poet hears a child in the street singing "O bella libertà". Karlin points out that no record of that phrase "has been found in any Italian song or poem of the period". But, he adds, "It is plausible without being documented".

Other questions occur. The Brownings were not living in Casa Guidi when she started writing the poem. Various versions of the poem have different titles, and so on. Does it matter? The test is whether or not the finished poem achieves the effect the poet was striving for? : "The child singer is a made-up figure; he is not there by accident". The poem is a construct, meant to impart a message about liberty, and, as Karlin notes, it is something of a riposte to those poets and others who indulge in a "self-indulgent, lettered tradition of melancholy, of lamentations over Italy's fallen greatness". EBB had a more positive view of the potential for change, and understood that "It is necessary that the song of Italian freedom should come from a child, and from the street".

I have to say that Karlin's attention to the historical and political background in the work he discusses is extremely helpful. I don't imagine that all that many people are familiar with the intricacies of nineteenth century Italian history before unification. They may know a little more about events in Ireland, as they crop up in references in James Joyce's *Ulysses*, though I do wonder how many people have actually read it? It took me a long time to complete it in the 1960s, and I can't honestly claim that I've done more than glance at it since.

In *Ulysses* a one-legged sailor wanders the streets and sings a few words from "The Death of Nelson", a "well-known ballad". Other songs and poems – around 400, according to Karlin, quoting Don Gifford's *Ulysses Annotated* – are scattered around Joyce's book, though not in an arbitrary fashion. They are mostly there to buttress the narrative by illustrating what is going on in the minds of the characters, who, as Karlin says, remember occasions when they heard the song or poem in question. And there are songs that are performed on the streets in varying circumstances.

The one-legged sailor singing "The Death of Nelson" has already been mentioned. "The Boys of Wexford" is an Irish rebel song, with its roots in the failed 1798 uprising and the battle of Vinegar Hill. A prostitute sings a bawdy song about "the leg of the duck" that hasn't been identified, though Karlin doubts it was something that Joyce made up. A popular song, "My Girl's a Yorkshire Girl", is played on a pianola in a brothel. Is its use an indication of the presence of British soldiers in Dublin, and who might be expected to patronise the bars and brothels of the city?

 It's fascinating to follow Karlin's line of analysis as he places these songs in context and explains their relevance to the development of the novel. And instructive for those, like me, who love to read about the origins of fragments of songs that crop up in novels. When Molly whistles the tune of "There is a charming girl I love", Karlin says that the correct title is "It is a charming girl I love", and it derives from *The Lily of Killarney,* a light opera based on Dion Boucicault's high Victorian melodrama *The Colleen Bawn (1860)"*. Boucicault's play is still occasionally performed, but it's doubtful if *The Lily of Killarney* will see the light of day again.

What enhances Karlin's close textual analysis of the poems and books he studies is his enthusiasm, something which is especially evident in his chapter on Walt Whitman. And what a pleasure it is to see someone paying attention to the American poet. Karlin looks at Whitman's poem, "Sparkles from the Wheel", in which the poet joins (not just observes) a group of children as they watch a knife-grinder at work. My own memories stretch back far enough to seeing what must have been one of the last of his kind at work in the street, and to being interested in what he was doing.

Karlin draws our attention to the fact that it was hard work. We talk about the "daily grind" and "keeping our noses to the grindstone", a phrase that brings to mind the knife-grinder bent over his wheel. There is an amusing passage which deals with a satirical poem, "The Friends of Humanity, and the Knife-grinder", in which a well-meaning liberal questions a down-at-heel knife-grinder because his impoverished appearance suggests exploitation "by the rich and powerful". The man turns out to be fiercely independent, rejects any interest in politics, and indicates that the liberal's concern and philanthropy ought to extend to giving him sixpence so he can buy a pot of beer.

In Virginia Woolf's *Mrs Dalloway,* an old woman is seen near Regent's Park underground station "singing" what seems to be a wordless and most probably tuneless song: "ee um fah um so/foo swee too eem oo", which puts me in mind of the Dada performances at the Cabaret Voltaire in Zurich in 1916, and of children chanting nonsense rhymes. But Karlin, quoting an "incomprehensible song" that some children sing in another work by Virginia Woolf, asserts that it is "fundamentally different" to the old woman's "song", being well in the compositional tradition of "innumerable ballads, hymns, popular songs, and nursery rhymes".

There is so much more packed into each page of *Street Songs* that it would be possible to carry on talking about it almost endlessly. Proust makes an appearance, and in *Remembrance of Things Past,* Marcel "may be thought of as a kind of aural *flâneur,* enjoying and consuming the sounds of the city as they are brought to his ears". He "hears or mentions a score of cries relating to food", and the cries of numerous other street traders, such as the old-clothes man, the knife-grinder, and many more. There is an "erotic energy of the great city" and street cries suggest this. Karlin brings in references to Charpentier's opera, *Louise,* in which Paris and its temptations are highlighted. I remember seeing a performance of *Louise* in London some years ago and being intrigued by its musical portrayal of Paris street life.

Street Songs is clearly an academic work, thoroughly researched, with extensive notes, and intense analysis of its basic material. But it strikes me that it can be read to advantage by those who may not be involved in academic studies, but who have an interest in literature. It is clearly written, and even entertaining, which is not something that can always be said about academic texts.

STREET SONGS: WRITERS AND URBAN SONGS AND CRIES, 1800-1925 By Daniel Karlin
Oxford University Press. 195 pages. £30. ISBN 978-0-19-879235-2

THE TASTE OF MY MORNINGS: ESSAYS ON POETS, CRITICS & AMERICA

Some people perhaps prefer the critics they read to be acerbic, tearing into what they claim not to like and taking it apart. Young critics on the make often find it's a sure-fire way to success as they destroy a few careers on their way into the limelight. Nastiness becomes their stock-in-trade. Personally, I prefer the mature critic who looks for the best in what he is reviewing and generally writes about what interests him. It's much more satisfying to read measured commentary, and experience enthusiasm, than encounter the quick and glib that is designed only to draw attention to the reviewer rather than the work supposedly being reviewed.

Tony Roberts certainly never gives the impression that he is determined to make the reader notice him instead of what he is writing about. He is genuinely interested in the writers and the books he focuses on. The first essay in his book, "With the Topnotch Tates at 'Benfolly', 1937", is an entertaining account of a gathering of writers, including Allen Tate, his wife, the novelist Caroline Gordon, Ford Madox Ford and his companion, Janice Biala (sister of the abstract expressionist artist, Jack Tworkov), and Ford's secretary, 'Wally' Tworkov. A young Robert Lowell arrived out of the blue and camped on the lawn. Getting a bunch of writers together can often lead to a certain amount of friction, and there was a degree of it here, though Roberts handles it lightly. What does come through in his account of events is his fondness for the people concerned. He can evaluate their work as writers and look sympathetically at any human failings they may have. But on the whole it does seem that nothing very disturbing happened, though Tate thought that Lowell might become a nuisance.

The interest in Tate, Ford, and Lowell runs throughout the book, and several essays touch on aspects of their lives and work. Tate spent some time in Paris, though he's not often noticed when people write about the famed expatriates of the 1920s. Hemingway, Robert McAlmon, Malcolm Cowley, Hart Crane, Kay Boyle, and others like them normally attract attention, probably because they wrote novels and stories about their contemporaries, and in some cases got into trouble of one sort or another. Books about the Paris of the expatriates often like to have a few fallings-out and even fist-fights to push the narrative along. Tate, a quieter and more-conservative person, didn't stand aside from visiting the Dome and the Rotonde, noted expatriate watering holes, and meeting Hemingway, and Scott Fitzgerald. But he worked on his writing, though later wondering whether he needed to be in Paris to produce the material that he did. It's to Roberts' credit that he gives substance to Tate's sojourn in Paris.

As a good essayist should, Roberts draws attention to the overlooked, and his informative piece about Archibald MacLeish notes that "Few C20th American poets could boast of being as popular or successful as Archibald MacLeish (1892-1982) and few have had their readership collapse so quickly". He's likewise generous when dealing with James Dickey, once popular because of the film *Deliverance*, based on one of his novels, though probably less well-known as a poet, at least in this country. Dickey from all accounts wasn't an admirable person, being arrogant and aggressive. Roberts acknowledges these characteristics, but provides a close analysis of the poetry that recognises its shortcomings ("when not impressive it can at times be offensive") and also points to its better qualities.

Bad behaviour isn't a hallmark of every poet, but enough of them have shown signs of tantrums, breakdowns, mischief-making, and more, to provide material for several books. It might be that some people have expectations of poets in terms of misbehaviour and almost encourage them to go to extremes. And the poets, knowing that, like spoiled children, they will be indulged, take advantage of the situation. Dylan Thomas is a case in point, and "Dylan Thomas roars across America" recounts the Welsh poet's adventures as he drank, gave readings which could be spellbinding, drank more, insulted academics and propositioned their wives, drank even more, and left behind a legend of artistic outrageousness and a fund of anecdotes about his capacity for alcohol and boorishness. "There was a certain amount of poison in our goodwill", said the noted New York critic and novelist, Elizabeth Hardwick, and it neatly summed up how people hovered around Thomas waiting for him to be outrageous. It's the legend of the errant poet that has survived, while his poetry is mostly forgotten and his literary reputation, such as it is, largely rests on *Under Milk Wood*. Roberts is not unsympathetic towards Thomas, but notes his problems and limitations.

Other British writers visited America and left a better impression, at least in a few minds. Louis MacNeice was there and had an ill-fated affair with the novelist Eleanor Clark. She's probably little known here, though I recall reading her politically satirical, *The Bitter Box*, some years ago. Ted Hughes spent time in the United States, though he seems not to have liked the country, and its main attraction was Sylvia

Plath. And Charles Tomlinson, a quiet but impressive poet, was frequently in America and was influenced by American poets. The account by Roberts refers to Tomlinson's achievements, but I wonder how well-known he is in his home country? He's certainly never been what is described as a "popular poet", and it may be that his readership is largely limited to a few fellow-poets and some academics. Roberts is therefore providing a valuable service by devoting space to his work.

It's not all poets, and Roberts looks at the life of the exiled Russian political dissident, Alexander Herzen, at least insofar as his time in London was concerned. There is an essay on Richard Holmes, biographer of Shelley, Robert Louis Stevenson and Coleridge. It's easy to see why Holmes appeals to Roberts, his work as a biographer setting the style for successful biography. Roberts says that "all Holmes's biographical works are pursuits", and I very much have the feeling that it is what Roberts is doing when he delves into the lives and writings of his subjects. An essay on the novelist, William Styron, records the events of his career as a writer by looking closely at his novels, and relating them to his life experiences. Both the work and the life were flawed, as is probably the case with most writers, but Roberts paints a positive-enough picture to incline me to want to have another look at *Set This House on Fire*, which I read when it was published in the early-1960s but haven't looked at since. It's surely a sign of a good critic when what he writes makes the reader want to turn to the work under discussion, not turn away from it.

I was intrigued when I read the essay on Arthur Krystal, a man who from this account is a stickler for high standards and an opponent of what he sees as the dumbing-down of universities, literary criticism, and just about everything else. Roberts gives a balanced picture of someone who likes to employ a tone "described as provocative but not offensive". According to Krystal, "art has always been the product of talent, skill, inspiration, and labour, and so, to a degree, has been the appreciation of art". But, if Krystal is right, both creators and audience have failed in their duties, with the result that "the know-nothings, the politically suspect and the mercenary have taken over". It's difficult not to agree with Krystal, while at the same time feeling a bit embarrassed because one's own tastes are not always of the highest. Krystal says we live in "an age of diminished expectations" where, in Roberts' words, "taste has been reduced to a matter of personal preferences". The subversive thought occurs to me that it possibly always has been, though that might not make me feel any less guilty when I choose to watch an old episode of *Murder, She Wrote* instead of listening to *Two Gentle-*

men of Verona on the radio. I do know which is best when it comes to artistic qualities, but don't always feel the need to be demonstrating it.

There is so much more in *The Taste of My Mornings* that is worth reading besides what few examples I've referred to. An essay on Malcolm Cowley's poetry is useful, bearing in mind that his reputation rests on his work as a critic. Edmund Wilson and Lionel Trilling are discussed alongside each other, with Wilson as an example of a non-academic writer ranging over a variety of topics, and Trilling as a somewhat perhaps more-limited surveyor of life and literature. He, unlike Wilson, had the security of an academic career, so perhaps didn't need to take on some of the tasks that Wilson faced up to. But they are not set up as opposites, but rather as two sides of the same coin. And, as Roberts points out, both fell out of favour as fashions changed and "theory" crept into the universities.

I can't overlook Roberts's love of Robert Lowell. Leaving aside his appearance in the essay on the Tates at "Benfolly", he has three pieces devoted to him. They all deal adequately with his troubled life as well as his poetry, with one essay, "The Lives of Robert Lowell", inspecting several biographies of the poet and showing how different interpretations of the same facts are arrived at. It's an effective piece in terms of persuading readers to not always be convinced by a single account of a life.

Before closing let me declare an interest. One of the essays includes a review of a book of mine, so I could be accused of a less than detached view of Roberts' book. Perhaps so, but I feel that I can honestly recommend it to anyone who enjoys reading good literary criticism and commentary. His writing is always clear, concise, and with a care for the facts of a writer's life. And Roberts is enthusiastic. He gives the impression that he cares for the people he writes about, even when they are less than perfect.

THE TASTE OF MY MORNINGS: ESSAYS ON POETS, CRITICS
& AMERICA By Tony Roberts
Shoestring Press. 299 pages. £12. ISBN 978-1-912524-26-6

AND MY HEAD EXPLODED : TALES OF DESIRE, DELIRIUM AND GYPSIES

I'm venturing into unknown territory by writing about what was being published in Prague in the 1890s and early 1900s. And I doubt that there are all that many readers in Britain who can claim an acquaintance with Czech literature generally, beyond Kafka, Jaroslav Hašek, Bohumil Hrabel, and later, Josef Švorecký, Václav Havel, Milan Kundera, and Ivan Klíma. The latter quartet perhaps gained a certain prominence during the Cold War years because they represented, in one way or another, elements of the dissident literature emanating from the Iron Curtain countries.

But every country has its traditions, and although its literature may only throw up a handful of major writers, there are always plenty of others who contributed to its variety and development. To be given an opportunity to see some of their work in translation, especially that of what might be thought of as minor writers, is always valuable and interesting.

I suppose it's inevitable that, coming across the term, *fin-de-siècle,* one tends to think of Huysmans and *A Rebours*, or of Oscar Wilde and the fragile English poets like Ernest Dowson and Lionel Johnson. But if we use *fin-de-siècle* simply to designate a period rather than a mood, a style, or a particular approach to creativity, then it's obvious that a variety of writing will have been produced during the years concerned. Not every author wanted to view the world as in decline, or subject to a myth of decadence, with madness and self-indulgence in drugs and other forms of escapism dominating. It's perhaps true that writers focusing on such subjects often tend to be remembered, and sometimes even held up as typical of a time.

If this is the case, Arthur Briesky's "Mors Syphilitica" might be an example to use to demonstrate how a subject can be viewed as signifying an aspect of a *fin-de-siècle* atmosphere. In it Death visits a syphilitic young man – the sores on his face and his attempts to cover them with powder are vividly described – and promises to spare him if he refrains from any further sexual activity. They go out, into the city, with Death occasionally pausing to gather someone to his fold – "an old woman huddled in a shabby coat", and an old man who has had a stroke – and eventually arrive at a wild party where the young man can't resist kissing a woman he meets and lusts after. With this act he seals his fate, and, in despair, commits suicide. With syphilis having an almost-plague like impact in many European cities in the nineteenth century (think of poetry, prose and art coming from London, Vienna, Paris - Brlesky's story takes its lead from an illustration by Félicien Rops) we are in a society that seemed doomed to fall because of its decadence.

A plague of the kind that swept Europe in earlier times is at the centre of Miloš Marten's "Courtigiana" ("The Courtesan"), in which a woman, famed for her beauty, takes revenge on men who have used and abused her. The city of Florence is in the grip of the plague and the rich have locked themselves in their castles and palaces in an attempt to escape the infection, while the poor, without any effective means of protection or medication, die slowly and horribly. There are references to the supposed causes of the plague, such as comets, magic spells, and more. I was reminded of the line, "Brightness falls from the air", in Thomas Nashe's 1593 poem, "In Time of Pestilence".

The courtesan is invited to a party being held so that the people present can, they hope, defy death. She declines at first, but then, knowing that she herself has been infected, decides to attend so that she can spread the disease among the people she despises. It could be that this story reveals some of the fear of women that was a hallmark of *fin-de-siècle* art and literature. Bram Dijkstra's *Idols of Perversity: Fantasies of Feminine Evil in Fin-de-Siècle Culture* (Oxford University Press, 1986) is a detailed study of the subject. The courtesan in Marten's story may have good reasons for what she does, but the fact that she is prepared to disperse the plague among both men and women, some of whom she probably doesn't know, points to a kind of perversity in her thinking.

And what is one to make of Donna Flavia, a cold but beautiful female sculptress in Julius Zeyer's "Inultus: A Prague Legend", who persuades a young man to model for her as she attempts to re-create the look on Christ's face as he was crucified: "Will you be the model for my King of the Jews in the hour of his death?". This requires the man to be suspended on a cross and leads to her really crucifying him and placing a crown of thorns on his head, then thrusting a dagger into his side. He dies, and she initially hides the body, but eventually regrets what she's done, and kills herself.

As I said earlier, *fin-de-siècle*, if applied loosely to a period, can encompass other kinds of writing outside those described above. Božena Benešová's "In the Twilight" is a fairly straightforward account of how a woman is disillusioned when the man she had assumed would propose to her after his wife dies, announces that he is going to marry his housekeeper. It has an element of irony in that the man, in his turn, has assumed that the woman will understand why the housekeeper is his choice and that they can still meet and be friends. She is naturally less than enthusiastic about the idea. The situation is recognisable and told in a way that extends sympathy to the woman.

František Gellner's "My Travelling Companion" is a light-hearted tale of the narrator being burdened with an unwelcome companion as he sets out to visit Bavaria. The uninvited companion can't help involving them both in embarrassing situations as he proceeds to upset other people, destroy things accidentally, and generally make a nuisance of himself. He is like the proverbial bull in a china shop. It's the kind of anecdotal narrative once used to fill up spaces in newspapers, not requiring a great deal of time or attention to skim through it. But it's entertaining.

There is also the brilliant "The Empty Chair: An Analysis of an Unwritten Tale" by Richard Weiner. With its discursive style, it purports to be "a pragmatic account of the non-existence of a literary work". Instigated by a fragment of overheard conversation, in which one man was insisting that another should visit him, it quickly moves into discussions about readers, the difference between "sensory and psychotic horror", reflections on 'Visite', a poem by Charles Vildrac, and a variety of other topics which have a bearing on why the story was never written.

There is an aside about how one of the writer's other pieces was inspired by a painting by František Kupka. And along the way, there is a long anecdote about how the narrator met a friend in the street, invited him home to have some tea, asked him to pop down to a local shop to get something to eat, and waited in vain for the friend to return. Edgar Allan Poe comes to mind ("The Man in the Crowd") when reading this story. The narrator says that the incident occurred when he was living in Paris in 1914, and that he did meet his friend again, but no mention was made of what had happened on the previous occasion, though the friend surprised him by saying, "I really must come and visit you sometime".

There are several other pieces in *And My Head Exploded* which can be read with pleasure, and there is an informative introduction and short notes on the various authors.

Gypsy by Karel Hynek Mácha moves further back in the nineteenth century (it was originally published in 1835) and takes the reader into a world of ruined castles, decadent aristocrats, gypsies, Jews, superstitious peasants, thunder, lightning, a madwoman, and all the other Gothic characteristics of the Romantic movement. Two wandering gypsies arrive in a small village and, in due course, proceed to upset the apple-cart. Things and people are not as they seem, and revelations about who the gypsies really are, and how they've found their way to the village, eventually tumble off the page. It's all very melodramatic, though somewhat lightened by Bárta, a heavy-drinking elderly veteran of the Napoleonic Wars who keeps up a running commentary on his supposed exploits, most of which are so exaggerated that they can't possibly be taken seriously.

There is a long, scholarly introduction to *Gypsy* by Geoffrey Chew which places it in context and points to its relevance to Czech history and folklore. He is informative on the subject of Gypsies, and their origins, and how they were, at one time, believed in Western culture to have come from the Czech province of Bohemia, hence the French applying the term Bohemians to students in Paris who dressed unconventionally, like Gypsies. And he suggests there was something of a bond between Gypsies and Jews due to both groups being outsiders, and having no fixed place in the wider society.

There are references to the novel's relationship to Romantic writers outside Czechoslovakia, such as Byron and Sir Walter Scott. It's possible to read *Gypsy* as a simple, routine Gothic novel, with all its coincidences and confusions, but having it analysed gives it a resonance that enables it to take on added meanings. Chew points to a passage where the young Jew, somewhat unhinged mentally by a combination of circumstances, pours out a curious stream of consciousness ramblings. It appears to have had a lasting influence, in that it "served as a model for the 'automatic' writing of the avant-garde Czech 'Poetists' before World War Two". Now what do we know about them?

AND MY HEAD EXPLODED : TALES OF DESIRE, DELIRIUM
AND DECADENCE FROM FIN-DE-SIÈCLE PRAGUE
Translated by Geoffrey Chew, Introduction by Peter Zusi
Jantar Publishing. 204 pages. £15. ISBN 978-0-9934467-1-9

GYPSIES
Karel Hynek Mácha. Translated and with an introduction by Geoffrey Chew
Jantar Publishing. 138 pages. £12. ISBN 978-0-9934467-6-4

DREAMERS: WHEN THE WRITERS TOOK POWER, GERMANY 1919

November 7th, 1918, and crowds of soldiers, sailors, and trade union-ists were pouring through the streets of Munich, many of them armed and convinced that it was time to seize power. Germany was generally in chaos, as units of the navy and army mutinied, and the threat of revo-lution hung over everything. The final stages of the Great War had brought near-starvation, with the Allied naval blockade preventing food from reaching an already-desperately hungry civilian population. Strikes, demonstrations, and other methods of expressing dissatisfac-tion, had almost brought the country to a standstill. At the front, ele-ments of the army were convinced they should carry on fighting and that they were being stabbed in the back by agitators at home and, in particular, by Bolsheviks and Jews.

Resistance to the would-be revolutionaries in Munich was light, or non-existent. To his surprise, and perhaps that of many others, Kurt Eisner, a drama critic, described by Anthony Read in *The World On Fire: 1919 and the Battle with Bolshevism* (Cape, 2008), as "the very epitome of the bohemian café intellectual", found himself elected Prime Minister of the new Republic of Bavaria. The King had fled, and the parliament, previously controlled by the Majority Social Demo-crats, had disintegrated. Eisner declared Bavaria "a free state", and a new government, based on a system involving Councils of Soldiers, Workers, and Peasants, began to take shape.

Wilhelm Herzog, a dramatist and journalist, was appointed Press Secre-tary and Chief Censor. Josef Staimer, a former warehouseman, became Chief of Police almost by accident. Eisner, realising that his govern-ment would need the support of the existing bureaucracy if it was to function efficiently, also inclined to the view that he ought to cultivate relations with members of the Majority Social Democrats (SPD). His own party, the Independent Social Democrats (USPD), "had very little structured support, particularly in more rural areas". The problem of trying to interest people in those conservative rural areas in radical change would become a key one. Munich depended on them for its food supplies. But, as Volker Weidermann, points out: "As much as he put on a Bavarian accent and emphasised his love for the state, the Ber-lin Jew Eisner had a very difficult time in the rural parts of Bavaria. More bluntly, he didn't stand a chance".

Eisner's difficulties were further increased by the fact that, though he claimed to be heading a revolution, he didn't move fast enough, or decisively enough, to satisfy the more-extreme supporters of the new order. When Eisner met Karl Liebknecht from the German Communist Party he was told that they wouldn't back what was seen as a "compromise regime......Socialism could only be introduced if everything else was first torn down. The country could only be built anew once the entire capitalist system had been destroyed". As was usual with the Left, different factions began to form: "A Russian-German student from Moscow, Max Levien, founded a branch of the communist Spartacist League". And the poet, playwright, essayist and anarchist, Eric Mühsam, started "a union of revolutionary internationalists". Levien later got out of Munich safely, but died in one of Stalin's purges in the 1930s. Mühsam died in a Nazi concentration camp.

When elections were held in January, 1919, Eisner's USPD made a disastrous showing, whereas the moderate SPD, with Erhard Auer at its head, and the conservative Bavarian People's Party, between them got the majority of the votes. So, who ruled in Bavaria? Matters came to a head when Eisner was assassinated by a disgruntled ex-army officer who declared "I hate Bolshevism". Whatever government existed virtually fell apart and the Workers and Soldiers Council attempted to take over. A Congress of Councils met to elect a new leader, though some of those proposed as candidates were reluctant to take on any responsibilities. One of them, Johannes Hoffmann, a former schoolteacher, had been a minister in Eisner's short-lived government, and had "instituted an anti-clerical education policy that had made the Catholic Church's blood boil". Weidermann says that he had "the threat of death hanging over him". Hoffmann may have been anti-Catholic, but he was also anti-Communist, and would later move against them when he thought they were becoming too prominent in Munich.

Referring to the "ungoverned city, in this ungoverned state," Weidermann describes the "arrival of dreamers, winter sandal-wearers, preachers, plant-whisperers, the liberated, and the liberators, long-haired men, hypnotists and those who have been hypnotised drifters". Gustav Regler says that he turned up in Munich with "scanty luggage and little money, confused but with the feeling of having reached a new and better land". Regler would manage to get out of Munich when the end came and, a committed communist, he fought in the International Brigades in Spain in the 1930s.

The Council Republic drew up a list of "People's Delegates" (the new name for Ministers) that proposed Erich Mühsam as responsible for Foreign Affairs, though as one of his colleagues remarked, "he was such a literary bohemian that no one could imagine him in a dignified official post". So, Franz Lipp was given the post instead and turned out to be insane. He sent numerous telegrams to the Pope and one to Lenin which said that the Bavarian proletariat was "as firmly joined together as a hammer", but also complained that his predecessor had taken the key to the ministry toilet with him when he left.

And there was Silvio Gessell, who claimed to "know how to reform the financial world" by keeping "money constantly on the move, circulating, working for the workers, not the capitalists who hoard it". His theories did have some merit, and several other people had similar ideas in the inter-war period, but it was not the time or place to try to put them into practice. Many ordinary citizens of Bavaria, hearing of Gessell's plans, were convinced that their savings, and their property, would be seized.

Ernst Toller, poet and playwright, became head of Bavaria's government, insofar as one existed, but he was besieged by hundreds of odd-balls and misfits insisting that their personal problems and beliefs be immediately dealt with. Weidermann lists some of their demands, relating to sex education, eating cooked foods, the arrest of personal enemies, and non-porous underwear. None of this had anything to do with the very real problems relating to unemployment in Munich, the failure of supplies of food to reach the city, and other practical matters.

There was a "hardening of attitudes" among the revolutionaries with the "humanitarian dreamers", no longer in charge. The communists were increasingly playing an active role and the government "was now working flat out to form a Red Army", though it was probably a little late in the day. There was a determination on the part of the authorities in Germany generally, and those in Bavaria, to put an end to the chaotic situation in Munich. The Freikorps, largely comprised of ex-officers and patriotic other ranks, was being armed, albeit surreptitiously, by the regular army and numbered around 22,000 experienced soldiers.

Berlin had also ordered units of the army into Bavaria, and some troops who had previously aligned themselves with the revolutionaries had switched to the counter-revolutionary forces. Meanwhile, the so-called Red Army could muster around 15,000 men, many of them just workers with guns and not trained soldiers. They were comparatively lightly armed when compared to the tanks, artillery, and other equipment that the Freikorps had access to. There was also a lack of discipline among the Red Army personnel that would affect their operational performance when faced with well-organised troops.

Toller had somehow been given command of the Red Army, and he did manage to have one or two minor successes when the fighting started. But the end was a foregone conclusion and by the 30th April, 1919, the Red Army had fallen apart. There had been rumours of the summary executions of prisoners and other atrocities by both sides, and when the Freikorps finally entered Munich they discovered ten bodies, hostages who had been executed on the orders of hard-line communists, who had effectively taken over under the leadership of Eugen Leviné. He is credited with the famous statement, "We communists are all dead men on leave".

The sight of the dead hostages was enough to send the Freikorps on a rampage of reprisals, with dozens of alleged supporters of the revolutionary government, and even some perfectly innocent citizens who happened to be in the wrong places at the wrong times, rounded up and shot. The luckier ones, including Toller, who had tried to be a voice for moderation, and was appalled at the killing of the hostages, were imprisoned. Toller eventually received a five year jail sentence. Eugene Leviné was arrested, tried, and executed by firing squad.

Volker Weidermann paints a broad canvas with a large cast of characters, only a few of whom I've been able to mention. There was Gustave Landauer, a great enthusiast for the works of Walt Whitman and with wide-ranging, provocative ideas about education and culture. Gusto Gräser. who wore "a kind of toga made of sackcloth, held together with wooden pegs", and "preached texts by Chinese philosophers, passages from Nietzsche's *Zarathustra*, and his own aphorisms". And Ret Marut, who managed to escape from Munich when the revolution collapsed and later turned up in Mexico, where, under the name of B.Traven, he wrote novels like *The Death Ship, The Cotton Pickers*, and *The Treasure of the Sierra Madre*.

Dreamers tells an intriguing story, but it's also a sad one. That the Munich revolution would eventually collapse was inevitable, given the circumstances. The insurrectionists had failed in Berlin, and two of its leaders, Rosa Luxemburg and Karl Liebknecht, were killed by the Freikorps. It must surely have been obvious from the start to people like Kurt Eisner and Ernst Toller, if not to some of the more-utopian minded individuals in the city, that the central government in Germany would never allow Bavaria to separate itself from the rest of the country. It's also more than probable that other governments had an interest in seeing the uprising crushed. The world was in turmoil in 1919 following the Russian Revolution, a short-lived communist take-over in Hungary, and what seemed like extreme radical activity in many places, including France, the United States, and Britain. The authorities everywhere probably breathed a sigh of relief when a revolution failed.

There is also the question of whether or not a revolution in Munich could ever have succeeded, given the nature of many of the revolutionaries. While they were often engrossed in theories about the role of the arts, financial reform, educational policies, and such matters, what concerned most ordinary people – jobs, food, security, efficient running of essential services, and the like – was being overlooked. It does seem that, in many ways, the focus of attention was solely on Munich. As noted, what happened there held little interest for the population of rural areas. And even in Munich itself, most citizens probably looked askance at the bohemians and weird characters who drifted into the city. It must have seemed to them that every crank with a cause had come to town. Once the Freikorps had taken over, there was a drive to get rid of those who wouldn't conform: "Death to the Reds. Death to the Jews. Death to the Russians". And anyone else who didn't fit in.

DREAMERS: WHEN THE WRITERS TOOK POWER, GERMANY 1919
By Volker Weidermann
Pushkin Press. 253 pages. £16.99. ISBN 978-1-78227-504-6

THE 19TH CENTURY UNDERWORLD: CRIME, CONTROVERSY & CORRUPTION

In many ways it's difficult to generalise about a whole century. The nineteenth encompassed a wide range of social, political, moral and other concerns, not to mention all kinds of technical advances and changes in the structure of society. But there may be some discernible variations in how people behaved at certain times. It seems to be an accepted belief that the early part of the nineteenth century was marked by excesses in behaviour, at least among certain groups (and even then perhaps among only certain individuals in those groups), whereas later standards were set higher and a wider sense of propriety came into effect. I'm not convinced that this was the case. There have been numerous studies of the Victorian period which have shown that underneath a supposedly polite and polished surface there was a bubbling sewer of crime, sexual deviancy, and social disorder. It may have expressed itself in somewhat different ways to the Regency period, but it was still there.

Stephen Carver doesn't attempt to survey every aspect of human activity in the nineteenth century, but rather chooses to focus on specific elements of it. One of his early chapters, "A Corinthian's Guide to the Metropolis", looks at the life and adventures of Pierce Egan, author of *Life in London or the Day and Night Scenes of Jerry Hawthorn Esq., and his elegant friend Corinthian Tom in their Rambles and Sprees through the Metropolis*, originally published in 1821. Popular in its day, and still seeing occasional revivals of one sort or another (it works well on the radio), it manipulated the reading public's taste for accounts of low-life and particularly the slang that denizens of the "underworld" employed. It also, Carver suggests, put forward the view that the "underclass of society has all the fun". It wasn't true, of course, but it may have touched on the lurking suspicion that many people had (still have?) that their own lives lacked colour and adventure, and were consequently dull. Reading about those living dangerously on the fringes of society may have provided a voyeuristic thrill for the settled and safe in their homes.

Egan, whose early career is described as that of "a jobbing hack in the age of Austen, unconnected with fashionable society", achieved some recognition in certain circles with his book, *Boxiana,* which purported to provide a mini-history of boxing. It was a brutal sport when Egan was writing about it, fought bare-knuckle style and with no limit to the number of rounds. The bout usually ended when one of the opponents was physically unable to carry on. Boxers died or were badly injured, but crowds gathered at venues where fights were about to take place, despite it often being illegal to do so. I would guess that *Boxiana* is rarely read these days apart from by historians of the sport.

Egan wasn't the only writer to play around with the jargon and mischief of the underworld. Harrison Ainsworth, a hugely popular novelist in his day, though few of his books are remembered now, and Edward Bulwer-Lytton, also ventured into this territory. What Ainsworth did was to almost glamorise criminals like Jack Sheppard and Dick Turpin, whose actual personalities and exploits were really far less convincing than the fictional accounts implied. Things probably haven't changed all that much when one thinks of the ways in which Hollywood has frequently given minor criminals a veneer of attractiveness they probably never possessed. Were the real Bonnie and Clyde anything like the characters that Faye Dunaway and Warren Beatty portrayed in the film about them? Was Billy the Kid a handsome hero and not the nasty psychopath he most likely was? But in the nineteenth century, as now, people liked to hear about supposedly colourful villains. And even when the number of readers was relatively small, and cinema not even thought of, theatrical productions of varying quality, and doubtful authorship, toured the country, pulling in crowds, and providing exciting and highly imaginative versions of the lives of Sheppard and Turpin. Today, most people don't read books and are content to watch chronicles of crime, fictional and real, on television.

With the growth of newspapers and magazines aiming at a newly-developing audience of working-class readers, real crimes could be reported almost as soon as they happened. Murder became a standard item. Carver chooses a few juicy items to investigate, including, perhaps inevitably, the murders attributed to Jack the Ripper. In its way, the Ripper "Autumn of terror" is more interesting than an account of a brutal killing as part of a robbery, or a poisoning for financial gain. It can be used to focus attention on the social problems encountered in Whitechapel. Poor housing, homelessness, unemployment and low-paid jobs when work was available, drunkenness, prostitution. The Ripper's victims, and others who weren't killed by him but died in similar circumstances, were women who had been driven to selling their bodies because of the need to find enough money to pay for cheap lodgings, food, and the alcohol they wanted to numb their senses to the awfulness of their situations. Diseases including syphilis, were rife, and easily spread.

Sex we are often told was a taboo subject in polite Victorian society, but it was present in many forms, including pornography in which there was a thriving trade. Under-the-counter publications catered for most tastes, with a particular demand existing for tales of flagellation, something often referred to as "the English vice". Titles like *The Whippingham Papers* left no-one in any doubt as to what they were about. An intriguing aspect of nineteenth century pornography is that some quite well-known authors, writing under pseudonyms, produced work that could only be sold clandestinely. The poet, Algernon Charles Swinburne, is said to have written various pornographic works. Carver says that Dickens' friend, the well-known journalist, George Augustus Henry Sale, co-authored *The Mysteries of Verbena House, or, Miss Bellasis Birched for Thieving,* "an erotic novel set in a girls' school". Carver also points to *Teleny,* a novel which throws some light on the gay underworld of London at a time when homosexuality was a criminal offence. It has sometimes been attributed to Oscar Wilde, but it's unlikely that he was involved in writing it, and it's probable that it was the work of several authors, with the manuscript added to anonymously over time.

The publishers who risked prosecution for bringing out pornography, and the booksellers who peddled it, were often curious characters. Leonard Smithers backed a literary magazine called *The Savoy,* which printed work by writers (Ernest Dowson, John Gray, Lionel Johnson, Arthur Symons) associated with the so-called Decadent Movement of the 1890s, but he also did a steady trade in risqué material. John Camden Hotton, a "publisher and lexicographer", was reputed to have written "a comic opera called *Lady Bumtickler's Revels",* though I can't imagine that it ever had any public performances. And there was William Dugdale, "eldest son of a Quaker tailor from Stockport", who published books with titles which, Carver says, "speak for themselves": *Intrigues in a Boarding School, The Confessions of a Lady's Maid, The Confessions of a Young Lady,* and *The Wedding Night.* Books like these didn't come cheap, and were often printed in limited editions, so circulation must have been limited to a mainly middle and upper-class readership.

One of the dark sides of the Victorian sexual underworld was the use of children, both boys and girls, to satisfy the cravings of sexual predators, and a famous court case highlighted it. The journalist and editor of the *Pall Mall Gazette,* W.T. Stead, published a series of articles under the general title, "The Maiden Tribute of Modern Babylon", in which, among other things, he asserted that a young girl aged thirteen could be bought for five pounds. To prove his point, Stead did actually engage in such a transaction, though without any intention of claiming his right to molest her. He had a midwife standing by to check that the girl had not been touched. His campaigning, besides causing a sensation and selling papers, was designed to attack the government of the day for not raising the age of consent to sixteen. The fact that Stead's reports prompted an outcry against the government, and that it was revealed that a prominent Tory MP who had opposed Stead's call for reform had a close friendship with the owner of several brothels, seems to have prompted action by the establishment and Stead was charged with abduction and indecent assault (the midwife's examination) and sentenced to three months in prison. It really does appear to have been a case of him being victimised for rocking the boat.

Burke and Hare, the infamous body snatchers who made a living digging up fresh corpses and selling them to medical schools for dissection purposes, make an appearance. They weren't the only ones involved in this macabre business, though they took it to new depths of depravity when they made up for a lack of ready-dead people by murdering a few so they could carry on meeting the demands for bodies. Carver paints a picture of gangs competing for corpses, armed guards at cemeteries, and the way in which the medical establishment turned a blind eye to where the dead came from. And the law was often reluctant to take action because stopping the body snatchers could lead to a lack of resources for medical students to use. Matters were only resolved when it was decided that the unclaimed bodies of dead prisoners and one-time inhabitants of workhouses could be used in the interests of research. Some might argue that it was another example of the poor always being exploited, even when dead.

And who was the real person behind Dickens's villain, Fagin? Debate continues about whether or not his presence in *Oliver Twist* added to the stereotype of a Jew, and so incited anti-semitism. Was the basis for the character of Fagin a man called Isaac "Ikey" Solomon? He was a Jewish criminal who is described as being, "one of the most affluent and successful fences in London", but who was eventually arrested, tried, and transported to Australia where, at the end of his life, he ran a tobacconist's shop and died impoverished.

The public's taste for the details of murders continued unabated throughout the nineteenth century. One that attracted a great deal of attention was the "Murder in the Red Barn", the victim being Maria Marten who was killed in 1827 by her latest lover, William Corder. She wasn't the innocent maiden widespread sentiment made her out to be.

But her story became the basis for a popular melodrama which retained its interest long enough for it to be made into a film in the 1930s. The villain was played by Tod Slaughter, an actor who could strut around a stage, or film set, and leer in a suitably evil manner. He certainly impressed me when I saw the film at a local flea-pit in the 1940s.

It should be obvious from at least some of my comments that *The 19th Century Underworld* is highly entertaining. That's perhaps a strange word to use when writing about a book that deals largely with murder, mayhem, and misery. But it's a fact that we like to read about such matters from a safe distance, sitting in the comforts of our homes and knowing that nobody we come across on the page is going to turn up to terrorise us. If people aren't fascinated by the crimes of the past why is it that the obsession with the Jack the Ripper continues to occupy the minds of film-makers, novelists, social historians, and the people who watch the films and read the books?

Stephen Carver has written an account that manages to guide the reader through areas of the nineteenth century underworld in an easy-to-read manner. He's done his homework, and there are plenty of notes, and a useful bibliography. I could say that he largely explores themes which are mostly well-known, but then it occurs to me that they may not be to readers unfamiliar with nineteenth century social history. How many people, apart from some of those around my age, will have heard of Maria Marten and the Murder in the Red Barn?

THE 19TH CENTURY UNDERWORLD: CRIME, CONTROVERSY
& CORRUPTION By Stephen Carver
Pen & Sword Books. 209 pages. £12.99. ISBN 978-1-52675-167-6

VICE, CRIME, AND POVERTY : HOW THE WESTERN IMAGINATION INVENTED THE UNDERWORLD

The "underworld" is something probably most associated in people's minds with a criminal fraternity of one kind or another. *The Underworld Story* is the title of a 1950 film I recently watched, and it did involve a shady gangster, though interestingly the corruption he stimulated had spread into the upper reaches of society and dragged down a supposedly-powerful newspaper publisher and his son. Perhaps this was always behind the fear of the underworld, that it was there waiting to break out of its disreputable habitat and move to disturb the respectable world and its conventions and comforts?

That certainly seems to have been the belief in the nineteenth-century when a widespread suspicion of the lower-depths engendered an understanding that, metaphorically and physically, there was an underworld comprised of various groups who, at some point, might join together to turn on the bourgeoisie and destroy its fragile social structure. The *bas fonds de société* (dregs of society) were a noticeable presence in the towns and cities that expanded as the industrial revolution developed in the West. The underworld was something that, in a definable sense, arose out of urbanisation: "Poverty, crime, rape, and incest did indeed dwell in the depths of the rural world - and perhaps especially there – but the lower depths and underworld existed only in large cities". And furthermore, the nineteenth-century brought a change in perception: "A whole system of representation that had been erected at the end of the Middle Ages around outcasts and marginals was being reordered into a more coherent scheme, now clearly inscribed in a social dimension".

Dominique Kalifa points out that in earlier times there had been laws to restrict the movements and activities of certain types who were deemed to be functioning in anti-social ways. Beggars, tramps, vagabonds, and others who didn't appear to have a steady job and a fixed abode, could find themselves subject to restrictions in terms of being banned from certain areas. They were looked on as a nuisance, but were not necessarily seen as some sort of overall threat to the continuation of an ordered society. They were not revolutionary, and in many ways existed almost as a parallel society, with its own hierarchies and customs. Victor Hugo's *Notre-Dame de Paris* delves into this world, with its Court of Miracles. Fake blind men, false cripples, prostitutes, con-men of varying kinds. It can be seen as amusing, as the blind suddenly see and the lame walk normally, but it had its dark side of vice and crime.

It was with the spread of slums in cities that a notion of an underworld caught the imagination of writers who were not slow to exploit the idea of a mass of people who could, given the right circumstances, rise as a body to present a threat to the wider society. At the same time, novelists could often impart a degree of glamour to the exploits of certain members of the underclass. There seems to have always been a fascination with criminals. Harrison Ainsworth wrote about the highwayman, Dick Turpin, in *Rookwood*, and about Jack Sheppard in a serialised novel of that name. Neither Turpin nor Sheppard were exactly pleasant individuals, and both were seemingly prone to violence when it suited them, but their exploits were given a veneer of almost-heroic amiability when fictionalised. The likeable rogue was to become a fixture in many novels. And John Gay's *The Beggar's Opera* was a hit in London and its songs whistled and sung everywhere.

Exploring the underworld by means of a book or magazine perhaps gave a vicarious shiver of apprehension to the comfortable and secure. The way crime and vice are reported now isn't much different, and may appeal to a deep desire to break out of the trap of conformity. "I wish I had the nerve to be a great thief ", said the American entertainer, Richard "Lord" Buckley, and his audience laughed approvingly, as if sharing the sentiment.

The nineteenth-century fear of the underworld was, however, largely derived from knowing that there was a very large segment of society that, though working when it could, lived in absolute squalor and in close proximity to the criminal class. Crime of a routine kind was often a way for working class people to survive. Louis Chevalier's classic study, *Labouring Classes and Dangerous Classes in Paris During the First Half of the Nineteenth Century,* is of key relevance in this context, and ought to be in the library of anyone interested in life in the French capital in the period concerned. It was Chevalier who pointed to the novels, plays, and other materials that can usefully throw light on the underworld and its denizens. Hugo, Balzac, and Eugène Sue are all mentioned. The latter's *Mystèries de Paris* has all the liveliness of a potboiler, but is also a mine of information about the "world beneath the world", as the Goncourts described it.

Pauperism, a word that came into use in England around 1815, and in France ten or so years later, sprang out of industrialisation: "It referred to a new form of poverty, a new social state produced by factory working conditions, one marked by low wages, structural unemployment, and the loss of complementary traditional income". It was "the forced condition of a large portion of the members of society". It was often the lower middle-class, those just a step or two away from the abyss of pauperism, who felt easily threatened by the underworld. Told sensational tales of it by an increasing number of opportunistic newspapers, they feared losing what little they had, and so could easily be aroused to look down on the underclass.

It wasn't just Paris that offered insights into an underworld of poverty and criminality for inspection, either by social commentators or novelists. Dickens was an obvious example in England, and there was also Elizabeth Gaskell, whose *Mary Barton* focused on the Manchester working-class. Kalifa quotes from a lesser-known novelist, Geraldine Jewsbury who, in her 1851 *Marian Withers,* described the city's lower depths as having "repugnant visions/sights and intolerable stench, where all the garbage, filthy water and muck of houses and basements were putrefying in the streets". A little later, Arthur Morrison's *Tales of Mean Streets* and *A Child of the Jago* would bring the reader back to London and its scenes of misery and vice.

There were social reformers, of course, and indeed the aforementioned writers of fiction had more than earning a fee in mind when they produced their novels and stories. But it was investigators like Henry Mayhew (*London Labour and the London Poor)* and Charles Booth (*Life and Labour of the People of London)* who truly drew attention to the facts of vice, crime and poverty. In New York, Jacob Riis did the same with *How the Other Half Lives*. There was even an exchange of ideas when the American Jack London came to England and produced the powerful *The People of the Abyss*.

It may be debatable as to how many people were influenced to favour reforms by fictional commentary on the underworld, and how many by the factual reporting on poverty and corruption. It's probably impossible to obtain exact figures of the readerships in either category, and in any case they wouldn't necessarily give a guide to influence. Perhaps both combined to shape thinking, in a positive or negative way, at various levels of society?

It may also be difficult to know how much people's thinking was manipulated by novels, and how much by sociological surveys, in terms of inculcating fears of a possible uprising from the lower depths. Was the savage repression of the Commune in 1871 partly due to perceptions that the insurrectionists were not the respectable working-class but were mostly drawn from a shifting and shapeless mass that, at one time might have been referred to as bohemia. Kalifa does discuss the relationship between the *bas-fond* and bohemia, and points to the fact that both begin to emerge as identifiable bodies around the same time in 1830s/1840s Paris. With regard to the Commune, Kalifa makes the interesting observation that: "Republican democracy was not really established in France until the 'rabble' of the underworld was definitively crushed after the Paris Commune".

We now think of bohemians as activists and hangers-on functioning in and around the arts, but earlier descriptions gave the term a wider implication. Marx had no hesitation in thinking of bohemia as including individuals who made a living at one or other of the hundreds of small trades to be found in early-nineteenth century Paris. And when the great illustrator Daumier produced a series called "The Bohemians of Paris" for the journal *Le Charivari,* he drew pictures of a second-hand clothes peddler, a cigar-butt collector, a beggar, a political refugee, a gleaner, and a pickpocket. As Marilyn R. Brown said in her *Gypsies and Other Bohemians: The Myth of the Artist in Nineteenth-Century France* (UMI Research Pres, 1985), Daumier's bohemians were "a repertoire of the various types of *déracinairés* to be seen wandering the gutters and quays of Paris". Gavarni also had a flexible approach to the types he thought of as bohemians when he drew pictures of them.

It's worth noting that Marx didn't have a high opinion of bohemians of the type described above and referred to them as a lumpenproletariat and a reactionary force that could be used by the authorities to suppress genuine protest movements. They were "the worst of all possible allies". But Kalifa makes an intriguing reference to some "young Milanese bohemians of the 1880s who came to Socialism through reading Sue, Vallès, or Zola (and) thought that from this shameful subproletariat, this savage society of beggars, the downgraded, pimps and prostitutes, would someday emerge the true people endowed with a real class consciousness".

This sort of misguided romanticising of the lower depths has not been unusual among bohemian intellectuals, writers, and artists. In some cases it came about as people's faith in the power of the working-class as a revolutionary force began to decline, and would-be revolutionaries looked around for another group they hoped to lead to the promised land. In other cases, it was because the bohemians themselves felt marginalised, and exalting the down-and-outs and drifters was a way of repudiating the middle-class that most of them came from. The 1950s Beat espousal of poverty, and expressions of admiration for hobos, junkies, juvenile delinquents, and petty thieves in an affluent, complacent society, might be an example of this.

The fear of the "unknown", which is how the lower classes were often seen, may have almost reached a climax towards the end of the nineteenth-century and early in the twentieth-century when a spate of novels appeared in which alien forces threatened life on earth. Kalifa refers to H.G. Wells (*The Time Machine)* and several other authors: "A whole vein (illustrated by Arthur Conan Doyle, Henry Rider Haggard, and especially Edgar Rice Burroughs) used forgotten worlds peopled with races and civilisations but also with vanished monsters". It's a personal choice, but perhaps I can also suggest William Hope Hodgsons' 1908 novel, *The House on the Borderland*, where a strange race of beings is about to burst out of its hiding place in the bowels of the earth and create panic and disease. Later, in the 1920s, H.P. Lovecraft built up a whole series of stories about the "others" beyond the known world but always waiting to gain access to it.

There was, of course, always a racial element to fears of alien invasions. The early 1900s were a time when talk of the "yellow peril", meaning the Chinese and other Asiatics, was widespread. And in Britain the 1905 Aliens Act was essentially designed to limit the number of Jews arriving in the country from Eastern Europe. They were often identified with anarchist theories, and anarchists were considered as much a part of the underworld as criminals and other anti-social elements. Anarchism of the deed, such as hurling bombs into crowded restaurants and assassinating politicians and related public figures, was very much in the air at the time.

Is there an underworld now? Some would say "yes", meaning the criminal world I referred to at the start of this review. But Kalifa has his doubts, and says that crime is now often in the open, with criminals mixing with politicians and celebrities. They sometimes are near-celebrities. Journalists are not averse to reporting on their life-styles, especially if they involve scandal and possible associations with the powerful. In the nineteenth-century, newspapers thrived on sensational stories about the lower depths, now they spread fear of a corruption that involves all levels of society. They do also throw light on individuals on "sink estates" who live on welfare benefits, but they are just that, individuals rather than a mass that presents a threat. The reports engender moral outrage, but not a panic about an underworld.

Vice, Crime, and Poverty is a fascinating book and raises many provocative questions about nineteenth-century society and literature. It is clearly written, and has extensive notes.

VICE, CRIME, AND POVERTY : HOW THE WESTERN
IMAGINATION INVENTED THE UNDERWORLD
By Dominique Kalifa
Columbia University Press. 278 pages. £27. ISBN 978-0-231-18742-8

MORE RIVALS OF SHERLOCK HOLMES

Arthur Conan Doyle's Sherlock Holmes stories have an established place in English literature, and have inspired many imitators, not to mention film, radio, and television versions of the adventures of the famous private detective and his friend, Dr Watson. The stories were originally published in *The Strand* magazine, the first one in 1891. But Holmes wasn't the only detective around in the late-Victorian and Edwardian years. However, I would guess that many of their creators were most likely inspired by Doyle's success to turn their pens to producing material for the mass-market publications which abounded at the time. Nick Rennison mentions a few of them: *The Windsor Magazine, The Idler, The Pall Mall Magazine, Pearson's Magazine, Harmsworth Magazine*, even the *Railway Magazine* when crime occurred on the rails. It perhaps wasn't just the Holmes stories that helped set the style. Some of J.E. Preston Muddock's "Dick Donovan" stories were published in *The Strand* in the early-1890s, alongside Holmes, so he can hardly be called a copier in any way.

Of the numerous stories that appeared in print in the period concerned, it has to be admitted that only a few have survived in terms of their literary qualities. And not many of the authors have been remembered in literary histories. You won't find their names in the indexes of John Gross's *The Rise and Fall of the Man of Letters: English Literary Life Since 1800* (Weidenfeld & Nicolson, 1969) or, Doyle apart, Nigel Cross's *The Common Writer: Life in nineteenth-century Grub Street* (Cambridge University Press, 1985), to name just a couple of examples I have on my shelves. One or two do sneak into Peter Keating's *The Haunted Study: A Social History of the English Novel, 1875-1914* (Secker & Warburg, 1989). The Sherlock Holmes stories are briefly discussed, and Arthur Morrison, Ernest Bramah, E.W. Hornung, and a couple of other names are mentioned.

There's no doubt that some of the writers were what are usually referred to as "hacks", churning out stories, novels, and anything else that would find a place in print. There were dozens of magazines anxious to keep their pages filled with entertaining accounts, fictional and otherwise, that would interest their readers. Rennison, in one of the informative introductions he provides for each of the stories in *More Rivals of Sherlock Holmes*, says that Elizabeth Thomasina Meade Smith, in collaboration with Eustace Robert Barton ("a doctor and part-time writer"), wrote crime stories, as L.T. Meade, featuring a female detective,

Miss Florence Cusack. Smith published almost 300 books, of one sort or another, many of them "for girls, often with a school setting". It's unlikely that any of them are read now, though some of her crime stories have stayed the course.

I have to admit that I find the notes about the writers often almost as interesting as the stories they wrote. Hugh Cosgro Weir had been a journalist, written for pulp magazines, set up an advertising agency, and produced screenplays in the early years of the film industry. The aforementioned J. Preston Muddock had travelled in India and the South Seas, and prospected for gold in Australia. But there was also Herbert Keen, who wrote a few stories about a detective named Mr Booth and his friend Mr Perkins, and then appears to have disappeared into obscurity. Rennison says he has been unable to find any information about him, but it is possible that he used a pseudonym, or that he only wrote the Booth/Perkins stories and moved on to other things.

The stories have survived because enthusiasts like Rennison have rescued them from the forgotten books and magazines they were in. He edited a previous anthology, *Rivals of Sherlock Holmes* (No Exit Press, 2008). The late Hugh Greene compiled four collections, *The Rivals of Sherlock Holmes* (Penguin, 1971), *More Rivals of Sherlock Holmes* (Penguin, 1973), *Further Rivals of Sherlock Holmes* (Penguin, 1976), and *The American Rivals of Sherlock Holmes* (Penguin, 1978). Michelle Slung edited *Crime on her Mind* (Penguin, 1977), which had stories about female sleuths, mostly from the pre-1914 period. *The Dead Witness* (Bloomsbury, 2012), edited by Michael Sims, was another focusing on Victorian detective stories. *The Edwardian Detectives*, edited by Greg Fowlkes (Resurrected Press, 2012) is a bulky collection from a publisher specialising in old detective tales. Michael Cox gathered together *Victorian Tales of Mystery & Detection* (Oxford U.P., 1992). Inevitably, there are duplications in some of the collections and others like them. I make no claim to completeness and have simply used the books I have in my possession when writing these notes.

Bearing in mind that the magazines must have been constantly looking for material, and the writers under pressure to meet deadlines, it's not surprising that the quality can vary a great deal. Richard Marsh's "Conscience" throws the spotlight on a young woman with the ability to lip read. Relaxing in Brighton one day she notices three men who are passing on information to each other about a well-dressed woman. The next day the woman is found dead. Some time later the lip reader is in Buxton and again sees the same three men exchanging details about a woman who soon dies. When the men are observed at Euston clearly up to the same trick, our sleuth intervenes. It's at this point in the story, if not earlier, that one's ability to suspend disbelief totally breaks down. It isn't as if the writing is particularly interesting in itself, and the coincidences are just too much to accept.

Another author, David Christie Murray, is held to task by Rennison for deliberately taking his cue from the Doyle stories about Sherlock Holmes. Like Holmes, and other detectives, Murray's "John Pym" has a faithful friend who tells the story. The detective smokes a pipe when weighing up the facts of a case, and experiments with chemistry. And, Rennison adds, "the plot of this particular story is so blatantly lifted from one of Holmes's most famous adventures, published a couple of years earlier, that it is a wonder Doyle did not sue Murray for plagiarism".

Along with the routine stories there are several examples of good writing. Arthur Morrison created two detectives, Martin Hewitt and Horace Dorrington, for a series of crisply written and entertaining stories that still have appeal. Interestingly, both examples rather turn conventions upside down, one by allowing a murderer to escape abroad, though with a hint that he will likely come to a bad end, anyway. The other has a twist in its tail when a jewel that has led to a murder, is thrown into the Thames by an irate woman who had thought to profit from stealing it. Although Morrison's most famous fictional detective was Martin Hewitt, Rennison suggests that his other one, Horace Dorrington, is perhaps more provocative as a character. He describes him as a "sociopath" who, while hunting for criminals, is not averse to getting in on the action himself. It could be that Morrison, who had grown up in a rough part of London, had come across types like Dorrington. He wrote two books, *Tales of Mean Streets* and *A Child of the Jago,* which are often referred to in accounts of nineteenth century English social-realist writing about criminals and the working-classes.

The story about Dorrington, "The Case of the 'Mirror of Portugal' ", is partly set in Soho and involves foreigners who are, clearly, a shifty lot. A short, narrow street has a café called The Café des Bon Camarades, and it is implied that it's probably little better than its surroundings, which are described as "even a trifle dirtier than these by-streets in that quarter are wont to be". Another reference in the same story refers to Soho's "foreign colony of that quarter". There is a thread of uncertainty about foreigners and their habits and ambitions running through several of the stories in *More Rivals of Sherlock Holmes*. The chief villain in Richard Marsh's "Conscience" is said to have spent time in the East when young. India and Indians are present in Headon Hill's "The Div-

136

ination of the Kodak Films", though not in a negative manner. But the Indian character is kept hidden away so as not to disturb the servants. India also provides some of the background to E.W. Hornung's "One Possessed", where an officer who served in that country has been affected by being too immersed in studies of the murderous Thug cult. Hornung, incidentally, is probably best remembered for having, in the 1890s, created Raffles, a "cricket playing gentleman-burglar". Some of his exploits were turned into a radio series which still crops up on Radio4Extra.

Other examples of foreign influences not being benign can be found in "The Jewelled Skull", a Dick Donovan mystery involving the case of a spoiled young man who has been stealing valuable items to ingratiate himself with a group of opium addicts. Going back to Headon Hill's story, it seems that even foreigners who aren't Indian or Chinese, or generally exotic, are likewise not to be trusted. The attractive and ambitious American socialite, Miss Stella Hicks, is said to have "an inordinate desire to marry a 'title' ", something which is "a weakness common to most of her fellow countrywomen". And although it's nowhere stated that Captain Vandaleur in "The Arrest of Captain Vandaleur" is not British, his name sounds suspiciously foreign. There is a dangerous "Spanish Brazilian fellow" in "The Case of the Muelvos y Sagra" whose "swarthy" appearance immediately puts the narrator of the story on his guard. R. Austin Freeman's "The Mandarin's Pearl" has an obvious Eastern connection.

"After Holmes, the deluge", said the American Sherlock enthusiast Vincent Starrett, who himself wrote detective stories featuring Jimmy Lavender, Chicago Detective, as well as an easy-going memoir, *Born in a Bookshop* (University of Oklahoma Press, 1965). And it's true enough. It's difficult to estimate just how many detective stories were published between 1890 and 1914, or how many now-forgotten scribblers wrote them. There are more than a few people writing crime novels, not to mention TV scripts, nowadays, though it's probably more difficult for them to place short stories in appropriate magazines. They simply don't exist in the same quantity as they did in the late-Victorian/Edwardian years. It may be more relevant to consider, as Rennison does, that TV has, in many aspects, taken the place of magazines in terms of constantly needing fresh material.

More Rivals of Sherlock Holmes is a fascinating collection, partly because of the ways in which the stories throw light on the social attitudes of the late-Victorian and Edwardian eras. What is quite noticeable is that most of the crime takes place among the middle and upper-classes.

Few working-class types make an appearance, other than as servants, cab drivers, staff at railway stations, and similar jobs. Working-class people didn't own much of value, so no jewels were likely to go missing. And they were not going to run into complications about wills and inheritances such as occur in Percy James Brebner's "The Search for the Missing Fortune". Murders in the slums and poorer parts of cities tended to be squalid affairs, often resulting from an excess of alcohol. They lacked the sophistication of a death in a country house occupied by a group of elegant guests, or in a town house owned by a man with a reputation for losing large sums at gambling.

A final note. In "The Jewelled Skull" a servant, describing the oddball son of the house, says, "I should say he has a slate off". The meaning is clear enough, and a modern equivalent might be to say of someone that they have a screw loose. But I'd never come across the expression, "he has a slate off", and can only assume that it was in general use in the 1890s or so. I could be wrong, and it's not an important point that has any bearing on the story. It just intrigued me.

More Rivals of Sherlock Holmes is great fun to read, and the stories often entertain and impress with their twists and turns. Nick Rennison has done a fine job in bringing them together, and his introduction to the collection, and his general comments, provide a good guide to what was evidently a lively period in popular literature. One wonders how those near-anonymous writers lived and what happened to them?

MORE RIVALS OF SHERLOCK HOLMES
Edited and introduced by Nick Rennison
No Exit Press. 351 pages. £9.99. ISBN 978-0-85730-260-1

THE POPULAR FRONT NOVEL IN BRITAIN 1934-1940

What is a "Popular Front"? One definition I turned up says it is "a broad coalition of different political groups usually made up of leftists and centrists. Being very broad (it) can sometimes include centrist Radical or liberal forces as well as social democratic and communist groups".

That's a general definition, but what about The Popular Front, a coalition as described above, that existed for a time in the 1930s, and was probably to be seen at its most effective in France and Spain, when Popular Front governments were elected. It had a presence in other countries, such as the United States and the United Kingdom, but never to the same extent. The Popular Front of the 1930s was largely a construct of the Communist Party, and though there were active Communist Parties in America and Britain, they didn't have the same power and influence as they did in France and Spain.

Depending on how one views the activities of the Communist Party it's possible to see the 1930s Popular Front as either a well-meaning and practical endeavour to resist the rise of fascism, or a cynical attempt to make up for the mistakes that, in some ways, had not only allowed, but even almost practically assisted the Nazi takeover in Germany. The "class against class" policies laid down by Stalin and his supporters, and slavishly followed by national communist parties, meant that there was a refusal to co-operate with social-democrats and socialists. They were, in fact, looked on as "social fascists", and more time was spent abusing them than in building a broad front that might have been able to withstand a Nazi assault on the German state. This is a contentious suggestion, and it's possible, even probable, that the levels of support Hitler had from banks and business leaders, and in the army and police, not to mention among large numbers of the general public, could have enabled him to come to power, anyway, even if faced by a Popular Front coalition of communists, socialists, liberals, and others.

Elinor Taylor points out that, though it was only in August 1935 that the Popular Front strategy became the official Party policy, communists in France had, in 1934, already decided to form an alliance with the social democrats. There was a strong fascist movement in France, and there had been an unsuccessful right-wing attempt to overthrow the government. By 1934, also, the Soviet Union's entry into the League of Nations "appeared to signal its willingness to work with the capitalist countries in the interests of collective security".

If a Popular Front proposal was to succeed it was necessary to amend ideas about such matters as national histories, literature, and even the "masses", as communist theoreticians liked to refer to the people whose interests they claimed to represent. Taylor quotes Georg Dimitrov as saying that those masses "must be taken as they are, and not as we should like to have them". She then comments: "This turn towards the popular and the historical displaced a rhetoric of class and of imminent revolution; instead, 'the outlines of a better future were now to be detected in the patterns of the nation's past' ". It seems certain that the notion of a Popular Front did lead, in Britain, to a social movement that expressed itself through readership of newspapers that supported the Popular Front, and with interest in the publications of the Left Book Club. How many of the masses shared in these activities is not easy to ascertain. I suspect that Left Book Club readers were largely drawn from the middle-classes, and even then only certain elements of a white-collar constituency.

I think it's important to add that the switch to a Popular Front policy ran alongside an emphasis on socialist realism as the dominant driving force in the arts. Experimentation was frowned on, and in the Soviet Union it led to purges of those writers and artists who did not toe the party line. Taylor says that Karl Radek "spelled out a stark choice for writers, 'James Joyce or Socialist Realism'.

Was it, in practice, as clearly defined as that? Taylor's contention is that, despite party policies, writers were prepared to use lessons picked up from Joyce and other modernists to deal with matters relating to communist activities, working-class concerns, and economic and social factors that affected people's lives. Georg Lukács had stressed that "the broad mass of people can learn nothing from avant-garde literature", but Bertolt Brecht "attacked the notion that only realism in the nineteenth-century mode could represent popular life".

John Sommerfield's *May Day* (1936) is, perhaps, the best example of a British politically-committed novel that was at least partially experimental in form. Taylor describes it as "a formally experimental novel that appropriates a number of techniques and themes closely associated with the literary modernism of the 1920s". And she refers to a "montage principle" which attempted "an expression of the social totality". Sommerfield was not alone on the Left in deciding that the lines laid down by Lukács needn't be followed too closely. A couple of novels by 1930s American writers that spring to mind might be seen as moving in the same direction. I'm thinking of Edward Dahlberg's *Those Who Perish* and William Rollins Jnr's *The Shadow Before,* both published in

1934, as examples of radical writing that didn't feel the need to adhere to "realism in the nineteenth-century mode". The example of John Dos Passos loomed large over all these writers, I would suggest. But it's also necessary to consider the impact of the cinema. As Andy Croft indicated in *Red Letter Days: British Fiction in the 1930s* (Lawrence & Wishart, 1990), when discussing Sommerfield's fast-moving images, the "borrowed cinematic technique gave a novel like *May Day* the feel and force of documentary non-fiction".

Arthur Calder-Marshall's *Pie in the Sky,* (1937), a novel heavily concerned with class and commitment, was, on the whole, less-adventurous in terms of the writing than Sommerfield's book. Taylor quotes an interesting passage from an essay that Calder-Marshall wrote in the 1930s which seems to suggest that he was more-inclined to follow Lucác's ideas: "(w)here the bourgeois novelists have been driven to the pursuit of the abnormal, the perverted or the minute, in order to find fresh material, the revolutionary is concerned with the normal and typical in his portraiture of society as a whole".

If the evidence of *Pie in the Sky* is anything to go by, it's certainly true that Calder-Marshall aimed to describe the "normal and typical" in his work: "We went to a dance once, given by a friend of mine at the Assembly Rooms. This was a few months after we'd been married. I was eighteen and still terribly in love with him. And this fellow who was giving the dance was a boy I'd known before I knew Charlie. There was nothing in it, but in the course of the evening I danced four times with this boy". It's easy to see how he is aiming to deal with a world that is mundane, but can still have tensions within seemingly ordinary situations. These tensions can be political, as when there are differences of opinions among family members, and when the urge to create a Popular Front might clash with the feelings of resentment and anger against another class which, given the appropriate influential circumstances, could be prepared to swing either to the left or the right.

Calder-Marshall, unlike Sommerfield, who had been a merchant-seaman and served in the International Brigades in Spain, became disillusioned with the Communist Party, and had left its ranks by 1941. Lewis Jones, a communist from the mining communities, wrote two novels, *Cwmardy* (1937) and *We Live* (1939), which dealt with life in the coalfields of South Wales. Jones sadly died young, but his books, largely traditional stylistically, can be seen as attempts to create panoramic accounts of a period stretching from 1900 to the 1930s, and thus taking in pre-1914 agitation, sometimes verging on syndicalism, the General Strike of 1926, and the dark days of the Depression and the

Spanish Civil War, in which a number of Welsh miners fought.

James Barke's Scottish novels, *Major Operation* (1936) and *The Land of the Leal* (1939), were also panoramic in intent, tracing the fortunes and misfortunes of a family driven to leave the countryside and move to the city. Barke was probably never a member of the Communist Party, though he appears to have been sympathetic to its aims. Curiously, he did have doubts about the notion of a Popular Front and its adaptation of what he thought of as liberal policies. Taylor has a few lines from a letter that Barke wrote to a fellow-Scottish writer, Lewis Grassic Gibbon, in which he referred to himself as "a hopelessly intolerant doctrinaire" and stated that "Toleration belongs to the period of toothless liberalism". He also claimed that the Communist Party was the "heroic vanguard" of the working class. Despite sounding like a loyal follower of Party ideology, Barke was happy to use modernist techniques in his fiction. Andy Croft came up with a good description of a passage in *Major Operation* which dealt with a National Unemployed Workers' Movement march in Glasgow: "It is a crazy picture, slapstick and satiric, allusive, inclusive and nonsensical, the life of the city caught in snapshots, snatches of conversation and thought; James Joyce writing about Glasgow wIth a Communist Party card in his pocket".

Historical novels were seen as a way of providing a good story with an insight into aspects of history that had often been ignored or altered by establishment historians to support their view of what took place. Jack Lindsay's *1649: A Novel of a Year* (1938) is "structured through multiple perspectives and short chapters, interspersed with original documents". It deals with the endeavours by the Levellers to obtain "popular consent for *The Agreement of the People*", their manifesto which outlined changes they required in the English constitution. Cromwell crushed the Leveller rebellion or mutiny at Burford Church in 1649, executing several men and breaking up what was essentially a small radical element within the New Model Army. Their demands were mostly met as British society developed over the next three centuries, but were hardly likely to have been agreed to at the time.

The problem of how much steady support the Levellers had is still debated, and it puts me in mind of a question that could be asked about the readership of the novels that Taylor deals with. Do we have any figures for sales? Admittedly, such figures do not necessarily tell us how many people actually read a book. It may have been borrowed from a library many times, or loaned among friends of the owner. But I suspect that most radical novels, especially if they could be identified as written by communists ("communist propaganda in the form of fiction", was the verdict of the *Times Literary Supplement* on *May Day*), might not have circulated widely, apart from among Party members and sympathisers. Surviving records for the workers' libraries in South Wales and elsewhere would indicate that, when it came to fiction, westerns and crime stories were the most popular books taken out on loan. Ken Worpole's *Dockers and Detectives* (Verso,1983) likewise asserts that most working-class men, if they read novels, were likely to choose a western or a detective story.

Leaving aside such questions regarding readership it's obvious that Elinor Taylor has produced a scholarly, well-researched and informative survey of selected novels from the Popular Front period of the 1930s, with added references to other left-wing writers. It's not a book designed for what might be termed a general readership in the way that Andy Croft's *Red Letter Days* was, but both can be usefully read to give a broad picture of an area of British fiction too often neglected by literary historians.

Taylor's analysis of the books she discusses is always thorough and she successfully combines the literary values of a novel with comments on its political content and context. She's also honest enough in her conclusion to consider that there was probably little that was revolutionary, in any sense of the word, in the Popular Front novels. She quotes one fellow-academic as describing Popular Front aesthetics as "Stalinised pastoral", and another saying that there was "little that was genuinely socially transformative in the Popular Front; instead its coordinates were liberal, not Marxist; it affirmed a valorisation of bourgeois culture" under the mask of 'humanist' Marxism, and required intellectual commitment to only the most minimal demands".

Her explanations of the edicts coming from Moscow are relevant, though I admit to backing away from sentences like: "Lukács developed Hegel's central category of totality into a vision of the social totality marked by 'the all-pervasive supremacy of the whole over the parts' ". Taylor's book is, presumably, her Ph.D thesis, so perhaps words like those are to be expected, and I can work out what she means. But they offer a contrast to how she writes elsewhere, when she can be concise and clear as she outlines a story or describes a character. At her best she made me want to pull one or two old novels from the shelves and re-read them.

THE POPULAR FRONT NOVEL IN BRITAIN 1934-1940

By Elinor Taylor
Haymarket Books. 224 pages. £19.99. ISBN 978-1-60846-046-5

COLD WARRIORS: WRITERS WHO WAGED THE LITERARY
COLD WAR

When Mary McCarthy, in an interview broadcast on American television in 1980, said that Lillian Hellman was a dishonest writer and "every word she writes is a lie, including 'and' and 'the' ", the infuriated Hellman took legal action to combat what she claimed was a libel on her reputation as a successful playwright, screenwriter, and memoirist. It was a late chapter in a Cold War feud that had its roots in the 1930s and the Spanish Civil War.

When we talk about the Cold War it's often assumed we're referring to the years following the Second World War. Churchill's 1946 speech in Fulton, Missouri, when he used the term "Iron Curtain" to describe what was happening as the Soviet Union tightened its grip on countries in Eastern Europe that had fallen under its domination, is seen as heralding the start of "hostilities" between Russia and its satellites and the West. But it could be argued that the real beginning can be traced back to the Bolshevik Revolution that overthrew the Czar and created a communist state.

There was even something of a "Hot War" when America, Britain, and other countries intervened, ostensibly to stop guns and ammunition that had been supplied to Russia during the First World War from falling into the hands of either side in the Russian Civil War. The real reason was most likely to frustrate Bolshevik advances. Communism was never going to be accepted by the ruling classes in the West, a fact that often led to dissension between individuals and groups in countries outside Russia. And, as the trouble between McCarthy and Hallman indicated, by the 1930s the battle lines were beginning to be clearly drawn.

Duncan White doesn't go back to the 1920s, but he does start his narrative of how writers on both sides got involved in speaking either for or against communism, in the events of the 1930s, and especially the war in Spain. George Orwell and Arthur Koestler had both experienced what it was like to have a commitment that went beyond words and put them in real physical danger.

Orwell had gone to Spain as a volunteer anxious to help the Republican Government defeat Franco's Nationalist army. The International Brigades, which most foreigners wanting to fight for the Republic would join, were dominated by the Communist Party. Orwell instead joined the POUM militia, an independent Marxist organisation that was la-belled Trotskyist by the communists and so viewed with suspicion. The story of how he eventually had to flee from Spain as the POUM was suppressed and its members arrested, and in some cases executed by the secret police, is well-known, and written about in his *Homage to Catalonia*. It was a book he had some difficulty in getting published, its account of communist machinations as they hunted down anarchists, Trotskyists, liberals, and anyone else not agreeing with their ideas, not being to the liking of many left-wingers in Britain.

Orwell, as we know, wrote two other books, *Animal Farm* and *1984*, which presented negative views of communism, though he continued to be a supporter of democratic socialism. But his books were often em-ployed by conservative ideologues as weapons in their war against the Soviet Union. He doesn't appear to have ever become a fanatic in the fight against communism, though his reputation was slightly tarnished in later years when it was revealed that he had provided a list of people he knew and suspected of being communists, or fellow-travellers, to the Information Research Department, a somewhat shadowy government organisation.

Arthur Koestler's adventures in Spain were even more-dramatic than Orwell's. Posing as a reporter covering the war from the Franco side, he was, in fact, a member of the Communist Party and a spy feeding information to Moscow. His cover was blown and he was arrested and in danger of being executed. High-level interventions on his behalf se-cured his freedom in a prisoner exchange, but the whole experience had its effect on Koestler, one result being that his faith in communism had started to crumble. Further misadventures followed and when Koestler finally left the Party he wrote a novel, *Darkness at Noon*, which ques-tioned the purpose of the Show Trials in Russia, and the actions of old revolutionaries who supposedly confessed to their alleged misdeeds. Like Orwell's books, it could be used by those wanting to highlight the drawbacks of a totalitarian system, though in Koestler's case he was more than happy about it being employed in that way. He became, in some people's opinion, almost a professional anti-communist.

Stephen Spender also turned up in Spain, though not in a manner that was likely to place him in much danger. I recall many years ago talking to an old Party member who had been active in the 1930s, and who, when I mentioned Spender, referred contemptuously to him "poncing" around in Spain looking for his boyfriend, Tony Hyndman. After fall-ing out with Spender he had run off to join the International Brigades. White devotes a fair amount of space to Spender, though not necessarily about the Spanish episode. In the context of the Cold War, he might be more notable for his links to *Encounter*, the magazine founded in the 1950s and which, it was later revealed, had been financed by the CIA, along with various other publications.

Spender always claimed that he didn't know where the money to enable a publication like *Encounter* to be published on a monthly basis came from, or at least he didn't think it was from the CIA. Operatives from that organisation, who had been involved in promoting cultural activities to present the West as intellectually and artistically superior to Russia and the Iron Curtain countries generally, smiled when they heard his protestations of innocence. Perhaps White has it right when he suggests that Spender probably didn't want to know too much about the money side of *Encounter*, and was prepared to convince himself that the "fronts" through which it was channelled were genuine?

The question of the CIA funding the publication and distribution of magazines and even books is documented in *Cold Warriors*. There don't seem to have been too many occasions when influence was brought to bear on the editors of *Encounter* (Spender and Melvin Lasky, who almost certainly did know where the money originated) when it came to what they published. Of course, the counter-argument could be that they weren't ever likely to print anything that really rocked the anti-communist boat, which is why they were financed from the start. But I think it's only fair to point out that a lot of first-rate material did appear in *Encounter*. I read it on a fairly-regular basis in the late-1950s and early-1960s, and always found much of value in its pages.

There have been suggestions that the CIA may also have partially supported the literary magazine, *The Paris Review*, which was founded in Paris in 1953, with one of its editors being Peter Matthiessen. He admitted some time later that he had belonged to the CIA and may have been feeding information about American expatriates in the city to the authorities. White doesn't mention it, but Matthiessen's novel, *Partisans* (1955), is set in Paris and has a plot that involves communist subterfuge. It's worth noting that another novelist around when *The Paris Review* was born, was H.L. Humes, whose large *Underground City* (1958) took in events involving communists and the Resistance in the 1940s in France. Humes, whose career came to a sad end in madness, was called paranoiac because he was convinced he was being watched. It was only after his death that it became known that the FBI and CIA had files on him.

Paris was obviously a key city in the early days of the Cold War, and the French Communist Party then had a membership and an influence that particularly bothered the Americans. In this connection it might be worth noting that E. Howard Hunt, described as "spy, novelist, and future Nixon 'plumber' ", made a contribution towards anti-communist literature, albeit of a popular kind, with pulp novels like *The Violent Ones* (1950) and *The Judas Hour* (1951). *The Violent Ones* had a Paris setting and a gallery of communist villains. It could be argued that novels like these, clearly designed to reach a mass audience, may have had more effect in terms of convincing people that communists were almost akin to gangsters than some more-literary novels that wanted to show what the evils of communism were.

White's informative chapters on Grahame Greene and John le Carré (real name, David Cornwell, and a one-time member of MI6) similarly demonstrate how fiction can shape views and attitudes. Greene was not unsympathetic towards genuine liberation movements and his opinions about American policies, in particular, were often caustic in emphasising their shortcomings, as in *The Quiet American*. As for Cornwell, his characters in the John le Carré books often had doubts about the methods their own side used to confront a ruthless enemy. I think it's only right to say that both Greene and le Carré were far better writers than Hunt in his pulp mode. He wrote around 70 books in total, and I've only read a few of the pulp fiction publications, so he may have been more skilful in other areas.

All the writers mentioned so far were, in one way or another, in the anti-communist camp, but the American author, Howard Fast, was a staunch member of the Party for many years. Let me admit that, without sharing his political leanings, I've always had a sneaking admiration for Fast. He was reviled in the press during what has become known as the McCarthy and HUAC years of the late-1940s and early-1950s, his books were banned from some libraries, and his publishers quickly dropped their options on his novels when leaned on by the FBI.

Fast also spent time in prison, along with the crime writer Dashiell Hammett, because he wouldn't co-operate with HUAC. Had all that happened to a Russian writer we would naturally have said that it was an example of what literary life is like in a dictatorship. But Fast wasn't living in a totalitarian society and there was no excuse for the United States sliding dangerously close to some aspects of one. On the other hand, Fast was free to do what he did. He set up his own publishing house and distributed his books outside the usual networks that commercial outfits used. He had been a very popular novelist, often taking historical episodes as a basis for his books, and he eventually regained

148

his status as a successful writer.

He's probably mostly remembered now as the author of *Spartacus*, which provided the basis for the Kirk Douglas film of that name. It had a screenplay by Dalton Trumbo, another blacklisted writer who had been imprisoned when he defied HUAC. Fast's total output was extensive, and while no-one is going to claim that he produced major literature he did, on the whole, aim to write books that were popular but also had something to say. They're not likely to ever be reprinted, but his non-historical novels like *Clarkton, Silas Timberman* and *The Story of Lola Gregg*, attempted to comment on what was happening in American society at a time of reaction and do it in a readable and not overtly didactic way. There was never any doubt where Fast stood politically, but he liked to tell a good story to put across his message.

It would have been a brave soul in Russia, or any of the Iron Curtain countries, who even thought of doing what Fast did in terms of criticising the authorities and publishing his own books to circumvent censorship. Writers were closely watched and any deviations from style or content were punished by internal exile, imprisonment, restrictions on publishing, and at the height of Stalinist terror, death. White's chapters on Anna Akhmatova, Boris Pasternak, and others who fell foul of the restrictions placed on writers make for grim reading. Akhmatova couldn't publish for years and was harassed by the secret police. Stalin himself seemed to take some perverse pleasure in ordering her son and her friends arrested, while refraining from having her sent to the Gulag but leaving her to live in poverty and with a constant awareness of how close to being detained she was.

Boris Pasternak was likewise always under surveillance, and once his novel, *Dr Zhivago*, had been smuggled out of Russia and published in the West (a fascinating story in itself), with encouragement and some financial backing from the CIA, he was watched even more. He was lucky to have lived and have died naturally, though the tensions he experienced as a marked man no doubt contributed to his declining health. Earlier writers, such as Isaac Babel and Osip Mandelstam had either been shot or disappeared into the camps and died there in circumstances that were never properly explained. A later survivor, Aleksandr Solzhenitsyn, came out of the camps and his *One Day in the Life of Ivan Denisovich* and *The Gulag Archipelago* created sensations when they found their way to the West and appeared in print there. The embarrassment they caused the Soviet authorities led to Solzhenitsyn being deprived of his Russian citizenship and exiled to the West.

It wasn't only in Russia, nor among just a few well-known writers, that surveillance and censorship created an atmosphere of suspicion and fear. The subject is probably far too extensive for any writer to deal with it in total, and there must have been numerous novelists, playwrights, and poets in East Germany, Hungary, and elsewhere, who came up against Party instructions about what they could publish. It's my own suggestion, but the life of Stefan Heym might be a good example. He left Germany when the Nazis came to power in 1933, spent time in America and served in the U.S. Army during the war. He had problems with HUAC in the late-1940s, moved to East Germany and, though continuing to publish, was not always looked on too kindly by the Party leadership.

 White does give us an insight into what it was like in Prague when Václav Havel was involved with Charter 77 and his work was banned. Like some others of his fellow-countrymen who had believed in Alexander Dubcek's Prague Spring, and then wouldn't conform when it fell apart as the Russians invaded and the Czech Communist Party started to "normalise" the situation, Havel became a thorn in the side of the authorities. He was imprisoned and on release forced to work at menial jobs. The world was watching what was happening in Prague and other places in the 1970s and 1980s, and it wasn't as easy for the police and the Party to get away with an excessive use of force. But systems of surveillance and harassment of writers and their families could take a toll and soon wear down all but the most-determined of dissidents. Havel held out until communism in Czechoslovakia collapsed, by which time he had become something of a symbol of resistance for his fellow-countrymen and was elected President of the new Republic.

Cold Warriors is a large book and Duncan White covers a fair amount of literary ground, much of which I've moved across quickly. He has things to say about Richard Wright and his days in the Communist Party, his life in Paris in the 1950s, and his tangled relationship with the American authorities. He was always under suspicion, even though he had left the Party years before. Wright was one of the contributors to an important 1950 anthology, *The God That Failed: Six Studies in Communism*, along with Koestler, Spender, Ignazio Silone, André Gide, and Louis Fischer. But as an ex-communist, and a black whose books were often critical of racism in America, he was still a candidate for surveillance.

And there was Allen Ginsberg, perhaps a minor player in the Cold War game, but who put in an appearance in Prague, was feted by students and deported by the police. Kim Philby, Hemingway, James T. Farrell

150

(some of his novels and short stories concern the American Left and the struggle against Stalinism), and a few others, have their Cold War activities examined, and though it sometimes might be thought that little new is revealed, the fact of it being carefully brought together gives it relevance. A broad picture of the literary side of the Cold War is skilfully constructed. Duncan White has written a book that will appeal to those who lived through the turbulent years it covers, but should also be of immense interest to anyone who didn't directly experience the Cold War (for the record, it kept me in uniform in Germany for almost three years between 1954 and 1957) but is eager to know about it.

COLD WARRIORS: WRITERS WHO WAGED THE LITERARY
COLD WAR By Duncan White
Little, Brown. 736 pages. £25. ISBN 978-1-4087-0799-9

PRAGUE SPRING 1968: WARSAW PACT INVASION

1968. The year when students fought the police on the streets of Paris, hippies in America frolicked in the streets of San Francisco and protested against the war in Vietnam, and pop music seemed to dominate the airwaves. Some people now look back nostalgically and dream of their lost youth. Did it all really change anything? Arguably, the situation in France only got serious when the workers began to bring the country to a halt, and action in America to curtail the Vietnam tragedy only took on a major dimension when discontent spread to the wider public. And the underlying political and economic systems in both countries were largely unaffected. We only need to sit quietly and survey the current malaise in France and America, and in Britain too, for that matter, to realise that "sex, drugs and rock and roll", along with student rebellion, had few long-term effects.

But what of Czechoslovakia? What happened there in 1968 may have had greater relevance in that it did play a significant part in the eventual collapse of the wider communist set-up. It led to changes which had an impact on how the balance of power in the world was structured, and how that, in turn, affected national economic patterns in Western Europe as well as those of the former Iron Curtain countries. Technological advances have no doubt created problems in terms of the range of jobs available and consequent employment difficulties, but it may also be true that, with the decline of socialist ideas, the state and employers no longer feel that they need to keep people contented in order to stave off communist influences. Union membership in most countries is at an all-time low, so there is no need to negotiate with them in a meaningful manner. Many people have no choice other than to accept what's on offer. And the state is increasingly reluctant to support them to any great extent.

Be that as it may, there is no doubt that what happened in Prague did have an effect on later developments in the Iron Curtain countries. Changes didn't immediately take place, but they began to take shape. And when they happened they did so with a remarkable speed that took almost everyone by surprise.

Czechoslovakia was a curious country in some ways and only came into existence after the First World War when the old Austro-Hungarian Empire was carved up into separate states. The fact that it was two countries, the Czech Republic and Slovakia, pulled into one, was always a matter likely to lead to dissension. And that a large portion of the populace spoke German, and thought of themselves as kith and kin to their near-neighbours, created further problems. The 1938 Munich Agreement allowed Hitler to annex the Sudetenland, and then little or no opposition was encountered by him when he took over the whole of Czechoslovakia. Britain and France effectively bartered Czechoslovakia for a nebulous peace that wasn't going to last.

When the Second World War ended in 1945 the country had been "liberated" by the Red Army. But if the Czechs expected to have regained their independence they were quickly disabused of that idea. It was true that communism was initially strongly supported, and elections in 1946 saw communists selected by democratic means. Come 1948, however, and a communist coup established a dictatorship that was essentially just a tool of the Soviet Union. There would be no free and fair elections again until 1989 when the communist system throughout Eastern Europe began to splinter and break up.

Communist rule in Czechoslovakia was, on the whole, hardline. Little or no opposition was tolerated, and anyone likely to act as a figurehead for dissidents was quickly eliminated. The death of Jan Masaryk, the foreign minister, in highly suspicious circumstances perhaps signalled the determination of the Communist Party to maintain control by any means necessary. There were other signs of communist ruthlessness in 1952 when a wave of trials across several countries, including Czechoslovakia, purged the ranks of those suspected of deviations from the Party line. The fact that many of those accused were Jews was not without relevance.

The hardliners, under Antonin Novotny, the First Secretary of the Czech Communist Party, continued with their policies, usually under directions from Russia until the 1960s. There was then some easing of the restrictions on travel and freedom of expression, but Novotny was always unpopular, and looming expressions of dissatisfaction became apparent when students took to the streets to protest against poor living conditions. The police reacted brutally and many of the students were injured. Novotny then reinstated the restrictions he'd earlier loosened. He was desperate to stay in power.

Novotny was ousted and Alexander Dubcek became First Secretary in his place. It is essential to note that Dubcek was very much a Party man. He had spent three years studying in Moscow and had worked his way up the Party ladder like any other good bureaucrat. But he was a basically decent person, and was not without the imagination to realise that a degree of liberalisation was necessary. His slogan was "Socialism

with a human face". To this end, he again eased travel restrictions, reduced censorship of the press, allowed Western newspapers and magazines to circulate in Prague, and cut down on the blocking of radio
broadcasts from outside Czechoslovakia. Clandestine listening had introduced many young Czechs to pop music from America, Britain, and
elsewhere, and records flooded in, along with highly-prized jeans and
other forms of apparel favoured by the young. It was, for a time, a
heady experience for many Czechs.

It was never going to be all plain-sailing. There were always people in
the Czech Communist Party who looked askance at what Dubcek and
his supporters were doing, while in Moscow misgivings about the
seemingly-apparent relaxation of Party control were beginning to bother Leonid Brezhnev, head of the Russian Communist Party, and therefore effectively head of the Warsaw Pact countries. There had been
earlier rumblings of discontent in East Germany, Poland, and most of
all, Hungary in 1956, and the Russians were determined not to let the
situation anywhere behind the Iron Curtain get out of hand. The idea
that Dubcek might be moving towards a system of freely elected democratic socialism was never going to be tolerated by Moscow.

In retrospect, Dubcek has sometimes been criticised because he chose
to tread carefully as he slowly created what became known as the "Prague Spring". He was always ready to insist that he was functioning
within a Party framework: "Censorship would yield to a new openness,
but no one was to articulate an ideology hostile to communism. Market
forces would replace rigid central planning but there was to be no
large-scale private ownership or de-collectivisation of Agriculture". He
knew that changes could only come about over a period of time, but
some of his supporters wanted immediate alterations to the communist
status quo. They weren't prepared to temper their comments about
communist drawbacks, nor their hostility towards Russia. Or their dis-
like of Czech communist politicians who were not in accord with Dubcek's policies.

Phil Carradice paints a colourful picture of Prague in the summer of
1968 as foreign visitors poured in, pop groups performed, and what
seemed like a permanent party took place. There never can be a permanent party, of course, and the signs that it would have to come to an end
were already in evidence. There were reports of Russian troops, along
with others from Poland, Hungary, East Germany, gathering along the
borders of Czechoslovakia. Dubcek had been summoned to meetings
with Brezhnev where he was accused of allowing right-wing elements
to set the pace of reforms. It would only be a matter of time before a

rumour of intervention became a fact.

It happened on the 19th of August, 1968 with, according to Carradice, 165,000 troops and 4,600 tanks crossing the border into Czechoslovakia. The figures would soon increase to 500,000 troops and 6,000 tanks. The suddenness of the invasion took the Czechs by surprise, though it shouldn't have done had they not been busy celebrating their supposed new-found freedoms. There was no opportunity to mount any form of sustained opposition. It would have been useless, anyway, even if the Czech army had mobilised to take on the Russians and others. They would simply have been outnumbered and outgunned, and needless casualties would have been incurred. There were protests on the streets, with attempts to construct barricades and petrol-bomb tanks occurring in Prague and Bratislava, and more than a hundred civilians died in the fighting. But for the most part the occupying forces quickly assumed control of Prague and the rest of the country.

Dubcek and several of his supporters were arrested and taken to Moscow where attempts were made to force them into signing documents to say that the Russians had not invaded Czechoslovakia, but had only responded to calls from the local Party to help get the country back to "normal". In Prague, Gustav Husak took over as First Secretary when Dubcek realised that his position was no longer tenable. Husak had the support of the Russians and moved to "normalise" the country by rolling back any reforms Dubcek had instituted. It was to be another twenty years before Czechs enjoyed the kind of freedoms taken for granted in the West. In the meantime, purges were carried out among politicians, teachers, journalists, academics, writers, and others who were not considered reliable in the eyes of the Party. Dubcek himself was soon deliberately kept from obtaining any form of employment until he was eventually offered a job as a mechanic, maintaining machinery for the Forestry Commission near Bratislava. He was a Slovak and not a Czech, so had some relationship to the area.

Carradice has a number of brief quotes by people who, though not from Czechoslovakia, recalled how the suppression of the Prague Spring had made an impression on them. A one-time American diplomat, says that he was in Prague between 1985 and 1989 and took note of the "lack of essentials" and the "feeling of hopelessness that the population seemed to share". I spent a few days myself in Prague in 1984, mostly to honour the memory of a Czech friend who had been out of the country when the Russians moved in and would never go back while they were there. Sadly, he died long before communism came to an end in 1989. In 1984 the lack of goods in the shops was obvious. The only thing that seemed of quality and was cheap and in plentiful supply was the beer.

I suppose Dubcek was lucky to survive. The examples of the 1950s trials, and the harsh treatment of those involved in the 1956 Hungarian uprising, showed how ruthless the Russians, and their Party minions in countries under Moscow control, could be. But in 1968 condemnation of the invasion of Czechoslovakia came from many quarters, including communist parties in the West. And Brezhnev was more sensitive to criticism from outside than Stalin and his henchmen had ever been.

It would be easy to suggest that Dubcek failed. He was certainly criticised for not moving fast enough with his reforms, and for backing down when Bezhnev demanded that he agree to retract them. But what else could he do? The Russians held all the cards and could simply have disposed of him, in one way or another, any time they wanted to. But, in fact, he ought to be given credit for attempting to provide communism with a human face, and so starting something that finally came to a head in 1989, though he may not have been overjoyed at the almost-total disappearance of communism. It might have happened anyway, but the Prague Spring surely helped it along. There is, of course, always the question of what might have taken place had Dubcek been allowed to make his reforms and other Warsaw Pact countries had followed the same path? Could communism have survived in a more-liberal form, or was it inevitable that it would collapse because of its internal contradictions? And would the West have allowed it to function, even if it had managed to provide its citizens with a standard of living and the kind of basic freedoms applying in the United States, Britain and elsewhere? We can never know for sure.

One mistake needs correcting. On page 78 Carradice refers to "Senator Eugene McCarthy, he of 'witch hunt' fame". It was the notorious Senator Joseph McCarthy who did so much damage with his often-outrageous suggestions of communist connections. He died in 1957, so wouldn't have been around to condemn Russian actions in 1968. Eugene McCarthy's middle name was Joseph, but he was careful not to use it so he wouldn't be associated with the smears that Joseph McCarthy spread.

PRAGUE SPRING 1968: WARSAW PACT INVASION
By Phil Carradice
Pen & Sword Books. 127 pages. £14.99. ISBN 978-1-52675-700-5

LOST GIRLS: LOVE, WAR AND LITERATURE 1939-1951

According to Peter Quennell, the "Lost Girls" who are the subject of D.J. Taylor's book, were "adventurous young women who flitted around London, alighting briefly here and there, and making the best of any random perch on which they happened to descend".

It's a description which attracts attention, but is at bottom less than fair to certainly the main protagonists in Taylor's informative and entertaining account of various women who were all, in one way or another, caught up in the world of Cyril Connolly and *Horizon* magazine. They were all thrown into the uncertainties of what he refers to as "the notoriously rackety 1940s", and it's perhaps inevitable that, as a result, aspects of their lives gave an impression of "waywardness and loneliness".

But there was always more to them than that. The experiences of Janetta Woolley, Lys Dunlap, Barbara Skelton, and Sonia Brownell demonstrate that they all had character and often made a valuable contribution to whatever activities they were involved in. One thing that does need to be made clear is that they were not representative of a generation, group, or of the many young women drawn into London during wartime. Taylor's "Lost Girls" had a "far more exclusive status in which a whole host of factors, ranging from looks to social connection, combined to produce a figure who is more or less unique".

Janetta Woolley perhaps wasn't born into a wealthy family, but it was certainly a comfortable one in financial terms, if not in its domestic arrangements. Her father and mother soon separated, and Janetta spent some time in Spain in the 1930s with her mother. When they returned to England following the outbreak of the Spanish Civil War, they were taken up by Ralph and Frances Partridge, survivors of the Bloomsbury set. They were to play a big part in Janetta's life as she encountered a variety of men, often of a literary or artistic bent, who were attracted to her striking good looks. When she was seventeen she fell in with Hugh Slater, a veteran of the International Brigades in Spain. Mixing in his circles brought her into contact with a loose group of bohemians, including Cyril Connolly and the selection of women who appeared to be sufficiently attracted to him to provide the usual comforts, and help in publishing *Horizon*.

Slater was much older than she was, and she later had a relationship with another older man, Kenneth Sinclair-Loutit, who interestingly was

157

someone else who had served with the International Brigades. Taylor documents Janetta's adventures as she made her way through liaisons with several men, including Arthur Koestler, Robert Kee, Patrick Lee-Fermor, Lucien Freud, and the Duke of Devonshire. I've left out a couple of names. I'm not sure that any real purpose is served by listing all her lovers and others. She eventually married a Spanish nobleman in 1957 and lived until 2018. Taylor has a lively chapter about a visit he made to interview the elderly Janetta, and the crisp manner in which she quickly dismissed a suggestion that she was one of "the *Horizon* team". Nor had she been over-impressed by some of the people who were. Lys Lubbock "really was a bit of a nightmare" and Barbara Skelton "incredibly selfish", and "a menace".

Lys Lubbock stuck with Connolly for many years, and only finally gave up on him when his general behaviour, and failure to seriously consider marrying her, brought matters to a head. Despite what Janetta said about her being "a bit of a nightmare", it does seem that Lys was often largely responsible for getting *Horizon* out on time. I suppose what might arouse curiosity is why an obviously attractive and intelligent woman should be so besotted with someone like Connolly? He appears to have been lazy, selfish, largely indifferent to the problems of others, and arrogant. He was clever, and had the knack of making himself seem intellectually superior to people in his presence. From what Taylor says, none of the "Lost Girls" had what might be called a good formal education, and as a consequence could have been over-impressed by someone like Connolly with a gift for what came across to them as brilliant conversation full of classical quotations.

Barbara Skelton was the one "Lost Girl" who had some literary talent, and she wrote several novels and autobiographical accounts of her misadventures. She married Connolly in 1950, though it wasn't a match likely to last. *Horizon*, like so many magazines in the post-war period, had finally thrown in the towel, largely because Peter Watson, its long-suffering financial backer, had called it a day. And Lys Lubbock had moved on, though Connolly couldn't quite accept that she had. After years of using her, and ignoring her emotional needs, he was convinced he couldn't live without her, despite having married Barbara Skelton. Barbara herself had something of a long track record when it came to lovers, one of them being King Farouk of Egypt. There were others, such as Peter Quennell and the artist, Felix Topolski. They came to blows as they contested for her affections.

As for Sonia Brownell, she may be best remembered for her marriage to George Orwell when he was dying. She had met him while working in the *Horizon* office, where she was reputed to have been energetic and efficient, and probably responsible for putting the final few issues into print. Connolly, as always, was increasingly lacksadaisical about the practical work required to keep a publication operating to schedule. Late-rising and long liquid lunches don't make for efficient editing.

But there was a question about Sonia that Taylor phrases as "What did Sonia want?" He quotes Stephen Spender who thought that she had "always been on the look out for a great man, a titan of art or literature, to whom she could devote herself and whose interests she could self-denyingly serve". Before Orwell, she had relationships with the painter William Coldstream and the French philosopher, Maurice Merleau-Ponty, though neither was ever likely to leave his wife. Orwell was unmarried and riding high following the success of *Animal Farm* and *1984* when they married in 1949. After he died, she worked hard to keep his name alive. I think it's worth noting that in the 1960s she was involved with the very fine magazine, *Art and Literature*, which survived for a dozen first-rate issues.

I've given a brief summary of the four women that Taylor mostly focuses on. There were others he deals with, and there were moments when I almost lost track of who was who and doing what. I did like the comment he ascribes to "Glur" (Joyce Francis Warwick-Evans), who he says, "had no ambitions to run a magazine office, marry that elusive great man or go to literary parties". She did marry Peter Quennell, however, though she later plaintively said, "I thought it would be fun being married to a writer, but he's always writing". It's a complaint that many a weary wife has no doubt expressed over the years.

The Lost Girls is clearly designed to throw light on the personalities and activities of the women at the centre of Taylor's book, and he does that in a splendidly informative and entertaining manner. But the fact that all, or most of them, were involved with Cyril Connolly in one way or another, or even in several ways, means that he also looms large in the story. As does *Horizon*, though not too much is said about its contents. A reader wanting to know more about that side of the magazine's history perhaps ought to turn to Michael Sheldon's *Friends of Promise; Cyril Connolly and the World of Horizon* (Hamish Hamilton, London, 1989) for a full account. Or better still, try to have a look at a few copies of the magazine, or at least the anthology, edited by Connolly, of some of the best work from it, *The Golden Horizon* (Weidenfeld & Nicolson, London, 1953). It's easy to see why it was considered of importance at a time when civilised living seemed to be almost on the brink of extinction. To launch a publication like *Horizon* as war started, and keep it running through the years of hostilities and the period of austerity that followed, was no mean feat. There are some who might say that *Penguin New Writing* offers, in retrospect, a wider and better portrait of the 1940s. It was surely more representative of the democratic beliefs and aims that characterised the times, but there's no denying that *Horizon* had an air of being concerned to preserve the high-minded approach to examining the arts and society.

I have to admit that, reading about Connolly, I was inclined to think that he was not a very nice person. He seems to have been something of an opportunist, and always ready to cultivate friendships with the wealthy who would then invite him to spend weekends with them. He was not alone in this, of course, and reading about several others makes me suspect that it was rather expected that the rich, if they had any pretensions towards an interest in the arts, would provide support for indigent writers and artists. As for his treatment of the women he was involved with, I doubt that much positive can be said about it. He usually had more than one affair developing, and had no conscience when it came to brutally abandoning a lover if he thought that she stood in the way of his relationship with another. And he expected the cast-off party to both understand and tolerate what he had done. He was what in earlier days would have been called a cad or a bounder.

The Arts Council, once it came into existence, took on the role of stepping in to give grants and awards to individuals, as they did with magazines. But *Horizon*, as far as I can make out, existed solely thanks to the goodwill and generosity of Peter Watson. He comes across, in Taylor's telling, as one of the more-sympathetic characters in the book. A homosexual, at a time when to show it was to invite attention from the police, he put up with a lot of Connolly's indolence, rudeness, and other failings until it all became too much, and he finally pulled the plug on the financial support he provided. It probably came as a shock to Connolly, who had become used to having a steady supply of funds he could rely on for the magazine and some of his personal needs.

D.J. Taylor has written a fast-moving and colourful book about years when everything was said to be seemingly dull and dreary. As well as the main actors, a wide range of writers appear on stage, including Anthony Powell, Evelyn Waugh, Brian Howard, Julian Maclaren-Ross, Raymond Mortimer, the heroin-addicted Anna Kavan, and John Davenport. Taylor sets them all in context, and provides details of how their novels, stories, and memoirs recorded the events and atmosphere of the period.

I suppose a purist might find the thought of people enjoying themselves, sometimes with black market food and wine, at a time when many were going hungry while in situations of great danger, unpalatable. Why celebrate these people? And certainly with someone like Connolly, who was inclined to whinge and whine instead of being grateful that he wasn't in uniform or limited to basic foodstuffs, it's easy to be contemptuous. But history will no doubt remember him for his literary accomplishments, rather than his personal follies and foibles. And Taylor's "Lost Girls" may also have a place in the sun thanks to the diligent work he has done on their behalf.

LOST GIRLS: LOVE, WAR AND LITERATURE 1939-1951
By D.J. Taylor
Constable. 387 pages. £25. ISBN 978-1-47212-686-3

BLITZ WRITING : NIGHT SHIFT & IT WAS DIFFERENT
AT THE TIME

What did I know about Inez Holden before receiving this welcome re-issue of two of her short novels from the 1940s? Only a little, I have to admit. I had read an amusing story, "Uncle Drunkle", in an old copy of *Writing Today*, edited by Denys Val Baker and Peter Ratazzi in 1943. And there was another, "The Flat Above Me", in *Penguin New Writing* 9 (1941), edited by John Lehman. These were publications I'd picked up in second-hand bookshops as I hunted for grubby copies of magazines from the 1940s.

Andrew Sinclair mentioned Holden a couple of times in *War Like A Wasp; The Lost Decade of the Forties* (Hamish Hamilton, London, 1989) but didn't include any of her work in *The War Decade: An Anthology of the 1940s* (Hamish Hamilton, London, 1989). Holden's "According to the Directive" was selected for *Wave Me Goodbye: Stories of the Second World War*, edited by Anne Boston (Virago, London, 1988). I picked up bits of information from the notes on contributors in these publication, but it was Celia Goodman's "Inez Holden: A Memoir" in *London Magazine* (December/January, 1993/94), edited by Alan Ross, that helped me to get a better grip on her personality and writing career.

Holden was born in 1903 or 1904 (her parents didn't bother to register her birth) into a financially comfortable but somewhat eccentric household. Her mother was a noted "Edwardian beauty who had owned fifteen hunters and was known as the second best horsewoman in Britain". Her father came from a family listed in Burke's *Landed Gentry*. According to Kristin Bluemel in her informative introduction to *Blitz Writing*, Holden didn't have a conventional upbringing. She seems to have been left very much to her own devices by parents who were constantly at odds with each other. In later years she rarely spoke of her father, who she remembered firing a shot at her mother but luckily missing. When she was 15 she ran away and went to Paris and then London, "living on her wits and her exceptional good looks". By the time she was in her twenties she was "considered to be a bohemian society beauty", and was sketched by Augustus John.

There was more to her than the frippery of the bright young things of the time. She had a talent for writing, and in the late-1920s and early-1930s she published three novels which recorded "the frivolous, absurd lives of the privileged characters who could have stepped out of the pages of Evelyn Waugh's *Vile Bodies*".

It's difficult to determine exactly when and how Holden became more socially and politically conscious, both in her life and writing. Like other writers, she probably reacted to the tensions of the 1930s as the Depression brought poverty to millions of people and fascism began its inexorable rise in Europe. She knew George Orwell and H.G. Wells, and as a journalist covered meetings addressed by Oswald Mosley, leader of the British Union of Fascists. Wells later broke off his friendship when he accused her of siding with Orwell over an article attacking Wells that he wrote for Cyril Connolly's magazine, *Horizon.*

When the war started in 1939 Holden, like many other people, either volunteered for, or was conscripted into, the work force required to replace the men from factories and other locations who were being called-up for the armed forces. She did some basic training as a Red Cross nurse and worked as an auxiliary in hospitals and first-aid posts during the blitz, and later spent time in an engineering works as a machinist producing parts for aircraft. Her experiences provided the basic material for *Night Shift* and *It Was Different at the Time.*

It Was Different at the Time was written in the form of a diary, though not with a strict series of daily entries. It moves through a period from April, 1938 to August, 1941, focusing on certain months in each year, and building up the approach to war, its start, and the onset of bombing raids on London. To give an idea of Holden's commitment to what can be described as "socialist anti-communism". she tells how she still had the kind of connections that got her invited to a weekend in a country house. But the seeming-indifference of many of the guests to anything other than their own personal concerns, often centred around money, disturbed her: "Distressed areas, malnutrition, and unemployment are all subjects before which the blinds of the mind must be drawn down quick". And she adds that "this is the gay Bohemian thanklessness of artists, writers, musicians, and the like".

She has a friend, Victor, who has just returned from Spain, and is addressing meetings to raise funds for the Republican government. It's probable that he's based on Hugh Slater, who was an officer in the British Battalion of the 15th International Brigade. Holden had what is described as "a troubled romantic attachment to Slater that lasted for years". But, at a party, she also meets "a German with some National Socialist's paid job", who says that Hitler is peace-loving", but with regard to Spain, comments that it is "good practice for our airmen" to be engaged in bombing towns and villages in Republican territory.

When war was declared, Holden took on work as a Red Cross Nurse, and her experiences began to widen. The descriptions of the hospital wards are brisk and to the point, and her quickly-established portraits of staff and patients soon create a wide picture that the reader can clearly see. People have personalities and are not just a faceless mass. Much of the work that Holden did was routine and designed to support the qualified nurses, but she seems to have been present during at least one operation. Taking down details from a patient she finds that he has no next-of-kin, no friends, but she is impressed by his "apparent happiness. He was uninhibited, without fear, smiling and strong".

Later, working at a first-aid post, she watches the "demolition men, rescue parties, and stretcher bearers" being called out night after night. Like the firemen, they work while the bombs are still falling and the fires raging, and don't always return. Harry, a popular officer – "Always there when anything's on.....Right on the spot at the start and, and the last to leave at the finish", in the words of a member of his team – goes out one night and is killed.

Night Shift picks up Holden's story after she left working as a Red Cross nurse, and obtained employment as a machinist in a factory. It covers a working week, Monday through to Saturday, with the actual work being repetitive and seemingly needing only basic instruction before the operative is left to get on with the job. The employees were mostly women, though the foremen and supervisors were all men. Pay and conditions were not good, and the long hours (up to 60 a week) didn't produce hefty pay packets. Holden writes about the constant complaining among the workers regarding how little they earned. Some were lucky enough to do piece work and so could earn more if they produced the requisite amount of whatever it was they were working on.

There is a woman called Feather among the workers and she is clearly very much like Holden in being better-educated, if not in a formal way, and wider-travelled than her colleagues. She probably represented Holden, though the anonymous narrator talks about her as just being one among many. But, as in *It Was Different at the Time,* the workers aren't a nameless mass. Many of them are named and given certain distinctions of character that enable the reader to see them as individuals. They talk about their husbands and boyfriends, many of whom are already in the armed forces, and about what they do when they're not at work.

The hazards of factory work, especially at night, while the Blitz is at its height are outlined. Everyone is conscious of the fact that a bomb may hit the factory at any time. When one does while the Saturday night shift is working, the narrator is lucky in that she had been transferred to a Sunday night shift, and so is not killed or injured. Her situation brings out how much it was a matter of chance who lived or died. Another woman is doubly lucky. She missed the Saturday night shift because her house was damaged by a bomb blast and she survived but couldn't get to work. Death is all around, and people just get on with what they have to do.

In many ways, Holden's writing is much more convincing than later fictional recreations of the Blitz. Written while the events she describes were taking place, it still has a fresh feeling that gives it an immediacy. She keeps her prose simple and describes what she has seen without fuss:

"I went up to the top of one of the empty houses and looked out over London. All around us there were fires, seven or eight of these bowls of flame were near, so that we seemed to be existing in a small camp. In the sky there were intermittent flashes of anti-aircraft gunfire. They looked like stars and took their place amongst the other stars which never went out".

It often strikes me that wartime circumstances led many writers to a direct and straightforward way of writing. There wasn't a mood or an inclination to experiment, in either prose or poetry. Communication was the key factor when writing a story or a poem, and the aim was to reach as wide an audience as possible. No-one, writers and readers, wanted to waste time. Short stories, short novels, short poems predominated. Little magazines with compendiums of stories and other material that might be read in the barrack-room, the factory canteen, or while waiting to be called out to a fire, were popular and sold in numbers that would astound editors of literary publications today.

What happened to Inez Holden after 1945? Despite being widely published in a variety of magazines, and with seven novels (two published in the early-1950s) and two short-story collections to her credit, plus writing film-scripts for J. Arthur Rank, she was never a best-selling author. Kristin Bluemel sums up her situation in these words: "During her lifetime, Holden achieved publication but not fame, her novels and short stories and journalistic work failing to attain the popularity or influence achieved by many of her writer friends". She doesn't appear to have ever earned a lot of money from her writing, and presumably may have had an income from her family background. According to her cousin, Celia Goodman, Holden wrote only short stories, many of them published in *Punch*, after her last novel appeared in 1956. She died in 1976.

I think it's worth quoting Kristin Bluemel again when she sums up what Holden achieved with the two works I've reviewed; "Despite a career that produced no best-sellers and earned no literary awards, she composed a life out of the colourful scraps of material that others left behind and wove from them stories of the everyday art of survival in a city that was falling down and in a country defying destruction".

A couple of final notes that may be of interest. A character called Felicity crops up in *It Was Different at the Time,* and was based on her friend, Stevie Smith. In return, Smith based someone called Lopez in her novel, *The Holiday*, and her short story, "The Story of a Story", on Holden. And, though it wasn't quite like Marcel Proust's experience, memories of my childhood during the war came flooding back when I read Inez Holden's reference to a meal of corned beef and fried potatoes in *Night Shift*. I thought it was a great treat at the time.

BLITZ WRITING : NIGHT SHIFT & IT WAS DIFFERENT AT THE TIME
By Inez Holden
Handheld Press. 194 pages. £12.99. ISBN 078-1-912766-06-2

LONESOME TRAVELLER

I read *Lonesome Traveller* when it was first published in Britain in 1962, and it has remained one of my favourite Kerouac books since then. It hasn't been given the kind of attention devoted to some of his other books, perhaps because it is a collection of short pieces mostly written for commercial publications at a time when Kerouac's stock was riding high and he could earn some money from magazines which, unlike the small literary magazines he also sometimes contributed to, could afford to pay decent fees. Publishing in magazines like these would also bring his name to the notice of a wider readership than he was likely to attract elsewhere.

There are eight items in *Lonesome Traveller*, six of which had been previously published. All of them seemed to me to represent the kind of Kerouac I preferred, where he looked at what was in front of his eyes and didn't spend too much time behind them engaging in rhapsodic reflections on life, nature, religion, etc. I know that, in a way, it's only to be expected that Kerouac does that, anyway, but I liked to concentrate on his marvellous descriptive passages relating to the real world, his practical experiences on land and at sea, the jobs he did, and his friends.

There are some passages of what might be called religious meditation in "Mexico Fellaheen" and these are presumably what were published as "The Statue of Christ" in the June 1958 issue of the Catholic magazine, *Jubilee*. They only take up just under four pages of the sixteen or so in *Lonesome Traveller,* with the rest largely devoted to Kerouac's experiences with drugs, his visit to a bullfight, the people he met, and some seemingly romanticised ideas about the virtues of the simple lives of the Mexican peasants – the "fellaheen", as he refers to them. I suspect that he was influenced by reading Oswald Spengler on how an antidote to the corruptions and indignities of life in supposedly more-advanced societies like the United States could be found among the fellaheen. As for his comment that "There is no 'violence' in Mexico", it's difficult not to think that he perhaps had a naïve view of life in that country.

With one exception, the other previously-published pieces in *Lonesome Traveller* all originally appeared in *Holiday*, a mass-circulation magazine that was in existence from 1946 to 1977. "Alone on a Mountaintop" had a place in the October, 1958 issue of *Holiday*. I haven't access to the archives of the magazine, so don't know if the essay as printed in its pages corresponds exactly to the version in the book. Leaving that aside, it related to Kerouac's experiences as "a fire lookout in the Mount Baker National Forest in the High Cascades of the Great Northwest". And it allowed him to come into his own in terms of writing about the forests and valleys and mountains he could see all around him, the effects of a violent lightning storm, and the pleasures of making simple meals. The seclusion does incline him to reflect on life – "For when you realise that God is Everything you know that you've got to love everything no matter how bad it is" –but it's in the context of where he was, and how the solitude influenced him, and so does have relevance.

There was something of a change in the October, 1959 *Holiday*, with "Roaming Beatniks" being excerpted from the longer "New York Scenes" in *Lonesome Traveller*. He tours the city with his friends – Peter Orlovsky, Gregory Corso, Allen Ginsberg, Ray Bremser are all mentioned – goes in and out of bars and cafeterias, and listens to jazz musicians like Don Joseph and Tony Fruscella, two trumpet players who were fixtures around Greenwich Village and had their share of problems with drugs. Artists like Willem de Kooning, Dody Muller, Franz Kline, and Robert De Niro (father of the famous actor of the same name) make an appearance, and it all adds up to a celebration of bohemianism, as practised around Greenwich Village in the late-1950s. Kerouac makes it seem colourful and exciting, and it was a vibrant and productive period for many poets and painters. Kerouac's racy prose matches the movements of the people he describes. One of them, less well-known than the others, was Bill Heine. He was an artist and musician, and a junkie. Probably one of his few claims to any kind of recognition was his presence as the drummer on a March, 1954 recording date by a Tony Fruscella/Brew Moore group. I'd guess that his association with them came about through sessions at the Open Door in Greenwich Village. It was a club that Kerouac frequented in the early-1950s and he featured it as the Red Drum in *The Subterraneans.* (see my article, "Open Door at the Red Drum" in *Beat Scene 38,* 2001, and in *Brits, Beats & Outsiders,* Penniless Press, 2012).

The story of Kerouac's 1957 trip to Morocco, France, and England came out in *Holiday* in February, 1960 under the title, "Tangier to London: A Beatnik Pilgrimage", though again I don't know if it was the complete text of what was published in *Lonesome Traveller* as "Big Trip to Europe". I suppose the fact that he was working for a magazine like *Holiday* influenced how he constructed the article, with an emphasis on the sights he saw, the meals he ate, and the girls he gazed at. Stylistically, it wasn't too far from how Kerouac generally wrote, though it did come across in an overall way as a quick trip around the locations concerned by an enthusiastic tourist, albeit one who did have a degree of awareness of French and English culture, if not of Moroccan.

The final contribution to *Holiday* was "The Vanishing American Hobo" in the March, 1960 issue. It was Kerouac's lament for a breed of men he pictured in almost the same way as he portrayed the fellaheen, as if they might possess some sort of inner vision that imbued them with a naturalness that city-bred people lacked. It's possible to understand Kerouac's somewhat sentimental concern for such men, and his sympathy for their fear that they are slowly being driven out of existence as police patrols increasingly harass them and city ordinances limit their ability to beg. Kerouac says that "in Paris bums are treated with great respect and are rarely refused a few francs", which, when I read it, seemed at odds with my own recollections of seeing them chased away from loitering around tables outside bars and restaurants.

Probably the strongest essay in *Lonesome Traveller* was the wonderful "October in the Railroad Earth", to my mind one of the most-sustained pieces of writing that Kerouac ever did. It was first published in *Evergreen Review* in issues 2 (1957) and 11 (1960), though with no explanation as to why there was such a big time-lag between the two sections getting into print. The magazine had presumably accepted the complete piece in 1957. Issue 2 was, of course, the famous San Francisco number, and Kerouac may not have been as well-known in 1957 as he was in 1960. It was, perhaps, an opportunistic decision to use the second part, 1960 being a year when the Beats were very much in the news and all kinds of magazines and anthologies were focusing on them. The whole thing, as published in *Lonesome Traveller,* is a fast-moving account of living in San Francisco and working as a railroad brakeman. It's a minor point, but in *Evergreen Review 2* it was called "October in the Railroad Earth", whereas in *Evergreen Review* 11 and *Lonesome Traveller* it was "The Railroad Earth". Thomas Parkinson included "October in the Railroad Earth" from *Evergreen Review* 2 in the 1961 anthology, *A Casebook on the Beat.* (See my article, "Thomas Parkinson: *A Casebook on the Beat*" in *Beat Scene* 89, 2018, and reprinted in *Books, Artists, Beats*, Penniless Press, 2019).

The two essays in *Lonesome Traveller* which don't appear to have appeared in print before their inclusion in the book were "Slobs of the Kitchen Sea" and "Piers of the Homeless Night", though I'm open to correction if anyone knows of their previous publication. "Slobs of the Kitchen Sea" was about Kerouac shipping out as a "bedroom steward" on the *William H. Caruthers* , "a Liberty ship black with orange booms and blue and orange stack", though he soon switched roles and washed pots and pans in the galley and served the officers with their breakfasts. It's colourful and has neat descriptions of some of the other crew members, a couple of whom seemed to share his liking for jazz.

"Piers of the Homeless Night" had something of a connection to "Slobs of the Kitchen Sea" in that it concerned Kerouac's attempts to be taken on as a crew member of a ship called the S.S.*Roamer*. A friend who was a crew member had promised to get him a job, but in the end he was rejected at the union hall because he had "no seniority". I don't think it's as good a piece as "Slobs of the Kitchen Sea", perhaps because it comes across as a little aimless in its intentions. It had the usual Kerouac energy and colour, and described some lively characters, but didn't really add up to a great deal. And I doubt that it would have appealed to readers of a magazine like *Holiday* or other commercial publications, such as *Esquire, Escapade,* and *Playboy,* that Kerouac contributed to around this time.

As I said earlier, *Lonesome Traveller* is one of my favourite Kerouac books, along with *On the Road, The Dharma Bums,* and *Maggie Cassidy*. I've indicated that it isn't perfect. Kerouac could be a variable writer at the best of times, but even when he was writing with commercial intentions in mind he could still come up with descriptive passages that are a pleasure to read. "The Railroad Earth" is easily the best piece in *Lonesome Traveller*, and it's probably significant that, unlike the other items, it was written at a time when thoughts of publication in *Holiday* and similar outlets were probably not a major consideration. Prior to the publication of *On the Road,* Kerouac's most significant magazine contribution was "Jazz of the Beat Generation" in *New World Writing* 7 in 1955. And that was a publication largely aimed at a literary and not a general audience, though it certainly had a larger circulation than the so-called little magazines. He had to wait until *On the Road* started the Beat boom on its way before he could make money writing for bigger magazines.

Lonesome Traveller was initially published in Britain by Andre Deutsch in 1962. It has been reprinted in various paperback editions, most recently in 2018 by Penguin Books.

Readers may like to refer to my article, "Kerouac Goes Commercial" in *Beat Scene* 60, 2009, and later reprinted in *Artists, Beats & Cool Cats,* Penniless Press, 2014. It provides a wider survey of the commercial magazines where Kerouac was published.

LOOKING FOR JACK KEROUAC

Questing for Kerouac is a minor industry these days. Academics do it in essays with titles like "Duluoz and Faust" and "Synaesthesia, Synchronicity and Syncopation". Young poets make their way to his grave and then knock out an obligatory stanza or two. And even pop musicians and fans try to find Kerouac in music that he probably would have ignored or derided. his own tastes running to the classics, jazz, and singers such as Sinatra, Dick Haymes, and Ella Fitzgerald. I suppose all writers worry about being misunderstood, but poor Kerouac seems to suffer more than most.

But how about Chris Challis's quest? A youthful enthusiasm for the books and then a Ph.D in Kerouac studies (surely one of the first in this country?) seems to have inclined him to start thinking of himself as a Beat of sorts. A recent small collection of his poems was entitled, *Jack Kerouac, Charles Bukowski, and Me*, which some people might think is overdoing it a bit. When Challis decided to write a book about Kerouac, he made a trip to America, partly to talk to surviving Beats (Lawrence Ferlinghetti, Carl Solomon, Michael McClure), partly to soak up some of the atmosphere of the places that Kerouac himself passed through. This wasn't a bad idea in itself, though Challis tends to spoil it in his book by placing himself too obviously in the scenes and situations he describes.

That he knows and likes Beat literature isn't in any doubt, and he's at his best when discussing the novels and poems that Kerouac and his friends wrote. Challis may have an academic background, but he talks about literature in a clear relevant manner.

In other areas, however, he's often inadequate. His overall account of Beat history is sometimes a little too generalised for comfort, and he's occasionally repetitious in his linking of facts and personalities. I suspect that Challis's own loyalties lie with the 1960s, whereas the 1940s and 1950s were the truly formative and productive Beat years. This could explain why he's shaky when he talks about jazz, a music of importance to the Beats. A book about Kerouac that mentions Mick Jagger and Jim Morrison more than Charlie Parker is guaranteed to make me suspicious..

The 1960s proclivities might also explain why Challis virtually ignores the political climate in America in the post-1945 period. The collapse of American radicalism in the late-1940s, and the onset of McCarthyism, helped shape Beat attitudes and certainly created the situation where they could be thought of as unusual. And someone like Allen Ginsberg, despite his links to events in the 1960s, had his roots in an earlier era of American dissent.

I have the impression that Challis, aware of the existence of a youthful, pop-influenced audience for some aspects of the Beats, angled his book to cater to that audience. As a result, he's produced something which, though lively and reasonably informative, leaves one thinking that Kerouac is still a misunderstood writer.

QUEST FOR KEROUAC by Chris Challis. Faber. 1984

UNDERGROUND WITH THE HIPPIES

Malcom Cowley once pointed out that "Bohemia is Grub Street romanticised, doctrinalised, and rendered self-conscious: it is Grub Street on parade". What he meant is that although writers have always faced the possibility of having to struggle to make a living, it is only a certain type of person who makes a virtue out of it. Bohemians are basically the products of industrial capitalism, and it is significant that Bohemia as an identifiable entity has only really existed since the beginning of the nineteenth century. Prior to that writers may have opposed aspects of the society they lived in, and even deliberately disaffiliated from it, but they were not alienated from its overall structure.

Paradoxically, it is precisely the kind of society hated most by the bohemians that allows them to flourish. Affluence encourages the dabblers and poseurs to imitate penniless artists. This is true of our own time – it was no mere coincidence that the publicised Beat phase came at a time when there was more money around to spend on non-essentials – and it was certainly true of nineteenth century Paris, where Bohemianism had its origins. Joanna Richardson's study of bohemians in France between 1830 and 1914 describes more than one would-be poet whose inheritance was squandered in the search for creativity supposedly arising from la vie de Bohème.

The problem with studies of Bohemianism is that one has to rely mainly on records left by writers who are self-conscious about their links to the life-style. Richardson quotes Arsène Houssaye as neatly summing up the dangers inherent in accepting writers' views: "I don't believe in the good faith of the literary Bohemian. His disordered life is only a journey in search of sensations, of the documents and observations he needs to produce his work. The real Bohemian is the one who has no communication with the public. He leads a vagabond existence for himself alone, not for any readers or spectators".

With the above in mind, one is inclined to look more kindly at Richardson's shortcomings. She primarily discusses literary Bohemia, and it's disappointing that she fails to provide – other than on a faintly moralising level – any commentary on the sociological or psychological factors behind Bohemianism. The writers lived oddball lives, but what made them tick? And who were the minor bohemians, those who never wrote more than an occasional poem or story or article, if that? It's an interesting question, but one will look in vain for answers in *The Bohemians*.

173

However, within the framework Richardson has established, she has written a lively and informative book. She discusses a number of now-forgotten writers, and it is useful to have the information about them available. It should be noted that her otherwise-valuable bibliography has missed a couple of comparatively recent books: Malcolm Easton's *Artists and Writers in Paris: The Bohemian Idea, 1803-1867* (Edward Arnold, London, 1964), and César Grana's *Bohemian versus Bourgeois: French Society and the French Man of Letters in the Nineteenth Century* (Basic Books, New York, 1964).

The Hippies are inevitability referred to by Richardson, and the best essay in Joan Didion's *Slouching towards Bethlehem* takes a hard look at these contemporary drop-outs. I'm personally wary of including them in any true history of Bohemianism, because despite their failures in life and art the earlier breeds did produce many works of an artistic nature, fragmentary and fashionable though some of them may have been. And the more-obscure bohemians didn't court the publicity-machine as avidly as the Hippies do. I doubt that genuine Bohemianism is ever a mass-movement.

If Didion is to be relied on and I've also recently read Burton Wolfe's *The Hippies* (New American Library, New York, 1968), a sympathetic account by a journalist which seems to back up many of her findings, the American scene is grim. Drugs, group sex, endless pop music, a few underground papers, pathetic attempts at street-theatre. One looks in vain for the virtues of earlier American Bohemias, even the Beats.

Where is the Hippie talent? And if they want to restructure society, where are their doctors, teachers, scientists, workers? If the Hippies have any activists, they are salesmen, promotion boys, gimmick merchants. One wants to be sympathetic to any group or individual opposing the status quo, but at the same time it's necessary to be ruthless about what they're offering.

One thing is for sure, you don't have to dig very deep to hit the underground these days. The books are rolling merrily from the publishers, and it's tempting to speculate just who they're aimed at? Not at the hippies, surely, because if the evidence in the books is reliable they don't read anything other than the underground papers. Jane Kramer's book on Allen Ginsberg has an account of a lecture given by the poet to a group of students in California which is worth taking note of. Ginsberg, surprised by the fact that no-one in the audience had heard of Ezra Pound, pointed out that the books they were studying must have references to Pound, and surely they followed up on them. A boy rose to his feet. "But that's bad, man, "he said, "You have to go to the library to look up references".

The same wilful know-nothingness often comes through in Richard Neville's *Play Power*, a guide to hippie culture. Not that Neville himself is less than shrewd. He knows precisely how to cater for his audience, and virtually gives us a manifesto in which all things bright and beautiful (assuming you see drugs, ear-splitting pop music, and sexual activity in which the woman always seems to be debased, in that light) are found among the flower children, and the rest of us are dull, ugly, and worst of all, over thirty. This will infuriate or delight, according to how you feel about the underground, but either way Neville keeps his name in the limelight.

Still, I have to admit that *Play Power* is quite honest in places. Nothing could be more damning than Neville's account of the hippies abroad. Are they trying to locate other cultures or philosophies to put into practice? Do they want to broaden their minds? Are they interested in establishing some sort of communication with the natives in the interests of world or even personal harmony? No, they're not. They cluster together, carry their pop records wherever they go, swindle the locals if they can get away with it, and generally make a nuisance of themselves. It's noticeable, too, that these drop-outs are not so far out that they refuse help from their square fellow-countrymen when they land in trouble.

As for their political or economic ideas, just how does the hippie traveller get along? "Fifty forged student cards printed in India cost one dollar, and you can sell them to fellow-travellers at a dollar apiece". Coming from someone who has rejected the rat-race that isn't at all bad as an example of capitalist enterprise. Daddy, at home with his stocks and shares, will be happy to welcome his sons and daughters back to the fold if he realises they're as profit-inclined as that.

It's not hard to suspect that it's the middle-classes which provide the types who make up most of the underground, and that it's a variant on the old game of the wealthy young man's year in Bohemia. A recession and they'll soon head home to the comforts oif a safe marriage or a job in a relative's business. These people aren't real misfits or rebels. Neville reprints a guide to "Free London" which was distributed among the hippies not too long ago. This has such gems as using the emergency exits of cinemas as a means of sneaking in without paying. No wonder working-class kids treat the hippies with derision. That trick was

old hat when Flash Gordon first came out, and it wasn't thought necessary to put it into print, either.

The contemporary underground hasn't produced many, if any, creative
writers, and the few who do appear in its publications are invariably
like Allen Ginsberg and have their feet in an older literary Bohemia.
Ginsberg served his time in the Greenwich Village/San Francisco scene
of the 1940s and 1950s, and Jane Kramer has some useful insights on
that part of his career, but in recent years he's hopped on the hippie
bandwagon. To be honest, it's hard not think that he prefers the new
underground to the old because the latter was never going to be over-
awed by his mumbo-jumbo about how to change society.

In a way, though, you can't help having a sneaking liking for the man,
and he has written some worthwhile poems, though I tend to the view
that they mostly date from the period before he became a public figure
associated with the hippies and flower power and protest. Certainly, his
gentleness and good humour seem sincere enough. As a picture of life
in the underground, at least as it's lived by some of its denizens (and
Ginsberg's cronies are often genuine misfits, reasonably talented writers, or both) Jane Kramer's well-written study has a great deal to recommend it.

Finally, *The Politics of Ecstasy*. Timothy Leary's collection of essays
in praise of the psychedelic life. There are some interesting pieces here
– a long discussion of Herman Hesse's work is worth reading – but,
like Ginsberg, Leary appears to lose all sense of proportion when it
comes to suggesting new paths for society to move along. It just is not
true that everything will work out fine if we all turn on and drop out,
and a man in Leary's position, and with his knowledge, ought not to
give the impression that it is. Common-sense doesn't seem to be one of
Leary's attributes, and his criticisms of contemporary society (often
valid, I agree) lose their impact because of the endless slogans written
in adman's prose. I'm suspicious of wide-sweeping statements and
want to see them backed by facts.

The underground, as it comes across in these three books, often oppos-
es the kind of people I view as my enemies, but I have to admit to a
growing feeling that it really hasn't much to offer anymore. There is
still a genuine underground, comprised of writers, social critics, political activists, and it could be that it is where the hope lies, and that it has
nothing to do with the publicity-seeking personalities who have thrown

in their lot with the hippies.

A lot of the fuss about the hippies has died down since the student militants captured the attention of the mass-media, and it's therefore inevitable that anything written about them now, but based on what they were doing a few years ago, will seem a little dated. Tom Wolfe's book neatly dodges the major pitfalls ahead of any writer starting out on this trail, and he doesn't attempt to chronicle the whole underground scene. Instead, he concentrates on the activities of a small group of bizarre West Coasters who may have been partly responsible for setting the pattern of much of the hippie life-style.

The leader of this group, and looked up to with almost-religious fervour, was Ken Kesey, a novelist who made a hit with *One Flew Over the Cuckoo's Nest*, and then produced a chunky and erratic book called *Sometimes a Great Notion*. Kesey was domiciled for a time among California's suburban bohemians, but after taking part in experiments with various drugs, decided to opt out and develop his interest in LSD. He soon attracted a small, but devoted following, and started to lay the roots of what later sprouted all over Haight-Ashbury, the Hippie enclave of San Francisco.

Among the Merry Pranksters, as Kesey's crowd was called, were one or two characters from earlier underground scenes. Neal Cassidy, the prototype for the frantic Dean Moriarty of Kerouac's *On the Road,* and Hugh Romney, an ex-Beat poet (his bearded face and his poems are in *The Beat* Scene anthology) turned up to take part in the fun.

Kesey bought an old bus, the Pranksters painted it in what became known as the psychedelic style, and in this travelling church (it was viewed almost like one, and Kesey's aphorism, "You're either on the bus....or off the bus" shows its importance to the Pranksters) the gang trekked across California, and then over to New York, and eventually, when Kesey was on the run from the police, into Mexico. In between times, they attended a Beatles concert, turned up at, and almost fouled-up peace demonstrations, and fraternised with the notorious Hell's Angels.

The Prankster association with the Angels is one of the more-curious parts of the book. There is a long description of the party held to celebrate the start of the "friendship" (another view of the gathering can be found in Hunter Thompson's *Hell's Angels*, and Allen Ginsberg has given it a place in poetry with his "First party at Ken Kesey's wth Hell's Angels", and Tom Wolfe is rightly sarcastic about the way in which the would-be hip academics who hung around with Kesey fawned over the opportunistic toughs who comprised the motor-cycle gangs.

The admiration was not returned, as anyone who has read *Freewheelin' Frank* by Frank Reynolds, a leader of the San Francisco Hell's Angels, knows. Reynolds says: "When it comes to the peace marchers, Kesey, Allen Ginsberg, and others, there is no connection of any kind of scene where we look up to them. If anyone looks up to the scene it is our scene".

The Pranksters gave LSD to the Angels – an irresponsible act, though it luckily didn't result in any really bad incidents – and also dished it out liberally at their various get-togethers. At one of these they went so far as to lace the Kool-Aid (an orange drink) with LSD, with the result that a number of unsuspecting people drank it, got an overdose of the drug, and experienced what the hippies called "a bad trip". There seems to be no intelligent justification for this kind of behaviour, especially when there's a strong possibility, as there is in a any kind of bohemian community, of some people being highly-strung, if not somewhat unstable.

Kesey's role as a kind of prophet/philosopher – following in the California tradition of homespun religious extremists – is dubious, and the handful of mundane sayings attributed to him are not likely to cause a commotion among the unconverted. The much-vaunted drug experiences appear to be virtually incommunicable to anyone else. Perhaps the main influence Kesey and the Pranksters had was on the way of life – the music, clothes, social attitudes – of the hippies. From a wider viewpoint, they were the more flamboyant protagonists of yet another attempt to find a way out of the mass mediocrity of contemporary society.

The Electric Kool-Aid Acid Test will not arouse a great deal of enthusiasm among the those who give their loyalties to the organised Left. Both the Pranksters and the Hell's Angels can be seen as expressions of Fascism (interested readers are referred to Warren Hinckle's "The Social History of the Hippies" in the March, 1967 issue of *Ramparts* for a lucid dissertation on the subject), though Kesey would clearly not identify with any political party or idea. But I've a strong suspicion that the hippie idea might mean more to some of the young than that of the political activists. Tom Wolfe's book is necessary reading for anyone concerned about contemporary society.

THE BOHEMIANS: LA VIE DE BOHÈME IN PARIS 1830-1914 by Joanna Richardson. Macmillan, London, 1969.

SLOUCHING TOWARDS BETHLEHEM by Joan Didion. Deutsch, London, 1969

PLAY POWER by Richard Neville. Cape, London, 1970

PATERFAMILIAS : ALLEN GINSBERG IN AMERICA by Jane Kramer. Gollancz, London, 1970

THE POLITICS OF ECSTASY by Timothy Leary. MacGibbon & Kee, London, 1970

THE ELECTRIC KOOL-AID ACID TEST by Tom Wolfe. Weidenfeld & Nicolson, London, 1969

EASY LIVING: A NOVEL BY MAITLAND ZANE

The Beat explosion of the late-1950s and early-1960s brought a general upsurge of interest in bohemianism, and the lives of hipsters, oddballs, misfits, drifters, junkies, and other groups who were around the fringes of the wider society. Old novels were revived and referred to, new ones were published to take advantage of the situation. Pulp publishers were not slow to get on the bandwagon. Have a look at David Markson's *Epitaph for a Dead Beat* (Dell, 1961) or John Trinian's *North Beach Girl* (Gold Medal, 1960) to see how quickly mass-market paperbacks could exploit the darker areas of the Beat scene – drugs, sex, crime – to their advantage.

Not all of the novels were necessarily exploitative in their approach to the subject of "alternative" living, though most of them inevitability brought in the drugs aspect of their characters' lives. It happened to be a fact of their activities, even when they claimed to be no longer users. In Maitland Zane's *Easy Living* (Dial Press, New York, 1959), Harry, an ex-junkie jazz musician, is living a somewhat aimless life in Paris. He has a circle of friends who, in one way or another, are of a similar nature. Their conversations reflect the jargon and attitudes of the time, with women described as "chicks" and largely considered for their potential as sex partners and their ability to hold down jobs to help support their male partners.

It's easy to place the period involved from references in the novel. Harry does look at the newspapers, though he doesn't feel any real involvement with the events they report: "I didn't have to know how many Algerians the French said they killed yesterday, or the name of that Cypriot the British hanged". The war in Algeria lasted from 1954 to 1962 and the "Emergency" in Cyprus from 1955 to 1959. Zane's book was published in 1959, so he was presumably writing about the mid-1950s, say the years 1956 to 1958, or thereabouts.

There are other references that relate to the mid-1950s. A pianist in a little club is playing "Bernie's Tune", a composition made popular by the Gerry Mulligan-Chet Baker group early in the 1950s. One of the women in the story says that her husband is a musician called "Chet" and that he's currently playing at the Black Hawk in San Francisco. Trumpeter Chet Baker had been in Paris in late-1955 and early-1956, and his first wife was French. This doesn't necessarily mean that he's the "Chet" named, but it's highly-coincidental if he isn't.

Naturally, with Harry being a musician (though he's not active as such in Paris) there are plenty of other remarks about jazz players like Charlie Parker (more than once), Stan Getz, Art Blakey, John Lewis and Serge Chaloff. He is referred to as "Serge the devil", because he was reputed to be responsible for introducing a lot of other musicians to heroin. It's mentioned that he's dead, and his death took place in July 1957, so that nudges the novel's timeline away from 1956 and perhaps locates it more in late-1957 and 1958.

Harry's life, like those of many of his acquaintances, seems fairly meaningless in terms of not appearing to have any ambitions about returning to music, getting a job, etc. He meets a woman called Dolores, who he genuinely likes, and follows her to London, where, in the coffee houses, the people are "younger and dirtier than the bohemians in Paris". And he goes into the York Minster pub (the "French", as it was and still is known), but is confused by the English licensing laws. At a party he watches couples "jitterbugging to godawful English Dixieland". London generally comes across as shabby and run-down, which it still was in some ways in the mid-1950s.

His experience of jazz in London is improved when he goes to a jazz club and listens to a "coloured" alto player "trying to sound like Bird". Harry is impressed because the musician may be playing in the Charlie Parker manner but is not merely imitating him: "Raw and broken the sounds were, twisted and bent, atrophied and distended, and from the horn came barrage after barrage that filled the long narrow wooden-walled room to bursting, so that there was no escaping from him, no choice but to surrender to the music". Harry also watches the drummer who, he tells Dolores, is clearly a junkie. But he's "good, very good; noisy, but sensitive to the soloists and quiet when he should be".

From my own observations around the London jazz clubs in the late-1950s and early-1960s, I'd identify the alto player as Joe Harriott and the drummer most likely Phil Seamen. There is a reference to a guitar player who could well be Dave Goldberg. All three were active in the London clubs like The Flamingo, and on records.

The relationship with Dolores doesn't work out, and the final, short chapter of *Easy Living* finds Harry back in New York two years later, living in his parents' house, practising his saxophone again, and playing casual gigs, not jazz but wedding parties and the like, while he works towards command of the instrument. He occasionally has a letter from Dolores, now in Paris once more and living with an older man.

I can't claim that *Easy Living* is an important novel from any point of view. It's competently written, and its main interest lies in the way that it portrays a time and a type. The Beat scene (I'm using the term in a general way, and not to refer to a specific group if writers) probably had more than a few people like Harry in its ranks. They weren't necessarily all jazz musicians or junkies, but the drifting nature of their lives was typical of how many of them got along.

Maitland Zane certainly doesn't appear to have been that kind of American expatriate, idling around Paris and London, though he presumably had observed, perhaps even mixed with, people who were like that. He made a living as a journalist, and as far as I know wrote nothing else of a similar nature to *Easy Living*. He worked as a reporter for the *San Francisco Chronicle* for over forty years, and died in 2009. As well, as his activities as a journalist, he had some proficiency as a jazz pianist and played with a local band in the San Francisco area. One of his colleagues at the newspaper described him as "a cool guy, the swinging old hipster".

Easy Living by Maitland Zane, Dial Press, New York, 1959. A paperback edition was published by Bantam Books, New York, 1960.

MIMEOGRAPHING *MOVE* (1964-1968)

In the early-1960s I had just started to publish a few poems in little magazines and was looking for kindred spirits, people with similar interests. I was living in a medium-sized industrial town in the North of England, and poetry wasn't exactly an activity that had much attention paid to it. But it seemed to me that something was happening in Britain in terms of breaking the stranglehold that literary London appeared to have. I decided that the best way to get in touch with the scattered individuals who I thought might have something different to say was by starting a magazine.

There were already several magazines (not mimeographed) that were publishing poets, both British and American, I found of interest. *Satis, Outburst,* and *New Departures* all broke new ground. The American connection was important, and I had subscribed to *The Outsider, Evergreen Review*, and *Big Table*, so I could find out what the Beats, and what were generally referred to as "the New American Poets" were doing. New York Poets, Black Mountain Poets, San Francisco Renaissance Poets; they all were of interest, even if I didn't necessarily like some of their work.

The magazine I took as my guide to what I wanted to do was Gael Turnbull's *Migrant*, which ran for eight issues, mostly from Worcester, in 1959/1960. It was mimeographed (or duplicated, as I recall we referred to such publications in those days) and was essentially designed to function as a kind of workshop, with poetry, short articles, and exchanges of ideas and opinions. Turnbull, a doctor by profession, had lived in Canada and California, and had connections with poets in those areas. But what I liked about *Migrant* was that it wasn't dogmatic. It didn't represent any one "school" or "movement" and Turnbull wasn't averse to using what might have been seen as somewhat idiosyncratic contributions to the magazine. It also impressed me from the point of view of there clearly being no commercial aim in its publication. It wasn't likely to be sold in bookshops, apart from perhaps a few specialist ones where they existed, and people just found their way to it, or it found its way to them, if they were interested.

So, with *Migrant* as a kind of inspiration, I ran off the first issue of *Move* in December.1964. My then-wife, Audrey, helped as I cut stencils on my old manual typewriter, fixed them to the equally old, hand-operated mimeographed machine I'd obtained from somewhere, and got ink everywhere as we cranked out ten sheets, printed on both sides (twenty pages), for each of the two hundred copies I'd decided was an appropriate print run. The sheets were then piled in sequence around the room, where the furniture had been pushed to one side, and Audrey and I collated and stapled them, and stuck a printed label saying MOVE on the blue (later pink) paper covers.

I'd solicited contributions for the first issue by writing to poets whose work I'd liked and asking them for poems. Roy Fisher responded, and so did Lee Harwood. I got poems from George Dowden, an American living in England, and Lionel Kearns, a Canadian poet I'd met in London. Anselm Hollo, who was Finnish and worked for the BBC, sent poems, and Kirby Congdon, a New Yorker I was in touch with, provided some prose and poetry. Later, in 1966, Congdon compiled a small mimeographed anthology, *Thirteen American Poets,* published under the MOVE imprint and including work by Charles Bukowski, Taylor Mead, Carol Bergé, and Jack Micheline.

I should add that the first issue also had poems from Dave Cunliffe and Tina Morris, who were then editing *Poetmeat*, a more-substantial mimeographed publication, from Blackburn, around ten miles from where I lived in Preston. They deserve a special mention, not only because of what they did with *Poetmeat*, which I think was quite influential in its way, but because, when my old mimeograph machine had fallen apart, they printed the last three issues of *Move* on their relatively sophisticated equipment. I recall that I went over with a suitcase on the bus to collect the printed sheets and bring them back for collating. In between, one issue had been mimeographed at the local branch office of a large union, though I doubt that the Branch Secretary knew about it, and another in the local Town Hall, thanks to a friendly oddball who worked there.

I mailed the first issue to people I thought might be interested, and to magazines I'd come across while prowling around bookshops in London, Liverpool, Paris and Manchester. *Move* was never sold, but all two hundred copies of each issue were always distributed, one way or another. I had the addresses of some American and Canadian publications and before long reciprocal copies began to arrive. People seemed to want to be in touch with each other. Many of the magazines were mimeographed, some almost as plain-looking and slim as *Move,* others bulkier and obviously with more money and better facilities to provide for more-ambitious contents. I can't recall all their names, but *Wild Dog, The Floating Bear* and *Intrepid* from the United States, *Open Letter* from Canada, and *Iconolatre, Origins-Diversions* and *Tlaloc* from Britain, come to mind.

And there was the excellent *Wormwood Review* also from the USA. I remember it with affection because it was attractively produced within its limitations, and its editor, Marvin Malone, had a wide-ranging frame of mind which meant that the contents were always varied. In an issue published in 1970 he paid tribute to the New York bookseller and poet, Harold Briggs, by printing a selection of his work. Not an important name, perhaps, but Malone knew enough to think his passing worth noting. Poets too often forget the essential work that independent booksellers like Briggs, and editors like Malone, did. Looking at an issue from 1965, there is a list of well over ninety magazines (including *Move* and *Poetmeat*) which were exchanging copies with *Wormwood Review*.

Move survived until its eighth issue in April, 1968, and by then it had published numerous British, American, and Canadian poets. A list of names probably doesn't provide a proper guide to its contents, but, as well as those already referred to in this memoir, there were poems by Gael Turnbull, John James, Gill Vickers, Pamela Millward, Max Finstein, Larry Eigner, Tom Clark, Fielding Dawson, Earle Birney, Daphne Buckle, and others. Andrew Crozier guest-edited the fifth issue and got work from Jack Spicer, Richard Duerden, and Robin Blaser.

I'd come to the conclusion that it had served its purpose in terms of helping to put poets in touch with each other, circulating information about different magazines, and publishing some interesting poems by new writers. By 1968 there were quite a few other magazines covering much of the same ground. There was a mimeographed collection, *An Anthology of Little Magazine Poets*, edited by Tony Dash and published by Asylum Publications in 1968, which had a cover showing a map of Britain with the locations of over forty magazines pinpointed. Not all of them were mimeographed, but many were, and it was a useful reminder of how the "mimeograph revolution" had helped diversify poetry in the British Isles.

Looking back, did I really think that two hundred copies of a small, mimeographed magazine were likely to change anything? I did at the time, if seen alongside all the other similar magazines, and that's what gave me the energy and curiosity to produce it. It put me in contact with other poets and their publications. And it surprised me how far it reached. America, Canada, all around the British Isles, and even the odd copy to Australia and Germany. The point, as far I was concerned, was that it was getting to people who were genuinely interested in, and involved with, poetry.

POEMS ABOUT LONDON

This excellent anthology perhaps refers inevitably to Johnson's famous comment: "No, Sir, when a man is tired of London, he is tired of life". Not that I disagree with Johnson. I've never lived in London, but on the other hand I have visited the city regularly since 1952, and can honestly claim never to have tired of it.

What is especially appealing about the anthology is that Christopher Logue hasn't been content to plump for the obvious. Instead, his choice ranges far and wide, and takes in work by Byron, Dryden, Shakespeare, and Wordsworth, but also by contemporaries such as Fleur Adcock, Adrian Mitchell, and the delightfully named Candida Lycett Green. Interspersed with the poems are obscure rhymes culled from 19th century magazines, children's chants, and an entertaining selection of off-beat stories and cryptic asides. It is, for example, noted that Winthrop Mackworth Praed "became a Member of Parliament and stopped writing good verse". And, in a reference to Bunhill Fields, a favourite burial ground for Dissenters, we are told that, "in the 1960s certain powerful busybodies had the impertinence to move Blake's remains to Westminster Abbey".

It is the mixture of humour, light verse (some of which is marvellously evocative of its period), and more-serious writing, which makes the book such a dellght to read. It can be dipped into at any time, and it's an ideal volume to entertain with over a drink or two. Drink, in fact, is mentioned in more than one of the poems. Here's an extract from Tennyson (and it's much more entertaining than the tub-thumping about the Light Brigade at Balaclava):

> O plump head-waiter at the Cock.
> To which I must resort,
> How goes the time? 'Tis five-o'clock,
> Go fetch a pint of port.

The hostelry is The Cock Tavern in Fleet Street, and if it's still there I can't recall ever having been in it, which is an error I ought to rectify. Or maybe I should follow in the footsteps of John Taylor, a Thames waterman whose decision to walk to Scotland was commemorated in verse. The first 28 lines cover three days and find him no further than Edgware, by which time he'd visited eight pubs, in all of which he seems to have drunk himself insensible. Did he, I wonder, ever get out of London?

I'm tempted to carry on quoting, but let me round off with a short poem by Sir Henry Bradford whch I particularly liked:

> As I came down the Highgate Hill,
> The Highgate Hill, the Highgate Hill,
> As I came down the Highgate Hill,
> I met the sun's bravado,
> And I saw below me, fold on fold,
> Grey to pearl and pearl to gold,
> London like a land of old,
>
> The land of Eldorado.

Having come down Highgate Hill more than once on my way to explore London, I feel that as well as see it.

LONDON IN VERSE edited by Christopher Logue. Penguin Books, 1984

NEW BRITISH POETRY, 1968-1988

Anthologies are always useful, though it's a mistake to assume that they represent the whole, or even a large part of what has been produced in the country generally. The Morrison/Motion *Penguin Book of Contemporary British Poetry* had a somewhat misleading title and covered only a highly-selective area of recent activity, and the Crozier/Longville *A Various Art*, fascinating though it was. likewise concentrated on poets largely drawn from a specific grouping. I'm not condemning either book by saying this, because both seem to me to contain much good work, and to be useful guides of their kind. But they don't tell the whole story, and need to be considered alongside other things.

One book which may provide a wider picture, though it does occasionally overlap with *A Various Art* is *The New British Poetry 1968-88*, edited by Gillian Allnut, Fred D'Aguiar, Ken Edwards, and Eric Mottram. It makes some claim to be a kind of follow up to Michael Horovitz's *Children of Albion*, published in 1969, though I have the feeling that Horovitz may have been more-genuinely eclectic in his choice of poets.

The anthology is divided into four parts, with each editor being responsible for one and providing a short introduction to it. There is, thankfully, no general introduction in which large claims are made regarding the importance of the poets and their relevance to the well-being of literature in the United Kingdom. The arrogance implicit in the Morrison/Motion stance is nowhere in evidence in *The New British Poetry*, though some short-sightedness is. I know that every anthology inevitably has gaps and curious omissions, but I looked in vain for work by Ian Macmillan, Martin Stannard, John Ash, Elizabeth Bartlett, Henry Graham, and several others who surely ought to be in a book called *The New British Poetry 1968-88*. And I couldn't help wondering on what basis their work has been overlooked or excluded? My jaundiced northern eye did notice that "all four editors live in London", but I don't think that was the problem. It's more likely that what happened is that they all tended to trawl for contributors in waters they already knew rather than venturing further out to sea.

The four sections of the anthology cover "Black British Poetry", "Quote Feminist Unquote Poetry", "A Treacherous Assault on British Poetry", and "Some Younger Poets". The first two and the final one are largely outlined by their titles, while the third, selected by Eric Mottram, focuses on poets whose work appeared in *Poetry Review* when Mottram edited it. It's a good selection, ranging from Benveniste to Fisher (Roy and Allen), Harwood, Pickard, Raworth, and others, also getting a look in. It may be slightly predictable if you're familiar with the work of the people concerned, but will probably be mostly new to many readers.

The other sections cover their topics usefully, though the "Younger Poets" could have been more adventurous. Still, the work is often taken from small press pamphlets and books, and little magazines, so it should be unfamiliar to those who don't keep up with all the latest obscure publications. Likewise, the Black and Feminist sections may help to focus attention on various little-known names, and that's surely one of the aims of any good anthology. A question does occur to me at this point. I suppose it's debatable whether or not poets from the Irish Republic should, or would want to be in a book called *The New British Poetry*, but I note that Eavan Boland (born and still living in Dublin) is among the feminists. I've no complaints about this – she's a good writer, and that's all that matters – but why then weren't the excellent Paul Durcan and Sydney Bernard Smith represented in one of the other sections? Both use language and technique with a great deal of skill and imagination and would have fully suited the anthology. Was it another example of the appropriate editor or editors not looking beyond certain journals or the lists of a few small publishers for suitable poets?

A few minor reservations, but otherwise this is an interesting , sometimes provocative, and always lively anthology. It's wise to bear in mind that it is only a selection of British poetry of the past twenty years, but it does often provide a good guide to some areas that other anthologies have neglected.

THE NEW BRITISH POETRY 1968-88. Edited by Gillian Allnut, Fred D'Aguiar, Ken Edwards and Eric Mottram. Paladin. 1989

SOME POETS

Well, here's Mike Horovitz, poet of the cities and the jazz joints, jogging through the countryside for the good of his soul, if not the soles of his feet, which occasionally land on a few ants, caterpillars, spiders, and snails, not to mention dozens of dandelions, daisies, and hollyhocks. He's a "freakishly blundering four-eyed goon" worrying about whether or not it's right to kill a fly, and if it isn't shouldn't he keep his cat chained up so it can't kill a bird or mouse? He notes "how much more neatly/vegetation/arranges and disports itself/than clumsy mankind," and even acclaims "the lusty blustering teams of weeds".

As we jog along with him we're invited to consider all these things, and to think of Clare and Keats, Hopkins and Herbert. The spirits of Blake and Whitman are hovering around, too, and Dylan Thomas gets a look in, though I somehow can't imagine him straying too far beyond the door of a pub, despite what his poems said about Fern Hill and all that. And, of course, bringing in all those names makes you realise that this is a literary man's appreciation of the rights of rats and crows. Ask your local Pest Control Officer or farmer what they think about them.

But I'm not intending to mock Horovitz or to quarrel with him. He's always an entertaining poet, and his *Jog Log* is fun to read. It moves along at a nice pace, and even if the countryside isn't your idea of heaven you might find it hard to resist Horovitz's celebration of it. The book is beautifully produced and is illustrated by Peter Blake.

There are poets who produce comparatively little, and whose work is often overlooked I the hustle and bustle about the latest group, the current fashion, or this month's literary gossip. Their poems appear here and there, the occasional small collection is published to little or no acclaim from the reviewers in the weeklies and Sundays, and their names are known only to a few. And yet they have qualities that enable their work to survive.

I think this is true of Frances Horovitz's poems. And this is not something said because we should speak well of the dead, I would not want to claim that her work was of major importance. She didn't break any barriers or introduce new ideas, and she may not merit a place when the lists are drawn up by literary historians of the 20th century. But she may well be read for pleasure by those whose interest is in the poems and not what surrounds them in terms of personalities, social matters, etc.

190

What is impressive about her *Collected Poems* is its consistency. Each poems stands on its own, but taken together they add up to a viewpoint that is convincing at all times. It's a gentle viewpoint, with people and places sharing the concerns at the centre of the poems. The tone is always sympathetic, and when there's probing or questioning it's never with malice. In a world where viciousness and vulgarity are often applauded, poems like these can make one pause and feel slightly ashamed at one's own past misjudgements. There is a kindness in them that can be extremely moving.

I've deliberately chosen not to quote from any of the poems, because it seems to me that to do so would be unfair. The book ought to be read in its entirety if its qualities are to be appreciated. It would be sad if it is neglected because it doesn't fit in with this year's fads and fancies. It would be good if it is read.

A sense of the city and, and of urban life generally, informs all of Roy Fisher's work, and it is this, I think, that often makes me link him more with European traditions in poetry than with local ones. An earlier sequence, *City*, made a significant statement about how to deal with ideas implicit in the title, and *A Furnace* carries on his exploration of the industrial cultures of the 19th and 20th centuries.

What is impressive about Fisher's work is the way in which it manages to talk about the industrial experience without falling into the usual English trap of nostalgia for the rural. It isn't afraid to get to grips with the real problems:

> Hard to be there, the place
> unable to understand
> even its own Whig history
> for what it was: teachers
> trained not to understand it
>
> taught it, and never fitted. Even less
> did the history of the class struggle
> reach down or along to the working-
> class streets where work and wages
> hid, as the most real shame.

Lines like those seem to me to be political in the best sense, and the poem frequently has a hard-edged awareness of what industrial society was about, and still is, for that matter. Talking about how everything is

191

a commodity, to be sold, rented, traded, etc., it says of "freedom":

> grant it,
>> asking in return no more than
>> war service, wage labour, taxes,
>> custodial schooling, a stitched-up
>> franchise.

I have to admit to choosing passages that have a special appeal, ant it needs to be noted that *A Furnace* operates on many levels. It offers not only an analysis of the philosophical aspects of industrialisation, but also a vivid picture of its physical appearance. Like the urban landscape it can be both provocative and disturbing, both appealing and worrying. It is real literature.

D.J. Enright is one of the most entertaining poets around, and I've always turned to his poems with usually-justified anticipation whenever I've seen his name in a magazine or anthology. He was, of course, linked to the "Movement" group of the 1950s, but not for him the Little Englandism of Kingsley Amis or the higher-Philistinism of Philip Larkin. Enright, no doubt because of his foreign adventures, is cosmopolitan and alert to what goes on in the world generally, both in life and literature. What does connect him to the best of the "Movement" spirit is his clarity. He is rarely, if ever, obscure, and irony is central to his poetic voice:

> My mother's strongest religious feeling
> Was that Catholics were a sinister lot;
> She would hardly trust even a lapsed one.
> My father was a lapsed Catholic.

You'll notice how relaxed it seems, and this also sets him apart from quite a few English poets. I always have the feeling that they're afraid to speak naturally, and that concepts of what constitutes literature hold them back. As a result they often seem stiff and strained. But Enright manages to sound as if he's just letting the poems flow in the manner of ordinary speech. It may be that his technique can only be described as functional, but on the other hand it could be argued that he has the best kind of technique, an unobtrusive one:

> I'm not one of those simpletons who believe
> That if only they had a large TV screen
> They would be able to see the naughty bits

That he relies a great deal on humour can't be denied, but the poems are not just good jokes. They're backed by a humanist philosophy, and they often hold up to ridicule the pompous and powerful. The less-fortunate and those who fail to make the grade are looked on in a kindlier fashion, though fools of any kind are not suffered gladly. Not too long ago I heard a bright young poet describe one of his colleagues as "very readable". It was meant to be a clever put-down. Well, D.J. Enright is "very readable", and I consider that a great attribute.

There's a down-to-earth tone to George Charlton's poems which makes them immensely appealing:

> Grandfather told me that Gala Day
> How during the days of the General Strike
> The miners' band played for the tranquil soldiers
> From regiments at bivouac in the meadows,
> How out beyond the ends of double-rows
> Expectant policemen simmered
> Frustrated in their function.

The lines end naturally, the language is clear and direct, and the subject-matter is invariably drawn from the industrial north. Shipbuilding, or the lack of it, mining, the street corner, the pub, lives built around these things. It may seem a daunting world to those who've never experienced it at first-hand, who weren't born to it, but it would be a mistake to assume that Charlton's writing is in any way "local". He establishes the feeling of real communities and their problems, and in doing so cuts through the limitations of the local and touches on the broad experience of people and places that we've all got. Some of his lines can probably sum up the common situation of quite a few people in various parts of the country:

> There must be hundreds like us now,
> Born since the war, brought up
> In terraced streets near factory yards
> And on expansive council estates.

Nightshift Workers is not full of fireworks. Its poems are mostly short and they rarely, if ever, aim for any major statements. The overall effect is, on the whole, fairly low-key, but it stays in the mind much longer than supposedly more important books.

Hugo Williams was one of the more interesting poets in the Morrison-

Motion *Penguin Book of Contemporary British Poetry*. His adept handling of free verse seemed to set him apart from at least some of the other contributors and their linguistic cleverness or technical conservatism. His work moves along without fuss and sounds like someone telling a good story:

> Out of work at fifty, smoking fifty a day
> my father wore his sheepskin coat
> and went to auditions
> for the first time in his life.

It's highly readable and the pace never comes across as forced. I do sense that Williams has opened up a little in recent years, both technically and emotionally, and the look of his poems on the page tends to reinforce this feeling. The earlier ones are often tighter in construction and less inclined to talk in the direct manner he's more likely to use now. Personally, I prefer the later poems, especially the selection drawn from his 1985 volume, *Writing Home*.

My liking for these later poems shouldn't be seen as an indication of a lack of interest in the earlier ones, however. It strikes me that the book is worthy of attention as a whole, and it adds up to one of the strongest selected poems I've seen from any of the younger British poets for some time.

Ann Ridler is one of those poets who has been around for many years, not perhaps prolific but with a solid body of work to her credit. Her name isn't as well-known as it should be in some circles, and that's a pity. She's a consistently good writer, and even a confirmed urbanite like myself can't help but be impressed by her splendid evocations of the seasons:

> The land takes breath; the iron grip
> That clamped upon her heart is slackened.
> On roofs the slithering snow-wrack
> Like tods of sheep's wool slowly drips.
>
> Earth's grey and foot-patched quilt of snow
> Is wearing thin; the green shows through;
> The carnival days of ice are gone,
> The godlike skater's but a man.

Which has a lovely sound to it and shows how much care Ann Ridler takes with words.

She also highly effective when dealing with matters of mortality:

> The death that we shall die
> Is here, we know, coiled like a spring inside us,
> Waiting its time.

And she can cast a cold eye on the political, as when in the poem "Red Square", she talks of "The sun-washed, guilt-soaked Kremlin". But she's compassionate with people generally, and throughout her work there's a strong sense of the religious commitment that inspires her. Even if you don't share it you can respond to the sincerity and gentleness implied.

One hundred pages from around fifty years may not seem a lot, but the rest of us should hope that we'll have a similar amount of such quality at the end of our writing lives.

It's a sad fact that Martin Bell's work is virtually unknown to many of the younger poets and readers around these days. He did get a certain amount of attention in the 1960s when he was included in the Penguin Modern Poets series and his *Collected Poems* appeared, but the 1970s were dismal days for him, and he died in poverty and obscurity in Leeds in 1978. It's frankly doubtful if his death was even noticed by most people, and since then there have been only occasional attempts to revive interest in him. One or two of his old friends have tried to keep Bell's name alive, Peter Porter among them, and it is Porter who edited this new collection. As he points out in an interesting and informative introduction which explains why Bell has been overlooked: "He would see the point but not admire the performance of today's dandies, the Martians, and he would be disappointed at the re-emergence of Oxbridge fashion as the dominating tone of English poetry". Porter also goes on to mention how a programme of Bell's verse that he completed for Radio 3 "merely earned censure from the network's cultural officers". Which alone ought to encourage those genuinely interested in skilled and provocative writing to turn their attention to Bell's poems. He seems to have made many of the right enemies.

Bell was a translator French surrealist poetry and it shows in his work, though idiosyncratically so. But what also comes through is that he was prepared to write about almost anything, and to use a variety of styles to say what he had to say. Much of his work has a relaxed, almost-conversational tone:

No pleasanter way to finish the war off
At the convalescence Depot at Salerno,
Scrounging, on the Education Staff -
Run Quiz, Tombola, Brains' Trust in the NAAF
Give left-wing lectures on the post-war world.

You can see why those BBC "cultural officers" didn't like Bell's work, but it surprises me that a lot of younger poets – those outside the establishment framework - haven't shown an interest in it. To be fair, they perhaps haven't had a chance, only a few of his poems being easily available in anthologies, so one hopes that this book will do what's necessary. His loose, though never sloppy, technique, and his willingness to write out of what he saw and experienced, have much in common with what is written nowadays in some circles, though not all the newer poets have anything like Bell's skill with seemingly-casual but always-precise lists. And Bell was of s generation which knew left-wing politics and war at first-hand, and his poems consequently contain references outside the range of most contemporary poets. But you can't whip the young for that. They have to write about what concerns them. I'm talking about the way Bell wrote:

Well, OK, he was wrong
Getting killed in Spain
Like that. Wal Hannington
Sat and tried to argue him out of going.
He was wrong, he was wrong,
The angel has not descended, the state
Hasn't the faintest chance of withering away,
And nobody is sure which way Hegel is up anymore.

It's marvellously readable stuff, but not likely to appeal to those Oxbridge boys. It's too vernacular and direct, and its rhythms don't always conform to those we're told are the true tests of English poetry. It also uses language in a way that goes against the grain of today's ornateness. But it would be wrong to assume that, because Bell seemingly chose to write in what appears to be a plain, matter-of-fact manner, his work lacks erudition. It is, in fact, loaded with literary and political references, and reflects his awareness of world literature (no little-Englander he), his communist links, and his involvements with other writers.

It's worth mentioning at this point, Bell's attitude towards the poetry boom of the 1960s. Peter Porter quotes from a manuscript found among

196

Bell's papers:

> Poetry is too popular. What occurred at the Albert Hall was
>   disaster.
> Poems should be detested, but irresistible.
> "Doing one's own thing" is as obscene pun as "doing one's bit
> Crowds are for contracting out of.

It's a point of view that is perfectly understandable, and throughout the book there are expressions of dismay at developments in both society and literature, the two being inextricable, as Bell clearly knew. Still, I would hazard a guess that he wasn't completely untouched by the poetry of the 1960s, and some of the later poems suggest a willingness to become even more-oral in his approach.

I've avoided saying too much about Bell's life. He could too easily be made into some kind of minor cult figure by those who think that the personal details are more important than the work. The two can't be separated, I know, but it's how it comes through in the poems that counts, not how many drinks were downed or affairs entered into. Porter's introduction does give us some information to help us find our way through the poems, especially those in the latter part of the book, which comprises poems not in the original *Collected Poems*. They're often personal, though not to the point of obscurity. And it is admittedly useful to know about Bell's background and interests to fully understand certain of the attitudes expressed in his poetry. But it would be a great pity if the poems became merely a back-up for a biography. He deserves better than that.

In one of his poems Bell says:

> After a week of fog, a mild bright winter morning.
> Here I am on the train, reading Wordsworth to work
> Without any impatience.

And, looking at my copy of *Complete Poems*, I see that it's already a little worn and creased from carrying it around and reading it on trains and buses. It is, to put it simply, one of the most enjoyable books of poetry I've read for some time.

Michael O'Neill manages to make neat poems out of very little. I say that not in a derogatory way, because most of us have limited experiences and ideas, and originality isn't in abundance among either poets or the populace generally. In O'Neill's case, his subject-matter – drawn from his childhood, academic involvements, and domestic concerns –

isn't very exciting, but he does construct short, carefully-written exercises around it. He was born in Liverpool, but seemingly lacks the distinctive hallmark of the accent, something he remarks on almost wistfully:

> Our Liverpool Catholic background?
> We boast it like a badge, but
> don't share the nasal twang which warms
> this pub to life. Just open your mouth
> and it's there, the spirit of the city.

He moved on to Oxford, and then a teaching post in a university, so we get the appropriate references:

> Today a student riled by Beckett left
> me fuming, smiling.

And, of course, he's conscious of the clash between the attractions of the ivory tower and the demands of the everyday:

> We'd meant to mooch off early that last Sunday,
> broach some serious talk – Rilke, God
> Instead, we found ourselves wheeling the kids,
> imperious in their buggies, to the Parks.

I'm reminded of those 1950s American academics who, it was said, could change a nappy with one hand and write an ironic poem with the other. You had to smile wryly and admire their little achievements if you were in a similar position. And perhaps that is the assumption behind so many of these poems, that the likely readers will be familiar with the situations they talk about?

> I'm tap-tapping words into this weird box.
> Trowel in hand, you kneel beside flowers.

The successful young academic at his word-processor, the good woman busy in the garden. All's right with their world.

Willem M. Roggeman is a Flemish writer, born in Brussels in 1935 and active as a poet, novelist, and journalist. Yann Lovelock's introduction to this book refers to his "verbal ease" and says that he deploys his sentences with the "rhythms of brush strokes". The link to painting is intentional and Roggeman uses "short dabs adding up to a general impression". Puns, allusions, buried quotations, and a liking for playing with the sounds of words are also mentioned as hallmarks of Roggeman's work.

Lovelock's introduction is valuable in itself, not only for what it says about Roggeman, but also for its short history of certain literary and artistic developments in Europe. He draws parallels between the work of poets and painters, something it isn't always easy to do in this country due to the two forms often tending to operate separately. The only doubt I had was about how successful the translations are, bearing in mind what Lovelock says. Verbal puns are sometimes notoriously difficult to translate, an allusion might well be lost, and so on. The only test we have, if we can't read the originals, is whether or not the English translations are reasonable poems in their own right. And they are. They move along smoothly and some of that "verbal ease" does come through, along with the "short dabs adding up to a general impression":

> I'd like to be able to write like this.
> The way the sun sparkles on the glass
> and the warm wine shines
> on the white table in the garden.

It's often good-humoured stuff, too, and though the world may be viewed obliquely, it's a real world, nonetheless, with real people and their problems.

This is an attractive book in which the combination of lively translations, apt illustrations, and Yann Lovelock's useful introduction, serves to focus attention on the work of a talented contemporary poet.

A MIDSUMMER JOG LOG by Michael Horovitz. Five Seasons Press. 1986

COLLECTED POEMS by Frances Horovitz. Bloodaxe. 1986

A FURNACE by Roy Fisher. Oxford University Press. 1986

SELECTED POEMS 1990 by D.J. Enright. Oxford University Press, 1990

NIGHTSHIFT WORKERS by George Charlton. Bloodaxe, 1989

SELECTED POEMS by Hugo Williams. Oxford University Press, 1989

NEW & SELECTED POEMS by Ann Ridler. Faber, 1988

COMPLETE POEMS by Martin Bell. Bloodaxe, 1989

THE STRIPPED BED by Michael O'Neill. Collins Harvill, 1990

A VANISHING EMPTINESS by Willem M. Roggeman. Forest Books, 1989

THE FORGOTTEN FORTIES

A jazz writer has to be careful when writing about the past. Nostalgia can blind him to the fact that the scene forty or fifty years ago wasn't as exciting as he likes to think it was. Most people live a large proportion of their lives doing quite ordinary things, and a handful of incidents and encounters selected from a four or five year period hardly back up claims that it was then more hectic and exciting. When I recall my own days as a young jazz fan I have to admit that a lot of time was passed in listening to second-rate musicians playing third-rate music. How else could I have made sure of being there when the good stuff was produced. But ask me now and I'll talk about the better and more-memorable experiences. Kenny Graham's Afro-Cubists, the Jack Parnell orchestra, Hank Shaw on an inspired night, Ronnie Scott when he was on a Getz kick. And I'd forget that I ever yawned my way through boring concerts by British dance-bands and scrappy sessions with groups of listless jazzmen.

Still, bearing that in mind, it does seem that the 1940s and early-1950s had more than its share of characters. People – both musicians and fans – had, or so it seems to me, sharply-defined personalities, and the bop movement spawned a whole generation of eccentrics, with admittedly disastrous results in quite a few cases. But generally there was a kind of semi-bohemian behaviour which seemed pervasive at the time. It perhaps didn't amount to much in the long run, and it may have been just a mild form of rebellion against the drabness of post-war Britain.

Let me quote Johnny Dankworth on the early days of the modern movement: "I remember we had our first concert at Manchester, and Cecil Gee's had promised to make us special suits. Well, when the time came we hadn't any money at all. So they offered to lend us the suit trousers and some windcheaters if we left a deposit of fifty pounds. We hadn't a fiver between us, much less fifty pounds. Eventually Les Leston, the former Ambrose drummer, offered to put up the fifty. He gave it to us in cash. Well, that was tempting providence. And by the time everyone had helped themselves to a fiver, there was only fifteen left. Gee demanded an instrument as an additional deposit. Poor old Don Rendell, who was guesting at the concert, got really lumbered. He left his clarinet with Gee's with the proviso that it would be forfeited if the trousers and windcheaters weren't returned by the following Monday. Needless to say they weren't. But somehow Don managed to get his instrument back".

This is relatively good-humoured when one considers some of the incidents enshrined in the history of bop. The environmental influences could, and did, lead many musicians and fans into minor criminal activity, mostly linked to the use of drugs.

Not all of the accented individuality of the Forties dissipated itself in zany or anti-social behaviour. There's no need for me to stress the great contributions of the musicians, and more than a few of the fans used their time and money to support and document the new music at a time when it wasn't fashionable to do so. Some had an-almost messianic determination to spread the word, others recorded bop musicians in clubs and concert halls, and so helped to preserve their efforts for posterity.

The atmosphere of the bop era encouraged this kind of devotion, as witness Ross Russell's novel, *The Sound,* with its seemingly-larger than life characters who are actually based on real-life people. There's The Record Man (selling the latest bop discs brought in to Los Angeles by staff on the cross-country trains from New York) in a Hollywood restaurant, and Royo, who fanatically records every performance by the book's central character. Royo had his origins in Dean Benedetti, a one-time alto player who worshipped Charlie Parker and followed him from club to club. His collection of Parker material, often recorded surreptitiously in less-than-perfect circumstances, was "lost" for many years, but surfaced years later. It frankly doesn't make for easy-listening. Benedetti only recorded Parker and switched off his machine when other musicians soloed, and the music often seems distant and disrupted by audience noises. But it does capture the atmosphere of the Forties bop revolution.

The point I'm trying to make is that non-musicians often added a lot of colour to the scene. They too often tend to be neglected by jazz historians, with the result that a lot of interesting material is overlooked. Many years ago (around 1953/54) the weekly *Melody Maker* devoted half-a-page or so to an interview with Jerry Newman. He was quoted as saying: "I was in on the earliest days at Minton's. It started in January '41, at the Hotel Cecil on 118th Street. They turned the dining-room into a club and built in a stage for seven, and a bar. Henry Minton ran the sessions. He was the first Negro delegate to the AF of M, and called the place Minton's Playhouse. I just went down there for kicks. I was a kid with a recording machine. I used to do an act. I'd play a record with Roosevelt, Bob Hope, Churchill, and a lot of other voices on it, and stand at the mike imitating them. For that, Minton let me make any records I liked".

Dan Morganstern, writing about Newman, also recalled that he was welcome with his machine because the would-be singers who sat in at the clubs often wanted to have a memento of their efforts (this was before the days of tape and Newman's machine recorded directly onto disc). And the musicians liked to hear their solos played back, so Newman got himself invited to Clark Monroe's Uptown House and other after-hours clubs.

It's for the recordings made at Minton's and Clark Monroe's that Newman is probably best-known. When some of them began to be issued on LPs in the early-1950s, "Swing to Bop" and "Stompin' at the Savoy" featured the legendary guitarist Charlie Christian and trumpeter Joe Guy. The latter was a seemingly-forward looking jazzman who faded from sight as the 1940s progressed and died in obscurity in the 1960s. (see my article about him in *Artists, Beats and Cool Cats*, Penniless Press, 2014). And "Stardust" and "Kerouac" spotlighted a young Dizzy Gillespie. Other recordings included music by Don Byas and Hot Lips Page. Charlie Parker was also to be heard in the clubs, but Newman wasn't keen on his playing: "But Parker, I really passed him up. He blew so wild I used to turn off the machine when he started playing".

It's worth mentioning how "Kerouac" got its name. Gillespie had been soloing on "Exactly Like You" but the question of paying royalties if the record was issued under that title came up. Jerry Newman suggested "Ginsberg" as a title, but Gillespie didn't like that, so it was called "Kerouac". Both of the Beat writers were friendly with Newman, and enthusiastic about jazz, and especially bebop. There are many references to jazz musicians in Kerouac's novels. (see "Jack Kerouac's Jazz Scene" in *Bohemians, Beats and Blues People,* Penniless Press, 2013).

Newman spent four years in the armed forces, and when he returned to New York in 1946 he found the jazz scene vastly changed. Bop had broken through, and Newman wasn't too sure how he felt about the new sounds. He did like Woody Herman's band, which he thought successfully synthesised swing and bop, and a friendship with Chubby Jackson, the band's bassist, led to him recording a number of young white modernists.

Newman recalled: "We arranged a rendezvous for 2am that night, and at the appointed hour I was ready with my recording equipment at my parents' home on 88th Street, when Chubby's friends began to arrive – Sonny Berman and Marky Markowitz with their trumpets; Al Cohn tenor sax; Serge Chaloff, baritone; Earl Swope, trombone; pianist

Ralph Burns, and Don Lamond who used only a snare drum. Ironically, Chubby himself never showed up, and we started the session at 2.30 without him. Everyone was having a high old time when the doorman came up and told us that unless we stopped making this noise the neighbours downstairs would call the police. Since nobody wanted to quit, and since there was another room where the music would be less likely to disturb the neighbours, the whole bunch of us hoisted the piano bodily into the next room and continued the session".

Newman's recordings may not have been technically perfect, but they captured for posterity certain aspects of modern jazz which were not then fashionable and hence not documented by major companies. The writer or collector wanting to study Serge Chaloff's early work, or hear some of the rare examples of the ill-fated Sonny Berman's solos, will have to refer to the material that Newman recorded. Newman also recorded items from a radio station WNEW jam sessions in 1947 featuring tenorman Allen Eager and trumpeter Fats Navarro ("Sweet Georgie Brown" and "High on an Open Mike") and Roy Eldridge and Flip Phillips ("Honeysuckle Rose" and "Flip and Jazz").

Jerry Newman died on January 8th, 1970, and another link with the brave days of the 1940s was severed. Prior to his death, he had operated a record shop and, and had worked as a recording engineer. He ran his own small recording companies, Esoteric and Counterpoint, mostly concentrating on contemporary classical music, with the jazz issues usually taken from his 1940s recordings. But he did record a superb date by pianist Al Haig in 1954. He lost money with his recording companies because he refused to compromise by issuing discs he personally disliked but which could have been commercially successful.

WHO REMEMBERS DOUG METTOME?

The Billy Eckstine band of the mid-1940s had in its ranks, at one time or another, most of the trumpeters who were identified with the bop idiom – Dizzy Gillespie, Miles Davis, Fats Navarro, and Kenny Dorham are obvious examples, but there were others, albeit the names may not be as familiar as those already mentioned. The legendary Freddy Webster played with Eckstine, as did Gail Brockman (featured with Gene Ammons later in the Forties), Shorty McConnell (who recorded with Lester Young), Leonard Hawkins (co-partner with Dexter Gordon on some sprightly sides for Savoy), and Doug Mettome. He's something of a mystery man to most jazz enthusiasts.

Mettome was born on the 19th March, 1924, in Salt Lake City. He studied piano when quite young, switching to trumpet at the age of eleven. His interest in jazz was reputedly aroused when he heard Roy Eldridge perform "Rocking' Chair" (presumably with Gene Krupa's band) and, prior to a three years stint in the army, he led a band of his own on a local basis. He joined the Eckstine orchestra in 1946, staying until the following year.

I can only assume that Mettome must have been proficient enough in the modern idiom by 1947 to have gained the respect of the young New York boppers, because it was in that year he recorded with Allen Eager for Savoy. Eager was in excellent form, and on "Unmeditated" Mettome can be heard playing a solo which outlines his main attributes – a pure, consistent tone, attractive ideas, and a good-humoured way of presenting them. His style is, to a degree, reminiscent of Red Rodney and Conte Candoli (the tracks Candoli made with Chubby Jackson in 1947 will, I think, demonstrate his tonal links to Mettome), and there are even touches of Fats Navarro, though without the elegant poise that distinguished his best solos.

Mettome joined a Herbie Fields group in in 1948 and then, in November of that year he was recruited for the new big-band which Benny Goodman was forming. The "King of Swing" had said some harsh words about bop, and its practitioners, but events had caught up with him and, besides hiring Chico O'Farrill to provide bop-tinged charts for the book, he brought in modern soloists like Mettome, trombonist Eddie Bert, and tenorman Wardell Gray. The band didn't last too long, and Goodman seemingly couldn't make up his mind about whether to let the musicians loose on the bop material, or whether to stick to tried and tested earlier scores. Recordings of broadcasts from this period point to the confusion that ensued. A fair percentage of the audiences probably expected Goodman to run through his old hits like "King Porter Stomp" and "Clarinet A La King", and were confused by "Chico's Bop" and "Undercurrent Blues". O'Farrill perhaps summed up the situation when he recalled: "I got a kick out of that rebop band. Possibly Benny was trying to keep up with the times – he may not have felt too comfortable. Whatever the reason, he didn't pursue it long".

Sufficient recordings exist to allow an inspection of Mettome's work with Goodman. The band recorded for the Capitol label, and on "Undercurrent Blues" there was a solo which helped to bring his name to the notice of a wider jazz public. If memory serves me right, this disc did enjoy a certain amount of popularity, at least in modernist circles. I recall that, during my army days in Germany between 1954 and 1957, it was the signature tune for a weekly jazz show on AFN (American Forces Network) which broadcast under the title, *Hot House*, late on Friday nights. It was sometimes associated with other big-band bop records, like Woody Herman's "Lemon Drop" and Charlie Barnet's "Cu-ba". Like them it managed to blend bop with easily-identifiable big-band sounds. Mettome's assured solo was an integral part of the arrangement and clearly designed to relate to the overall framework. It's interesting to note that an airshot version of "Undercurrent Blues" exists and has an essentially-similar solo by Mettome, almost as if he'd realised that there was little point in trying to improve on an already-successful formula.

There's a spirited Mettome solo on "The Huckle-Buck", another track by the Goodman band, but of even greater value are three small-group items which allowed the trumpeter, and Wardell Gray, to stretch out even more. "Blue Lou" is especially impressive, Gray's forthright lines being followed by Mettome with a solo which is skilfully constructed enough to put one in mind of Fata Navarro. It climbs towards a climax and then dances out with a dark-toned descending phrase which relieves the tension. Mettome's other solos – on the novelty "In the Land of Oo-bla-dee", and "Bedlam" (a tune also recorded by Gray under the title, "Stoned") are slightly less impressive, but worth hearing, nonetheless, being crisp and lively and perfectly complementing Gray's agile soloing.

That Mettome was a good partner for Gray was further demonstrated on several broadcast items from 1949. Surprisingly, a long "Blue Lou" has a somewhat diffident solo by him, but "After You've Gone" and "Sweet Georgia Brown" are livelier, and the muted trumpet work on the former is particularly good. I hate to keep relating Mettome to Fats Navarro, because it makes it seem as if he didn't have his own voice, but there are definite touches of the ill-fated bop star in both his sound and phrasing. In this connection it's relevant to note that the first choice for trumpet soloist with the Goodman band had been Navarro – he did record one track, "Stealin' Apples" with a small Goodman group – but that various factors, including perhaps Navarro's personal problems, eventually precluded this happening. Maybe Goodman then chose Mettome because of his full tone and melodic improvisation? He had earlier used Red Rodney – another trumpeter noted for these attributes – in a small group he led in 1948, and it would appear that his liking for musicians such as Wardell Gray and Stan Hasselgard, both melodic soloists, denoted a preference for the more-relaxed and tuneful side of bebop.

After his spell with Goodman, Mettome returned to Herbie Field, and then moved on again to Woody Herman's band. He was present at several Herman recording dates in 1951, and can be heard in a brief, muted solo on Gene Roland's bouncy "Hollywood Blues". Mettome takes the first trumpet solo and the second is by Don Fagerquist, another talented musician whose work with Herman, Gene Krupa, and Les Brown is generally overlooked. There is another bright Mettome solo on "Dandy Lion", a Sam Staff tune recorded by Herman's small group, the Woodchoppers.

In July 1952, Mettome recorded with clarinettist Sam Most, and turned in competent-enough performances on "Undercurrent Blues" (he doesn't make the mistake of trying to emulate his Goodman solo in this small-group context), and "First with the Most". He is, in fact, the one bright light in an otherwise dull session, and without him the tracks could easily be consigned to the archives. Most was at best an average soloist, and the drummer on the session, Jackie Moffit lacks imagination. As a result, one senses that musicians like Mettome, and the capable Chuck Wayne and Clyde Lombardi, were unable to do much in the face of the prevailing lacklustre atmosphere. I seem to recollect reading that these tracks were produced on an informal basis, and recorded in a hotel room, which may explain the variable sound quality, but even so they mostly lack any kind of imagination or invention.

1952 saw Mettome working with Herbie Fields again. He was in a big-band that Fields took into the Coral studio. As the 1950s progressed, he worked with the Tommy Dorsey and Pete Rugolo orchestras, and recorded with trombonist Urbie Green and again with Sam Most. The sessions with Green appeared to be to the trumpeter's liking, and alongside musicians like Green, Al Cohn, and baritone-sax player, Danny banks, he came up with some attractive solos. The gentle arrangements by Marion Evans may have had something to do with how Mettome played. His contributions to "On Green Dolphin Street", "Mutation" and "Just One of those Things" are delicately handled, whether he's soloing or functioning as part of the ensemble. Most important of all is his solo feature, "When Your Lover has Gone" which spotlights his tonal beauty and emotional depth. Kicking off wth a phrase which pays homage to his early idol, Roy Eldridge, he moves into a statement of the theme which is almost-passionate in its intensity. Green and Cohn take over and sustain the mood until Mettome returns to take the piece out with a precision that never becomes mechanical, but is, instead, a display of deep yet controlled emotion. It is an almost-perfect little per- formance, rarely departing from the main theme, yet implying a great deal through its restraint.

Mettome teamed up with Urbie Green again when both were members of a Nat Pierce group which recorded for Vanguard. I don't think the trumpeter produced anything as good as his work on the session re- ferred to above, but his mellow sounds helped shape the ensemble shadings on the attractive "Constance", and his bright muted playing on "Stomp it Off" and the more-outspoken statements on "Blues Yet?" added to the convincing atmosphere of the whole session. Mettome appeared to be at home in a big-band setting or in small groups which eschewed the frenetic and instead concentrated on a kind of modern mainstream style.

Little was heard of him after the mid-1950s, but in 1957 he was once again in the recording studios with Sam Most, and crested what were, to my mind, some of his finest solos. Most took a number of classic bop themes by Bud Powell, Charlie Parker, Thelonious Monk and Miles Davis, and asked pianist Bob Dorough to arrange four of them for a sextet and four for a big-band. Mettome is heard in a solo capacity on seven out of the eight tracks, sometimes riding high over the band riffs, sometimes dancing happily across the buoyant base supplied by the sextet's rhythm section. His work on "In Walked Bud" and "Ser- pent's Tooth" shows him to have been a very emotional musician, his sound at times taking on an almost searing quality. Some of the earlier purity of tone may have been missing, but in its place was a crackling warmth and occasionally fierce drive which more than made up for it. The music produced by many of the musicians associated with the New York scene of the 1950s is neglected these days, but it would be a great pity if this led to Mettome's excellence being overlooked.

Mettome died on February 17th, 1964 in his home-town of Salt Lake City. A brief obituary appeared in *Down Beat*, and bassist Whitey Mitchell was quoted as saying that the trumpeter "was an extraordinary musician, capable of playing lead trumpet or jazz, and in most bands he worked with, he had the responsibility of playing both......he was that rare find – a mainstream jazzman; that is one whose playing is at home with, and is a part of, every significant era in the long development of jazz".

Doug Mettome was not an innovator, but he was an individual, and he produced work of quality with a style identifiably his own. He left behind a small, but valuable body of recordings which back up Leonard Feather's description of him as "an outstanding modern jazzman".

THE GOOD OLD DAYS (the 1950s)

The first time I saw Julian was one Sunday night in a local cinema. That was in the days when there wasn't much else to do on Sunday, and everyone went to the cinema in gangs to see what kind of trouble they could cause and which girls they could pick up. Julian came down the centre-aisle a few minutes before the lights dimmed, and a lot of people cheered and stamped their feet and shouted comments. It didn't seem to bother him because he just smiled, swished his hips, and waved a hand, as if acknowledging some sort of tribute. I didn't know who he was, so I asked the girl I was with, and she said, "Oh, that's Julian, the queer".

After that I occasionally noticed him around the town centre, maybe talking with friends in the arcade, or going into the pub where they met. I wasn't in town the night he was thrown through a shop window, but I heard about it later. He'd got into an argument with one of the local hard-men who'd been joking about Julian, and this guy had picked him up, held him over his head for a moment, and then thrown him through the window of a dress shop.

I went into the army about then, and when I came home again three years later the crowd around town had changed quite a bit. I did see Julian. I was on a bus and as it slowed down to take a corner, I heard the conductor shouting and the two women on the back-seat giggling. The conductor whistled and asked Julian where his boy-friend was, and he smirked and waved his hand.

You know how it is when you get married and lose contact with people and the way you used to live. Well, that happened with me. I forgot about Julian until one Friday when I went to the station to catch the last bus home. As usual, the place was full of drunks and couples saying goodnight. A crowd of soldiers stood around one of their companions who'd passed out, and another soldier was leaning against a wall and puking. Greasy fish-and-chip papers were scattered around the floor.

A group of young men came through the entrance. Two of them had dustbin lids and were beating out rhythm and the rest were clapping their hands and chanting. When they got into the station they formed a circle and I saw that Julian was in the middle of it. He wasn't wearing a jacket and his shirt was unbuttoned and hanging outside his trousers. His face was sweaty and flushed, and he was trying to dance but was so drunk that he kept falling over.

All the boys were laughing and shouting obscene comments, but Julian smiled and twirled around and snapped his fingers. There was something desperate in the way he was trying to execute the movement without falling, and when he moved into the light I could see that he looked exhausted. The sweat had streaked his make-up and his face was haggard and lined.

One of the boys shouted, "The bus", and they dropped the dustbin lids and ran across the station. Julian danced on his own for a few seconds, and then realised they'd gone. He stood swaying slightly, his eyes blinking in the harsh glare of the lights. Two men in black leather jackets walked towards him and he smiled at them. The tallest butted Julian with his shoulder, and they both stopped and stared at him. He clutched his shirt across his chest and scurried through the exit and into the street.

THE BARMAID (the 1950s)

I once lived in a big, old house that was let off into rooms. It wasn't in a very good condition, and the district had a poor reputation, but the rents were cheap, so it attracted itinerants, young couples who'd had a baby too soon, old couples who had nowhere else to go, and all those who couldn't afford a house or a flat, or perhaps weren't considered acceptable in more respectable areas. If you have money, and no children, a good job without the inconvenience of having to get dirty, and a decent appearance and reputation, you will always find a place to live. On the other hand, if you belong to that loose group of people outside the main classes in our society, you will almost certainly gravitate towards certain areas of any town or city you live in.

I won't tell you about all the people who lived in the house during the three years I was there. The rooms often changed monthly, sometimes even weekly. Most of the occupants moved on to other towns and houses similar to the one I'm talking about. A few were allocated council houses, others perhaps even managed to buy one of their own. An elderly man died alone in his room. The two I remember most of all were a couple of long-time residents on the second-floor. One was a middle-aged bachelor with a nervous complaint which made his lips twist and jerk. His affliction had driven him into a shy and stuttering awkwardness, and I glimpsed him only on odd occasions as he hurried in with his string bag full of cans and packets. The other was the barmaid.

She was possibly around fifty, had dark hair going grey, and a body that sagged in the too-tight dresses she wore. Her face was heavily made-up and she used a lot of perfume. We knew her as Mrs Rawlinson, but if she'd ever had a husband she never mentioned him. According to some of the older men I worked with in a local factory she'd been a barmaid for as long as they could remember. There was a small group in the town who were professional barmaids, and I suppose they must have started in that line in the 1930s when jobs were scarce. Most of the younger barmaids were like my wife and just did it part-time for the extra money.

One Saturday night when my wife was working I was sitting in our room, and heard someone open the front door of the house and then walk through the hallway towards the stairs. A few moments later there was a scuffling noise and then a loud bump. I waited for a few minutes, but nothing else happened, so I began to read again. When I heard more noises outside the door of the room I decided I'd better make sure everything was all right.

The door was opposite the foot of the stairs, and I opened it and saw Mrs Rawlinson lying half on the stairs and half in the hallway. She didn't appear to be hurt and was trying to get up. When I bent over her I could smell the gin and cheap scent and had to turn my face away. I pulled her upright and helped her up the stairs.

"Where's your key?" I asked her, but she didn't answer. "The key", I said, and as she didn't seem to understand I took her handbag and started looking through it. I pushed my fingers into wads of worn envelopes and snapshots, feeling for the key, and eventually tipped the whole lot onto the floor and knelt down to sift through it. Mrs Rawlinson wavered above me, her slack face and dull eyes making me feel like an interrogator finally unearthing his worn-down victim's secrets. The snapshots showed scenes at the seaside. A laughing couple posed on the promenade. A young girl perched on the back of a donkey. A man and a young boy, their trousers rolled up, paddling in the sea. The blue and brown and white envelopes were a mixture of old private letters and income-tax notes, their dates going back several years.

When I finally found the key and opened the door, I scooped the various bits and pieces back into the handbag, and then helped Mrs Rawlinson into the room. It was small and contained a bed, an easy chair with a flowered cover, a hard, straight-backed chair, a small table, and a chest of drawers. The wallpaper had once been lightly-patterned, but had faded, and the light from the single bulb made it appear a plain, off-brown colour. Stockings, blouses, and other articles of clothing were scattered across the chairs, and dresses and coats hung behind the door. The curtains were closed, and the air in the room was heavy and stale. I could make out the faint smell of liniment. A couple of plates and a teacup lay on top of the old-fashioned, blocked-up fireplace, and a small electric heater stood in the hearth. A calendar with a scene of a lakeside village was tacked to one wall, but the rest of the room was bare of any kind of decoration or ornament. Like the rest of us, Mrs Rawlinson used a communal bathroom and a shared kitchen, if she did any cooking.

I managed to get her coat off, and I helped her onto the bed. As I was leaning over her she wrapped her arms around my neck and kissed me on the forehead. I was surprised and embarrassed and began to back away, but she said, "Oh, come here, love", and pulled me down again. She hugged me and kissed my cheek, and then let go, and said, "Thank

212

you". I removed her shoes and picked up a blanket and covered her with it.

Just before I switched off the light, I glanced back at her. She was lying quite still, but her eyes were open and I could see that she was crying. I closed the door gently and went back downstairs.

CORPORAL OLLERTON (the 1950s)

Ollerton, at least I think that was his name, was a corporal I knew when I was in the army. He was cook-corporal and everyone called him Olly, so I guess his name was Ollerton, or something like that. It's not important.

When we'd been out drinking Olly would unlock the cookhouse and make us egg and chips. It was against the regulations, of course, but Olly didn't care about those, drunk or sober. I remember he disappeared for two days, and no-one knew where he'd gone. I never thought it could be done, but one way or another we covered up for him. The CSM would come around, and someone would say, "Oh, he's gone to the stores", or "He's just gone to pick up some provisions", and so on. Everyone liked Olly, so no-one wanted him to land in trouble. We also liked our late-night fries.

I got to be reasonably friendly with Olly when his wife died. She was a German girl and had a hole, or whatever, in her heart. He knew she would die anytime, and she knew it, but she said she didn't care. He went home from camp one lunchtime and found her dead on the kitchen floor. He'd used up all his leave, and had no money, so we fiddled him a pass, and some pay, and he went off to see his wife's parents, somewhere in Southern Germany. He came back a day after he should have done.

Olly moved into the room where I slept. I was platoon-corporal, so had the room to myself, but it had a spare bed, so he moved in. He was tidy, and quiet, and didn't mind my listening to jazz on the little radio I had. I don't think he really liked me all that much, but I was probably no worse than the rest of the people in the unit, so we went drinking together. He spoke German and dressed like a German, and took me to clubs and bars where normally I'd never have gone. And that's when those late-night visits to the cookhouse took place.

About a year after his wife died, Olly married her sister and moved out to married quarters again. I didn't see him much after that, apart from in the cookhouse, and we didn't have a great deal to say to each other. The day I went back to England, Olly hadn't come back from a couple of days leave, so I couldn't say goodbye. I did get a brief message via a friend who was demobbed shortly after I was. I think Olly had said to tell me not to drink too much bad beer. Something like that.

I did send him a Christmas card a couple of years later, but I suppose he may have left the army by then, or perhaps been posted to another unit. Anyway, I didn't get an answer. Maybe he hadn't bothered going back after one of his leaves? Anything could have happened, and I don't even know why I thought of sending him a card. I didn't even know him all that well.

SWEET SATURDAY NIGHT (the 1960s)

He saw her standing by one of the pillars, and as she didn't seem to be with anyone he asked her to dance. Afterwards, he bought her a drink and they talked about work, and the town, and things like that. She was a typist and he was employed in a local engineering works. He didn't think she was very good-looking, but the clothes she wore were neat and fashionable, and her slimness somehow attracted him. She was shy and hadn't a great deal to say, and he guessed she was seven or eight years older than him, which made her twenty-nine or so.

The dance ended just before twelve and he asked if he could drive her home. She agreed, and when they were in the car he kissed her and she held him close. He had to fumble with the keys to get the car started, and she wanted to know if was all right. He hadn't drunk all that much. he said, and anyway would take it easy and the roads were quiet. She relaxed and let her head rest on his shoulder.

They drove for a short way and then he parked the car down a side-street, and they kissed and he let his hands stray over her breasts and along her legs. She didn't say anything when he unclipped her bra, but when he tried to slip his hand between her legs she objected and pushed him away. He tried again, and she pushed him again, so he decided it wasn't his lucky night so made the most of kissing her and caressing her breasts.

She said it was time for her to go home, so he started the car and drove slowly back to the main-road as she fastened her clothes and tidied her hair. When she said she'd finished he swung the car onto the road and headed for the part of town where she lived. The streets were deserted, and once they got into the suburbs, and away from police patrols, he started to press down on the accelerator. Be careful, she said, but he looked at her and grinned. When he glanced back at the road he started to haul wildly on the wheel in an effort to take the car around the corner looming ahead. He didn't make it and the car hit the kerb on the other side of the road, slewed sideways for a few feet, and then turned over several times.

The people from the houses nearby managed to pull the woman out, but the man was trapped behind the wheel and they were driven back by the flames. She died just before the ambulance arrived. Someone had put a coat down on the grass verge and she was lying on that with her head cradled in a woman's arms. She was conscious for a few minutes and whimpered softly and asked for her mother. And then she died.

The police checked the pockets of her coat to see if they could come up with something to identify her by, but all they found were a button, a torn ticket for a local dance, and a lipstick-stained handkerchief. It was all they had to work on until her mother reported her missing, and they took her to the morgue to identify the body.

ON THE SCENE (the 1960s)

I was only passing through that town when I met him. If he hadn't shouted and hurried across the street I don't think I would have stopped. The last time I'd seen him had been at a poetry reading in a bar, but I had a girl with me that night, so I didn't pay too much attention to what was happening among the poets on the little stage.

It was raining hard and the town depressed me, all those dirty buildings and the atmosphere tight and clammy. I was hunched In my overcoat, but he wore a pair of red trousers, an old brown jacket, and a frayed shirt. His hair hung down on his shoulders, and he had on a battered hat which looked like the one that Billy the Kid has on in that picture you see in Western history books.

He was selling a magazine, mainly filled with his poems and those of a couple of his friends, and asked me to walk down to the bookshop with him. "I'm flat", he said, "really cleaned out", but I didn't reply, and he went on to tell me that he'd just hitched a lift from Edinburgh, where he'd sold sixty copies of his magazine in two weeks. "That's good", I said.

He carried on talking. He'd been to a party the previous Saturday and everyone got high and drove into the hills and danced on the grass. Then he'd made his way home and written the opening two pages of his novel before going to bed. The following night he'd attended another party and sat on top of the piano, writing haiku, as everyone shouted and screamed and made love all around him. I asked him how far he'd got with his novel, and he replied, "Oh, it's taking shape".

He also mentioned that he was having his poems broadcast over the local radio station. He'd invited a journalist to a reading he'd organised, and they'd recorded him declaiming a manifesto and a poem. The money should be through for that very soon, but in the meantime he needed something to help him along until the end of the week. He took off his hat, scratched his head, and looked at his fingernails.

When we reached the shop I told him I didn't feel like going in, so we parted company. Through the window I watched him talking to one of the assistants. He had a beard and wore glasses with large white frames. Another man, with a blue denim shirt and flowered tie, came over and they went into a huddle with a copy of the magazine. I could see them gesturing and laughing, but I couldn't hear anything apart from the hum of the traffic and the soft hiss of the rain on the pavement. It was like watching three glittering goldfish in a bowl.

I turned up the collar of my coat and joined the crowds of people hurrying to catch their buses home.

THE DRIFTER (the 1960s)

John knew all the characters, all the people who he said did something "different". If he heard about someone odd he would make his way to where they lived and introduce himself. He once took me to a large, old house in the countryside, and we spent the day with a group of people who were supposed to be studying the causes of a lack of co-operation between countries. They let us sit in at their weekly meeting, and we listened to them argue about whose turn it was to wash the windows and clean the stairs.

John moved south, to London, and lived at various addresses. Whenever he came North he always brought two or three people with him, long-haired and dressed in colourful clothes. They'd sit around, talking about this and that, but always with an air of irreverence. A well-meant expression of belief was usually greeted with a howl of laughter, but at the same time they would never put forward a constructive suggestion about anything. As far as I could make out, they didn't read much, apart from a few magazines and paperbacks, and though they professed to like paintings and jazz they knew little about either.

John left London and drifted to the Continent. Then he went to North Africa, Israel, and a few other places. When he came North again he had a girl with him, and a boy, whose money they were travelling on. All three of them turned up at my house one night. The boy looked through the bookshelves, but obviously couldn't find anything of interest. The girl scanned the jazz records in the cabinet but seemed bored. John sprawled in a chair and rambled on about the various places he'd been to and the characters he'd met. I was restless and found myself glancing at the clock and dropping hints about the last bus into town.

They eventually left and I went back to the poem I'd been working on for a couple of days. I found it almost impossible to concentrate. The desultory manner in which they'd done everything, from commenting on politics, or planning what they were going to do next day, disturbed me. All their thoughts were fragmentary, and when I read through what I had written I noticed that the mood had affected me. The lines of the poem stuttered along and the ideas trailed off into a near-meaningless limbo. I felt like getting drunk, but it was too late to go out and I hadn't any wine in the house. It perhaps sounds crazy, but I opened the window to let in some fresh air.

Contents of Jim Burns' previous essay collections

Beats, Bohemians and Intellectuals *Trent Books 2000*

Radicals, Beats and Beboppers *PPP (2011)*

Brits, Beats & Outsiders *PPP (2012)*

Bohemians, Beats and Blues People *PPP* (2013)

Artists, Beats and Cool Cats *PPP* (2014)

Rebels, Beats and Poets *PPP* (2015)

Paris, Painters, Poets *PPP (2017)*

Painting, Poetry, Politics (*PPP* 2018)

Books, Artists, Beats (PPP 2019)

www.ingramcontent.com/pod-product-compliance
Lightning Source LLC
Chambersburg PA
CBHW061500030726
47503CB00005B/1757

* 9 7 8 1 9 1 3 1 4 4 1 2 8 *